The Twelve

D E McCluskey

*Thanks for your interest in The Twelve
The first eleven were rubbish*

D E McCluskey

The Twelve
Copyright © 2017 by D E McCluskey

The moral right of the author has been asserted
*All characters and events in this publication,
other than those clearly in the public domain,
are fictitious and any resemblance to real persons,
living or dead, is purely coincidental*

All rights are reserved

No part of this publication may be reproduced,
stored in a retrieval system, or transmitted in any form
by any means, without the prior permission, in writing of
the publisher, nor be otherwise circulated in any form of binding or
cover other than that of which it was
published and without a similar condition including this
condition being imposed on the subsequent purchaser.

ISBN 978-1977587688

A Dammaged Comics Production

www.dammaged.com

The Twelve

For Grace…
My constant inspiration who lifts me
from my darkest moments

Part 1

Present Day

1.

THE SCREAM THAT roared from the judge's chambers was unmerciful, like something hideous being torn from a womb from Hell. It was followed rapidly by another, similar scream. The only discernible difference was that this one sounded wet. Then came a slick, horrible rip, a sound akin to tearing leather.

'Stop! Please… please make it stop.'

This whimper was pathetic, in complete contrast to the energy of the scream preceding it. It was as if the scream's perpetrator had expelled all their breath, leaving none in reserve to help form words.

One final, bloodcurdling yell for help or mercy, it was difficult to tell, coursed unheard and unanswered along the deserted corridors, before suddenly falling silent, and the building was peaceful once again.

It was three-fifteen am on a cold, wet Wednesday morning.

2.

JOHN RYDELL AWOKE in his room, he was lost between the sheets of the massive king size bed he slept alone in. One side of the bed had been completely unoccupied through the night, the other side, his side, was a tangled, twisted mess. He was sweating heavily.

'Another nightmare…' He screwed his face into a grimace as he fumbled for the glass of water he always kept at the side of the bed. Twice he nearly knocked it over as the elusive container danced out of his reach in the dark. Finally, he grasped it and took a huge gulp, of fresh air. The glass was empty.

Through red, tired eyes he regarded the clock next to his empty glass. It read three fifteen am. He groaned, aloud.

'Shit… not again.'

For the last few weeks he'd been waking up at fifteen minutes past three every morning and then struggling to drift back off into anything that resembled sleep. Tonight, he realised the futility of merely lying there and allowing his mind to race, so he dragged himself out of the bed and stumbled his way downstairs to the kitchen. There was no point even trying to pretend to himself that sleep would belong to him again tonight.

He poured milk into a large cup and put it into the microwave. The light from inside of the square box almost blinded him in the gloom of the kitchen. It was the only source in the room and it shone like the sun. The cold, artificial light illuminated his tired, shattered face.

The Twelve

He regarded his reflection in the microwave door for a few seconds, his dark rimmed eyes and unkempt hair gave credence to the fact that he had a face that had been through too much just recently, too much for its own good. He looked much older than his forty-two years.

The microwave beeped, his warm milk was ready. He removed it and closed the door, relishing the blessed darkness that descended back over him, and the room. As if walking through a field of deep mud, he trudged his way back upstairs. He flicked on the TV; squinting his eyes as the illumination of late night rubbish filled his room. He watched it with disinterest, taking small sips of his cathartic drink.

Even without any soul searching, he knew, deep down, that he'd be sat here like this for at least the next couple of hours, and then in the morning, when the sun dared to peep in through his curtains, he'd be too lethargic to get up. He'd sleep through his alarm and hence most of the morning.

At this precise moment in time he didn't give one single fuck about any of that. He didn't much care for anything anymore; all he really wanted was sweet oblivion. A full night's dreamless sleep.

'Chance would be a fine thing,' he said to her, to the huge elephant that was, or more precisely, *was not* in the room.

At fifteen minutes past three, or there about, he always talked to her. She was the only one who would listen at that time, but then she didn't really have much of a choice.

'I can't believe it's a month... today.' He closed his eyes, as if in prayer, as if talking, pleading with some higher being who could hear him. 'Why wasn't I here? In the grand scheme of things, what was more important, a stupid works holiday to Chicago, or staying in London with the person I love, and maybe, just maybe keeping her alive?'

He looked down at his hot milk and was not too surprised to find that it was gone, the empty cup gazing up at him like one huge, accusing, milky eye. Tonight, was going to be a long night, one of those nights where sleep never actually came back to play.

He sat back on the bed and sighed. His mind rolled back to the events, of exactly a month ago.

The Twelve

One month earlier

3.

IT WAS PROMOTION time in the office. Every rat was happily running around in the perfectly designed maze, all wearing new suits and shoes, all trying their hardest to find the illusive cheese that smelt of promotion.

'You know it's just a ploy, don't you? Every year during the quietest period the exec gets us all running around like headless chickens, in the vain hope of having a shot of actually getting on the bottom rung of the 'partner' ladder.' John was making conversation as the two men hurried down a bland looking corridor towards a bland looking door with the words SERVER ROOM 1 written above it.

'I know,' replied his companion. 'But I still wouldn't mind a slice of that action man.'

He was smiling at John as he keyed in the numbers for the door lock. The blast of icy cold air from the built-in air conditioners inside washed over them both. 'Oh, don't you just love that.' Ian said lifting his arms into the air and turning around to get the full effect of the artificial winter storm. 'You know what we need to do? We need to get Lauren from communications in here. Can you imagine? Just that initial blast of cold air alone would set me up for weeks.' He popped his mouth and made exaggerated nipples with his fingers as they both entered the darkened server room.

John was looking and feeling rather sharp in his brand-new suit. Gill had bought it for him the week before, picking it out herself and paying for it from her own money. 'We've got to make you presentable if you're going to be partner.' She'd said while fixing his tie and planting a quick kiss on the end of his nose. Pretty much like what his mother used to do before she sent him off to school.

As they both logged on to the servers to perform the upgrades they had come here to do, John was looking a little troubled. He turned to Ian, with his face looking somewhat pained. 'Ian, mate I've got something I need to tell you.'

Ian's face dropped. 'You're not gay, are you?' He stepped back from John with his hands in the air. 'Because if you are man, I don't have an issue with it bro, but I do have to tell you that you're not exactly my type. Not that I have a type, but you know what I mean.' He was laughing but still looked more than a little uncomfortable in the tight environment of the small room.

John laughed. 'No, you dick... I *am* serious though. I do have something to tell you. I've been asked to go to Chicago.'

Ian stopped typing on his keyboard and looked at him. 'No way. No, fucking, way! Mate, that's brilliant news.'

His face told John that he was surprised but genuinely happy for him. This relieved him no end as he had been dreading telling him.

'Ok yeah. That means I can have your desk with the great view of Lydia.' He exaggerated huge breasts with his hands, before laughing again and slapping John on the back. 'Really mate, if anyone deserves it, it's you.'

John was taken aback a bit, after all Ian had been with the company for much longer than he had, and he'd made no secret about the fact that he longed for the Chicago trip. The trip meant promotion to just outside of the full first team. Not quite partner, but it was a kind of guarantee that you soon would be. At forty-two years of age John felt it was about time he began to climb that corporate ladder.

'I'm a bit nervous about it though; I haven't been away from Gill for more than three nights since we got married.'

'Man, you have to grow a pair! This trip will make you. Everyone in the first team makes partner. Just think of all the good times you two will have then.' His face changed, and he became a little pensive. He huffed a sigh and shook his head, a wry smile adorning his features. 'I'd have loved that trip though, but then, I'm not as young as you.'

'What? You're not old.'

He looked at John. 'Maybe not, but I can't give the level of commitment that they need. I've got three kids to look out for, and Jeanie. And well…' He pulled a knowing face to John raising his eyebrows, '…you've met Jeanie.'

For the rest of the day John was filled with mixed emotions, half excited at the prospect of Chicago, and half dreading telling Gill.

4.

THAT NIGHT JOHN arrived home around seven o'clock. He was tired and irksome, worrying about what he was going to tell Gill all day. As he was hanging his coat up a waft of smell crept over him, crawling into his nostrils, it was a smell of something that he loved. The fact that he could smell it tonight made his heart sink down deep into his chest.

Gill had made lasagne. She made the best lasagne that John had ever tasted. Home-made pasta, ragu sauce, not poured from a jar but created by her own fair hands, crushing real tomatoes, and the cheese sauce tinted with a little more than a hint of English mustard. Delicious, but tonight, ultimately heart-breaking.

The cutlery was already on the table when he walked in, and there were two large glasses of red wine airing in the centre. He loosened his tie and began to shrug off his jacket, he was hating himself already.

'Honey, I'm home. Dinner smells fantastic,' he shouted.

'It'll be ready in a moment, glass of wine there for you too.'

He walked into the living room, the places were set on their over large dining table, candles had been lit, and draped over the lamp was her red chiffon scarf, giving a pink-red hue to the room. It reminded him of an Eastern Boudoir from some cheesy seventies film. He knew exactly what all this was for, and it made him feel sad, almost empty inside.

The Twelve

'Right, you sit there and relax, take your shoes off and I'll be in in a moment with your starter,' she said as she bustled into the room, flashing him a gorgeous beaming smile.

John had always been in awe of Gill's beauty, even from the first moment they'd met. Her bright green eyes and dark auburn hair were striking, but when she smiled, *Jesus*, her whole face shone, to him she could literally light up his room. He felt truly blessed, and more than just a little lucky. But right now, none of that was helping, he was feeling awful. This meal meant that things had gone well at the fertility clinic today, and tonight was the night they were going to start their regime of trying for that elusive baby.

'Here we go... spicy chicken balls with rice noodles, your favourite, I do believe.'

She carried in the starters on two of their best plates. What she was wearing had not gone unnoticed by him either. It was the dress that she knew he could never resist; she knew it drove him wild. It was a tight fitting, figure hugging purple dress with buttons all the way down the front. It accentuated every curve she had, and she had many, delicious curves, every single one of them in the right place.

He knew the rules of the game she was playing right now. He wasn't to mention the dress, or the black high heels, or the alluring smell of her perfume. She'd make all kinds of excuses to go back and forth to the kitchen several times during this meal, making sure she wiggled, strutted and preened before him every time.

'Oh, my God, Gill these are incredible,' he gushed as he bit into the first chicken ball.

'I think mine need a little pepper.' She stood up and leant over him to grab the large, phallic looking pepper grinder that had been strategically placed on his half of the table. She tutted as her hands caressed the long wooden grinder, her green eyes flashed up to him, like a mermaid seducing her captain. 'This thing's almost empty.' As she stood up her hands slowly wiped down all the creases of her dress, delicately caressing the curves of her full breasts, all the while looking at him and smiling. She then turned and made her way into the kitchen, returning a few moments later with the large pepper pot and the top three buttons of her dress undone.

'More wine?' She asked innocently.

He gave her a knowing smile and nodded. 'You know I do.'

Another seductive smile, and another show of strutting into the kitchen ensued. When she returned with two refreshed glasses, her long, auburn hair was undone and was hanging around her shoulders.

This sight always took John's breath away, she knew the power she had over him. This was her game, and she was damned good at it.

He sat back in his chair, sipped his wine and looked at her. The starters were finished. He knew what was coming next and he longed for it and hated himself because of it, both in equal measures.

'You want your mains now? It's lasagne you know.'

He looked at her and tipped his glass. 'Oh please, I'm still starving.' He winked and took another sip of wine.

She picked up the plates and returned to the kitchen. When she was out of sight, he held his head in his hands, elbows on the table. He felt like such a shit. He knew that he was taking full advantage of this situation, because he knew what was coming for dessert, and then, the best part, instead of coffee. He had to tell her about Chicago and he had to do it soon, but finding the right moment tonight was going to be difficult. Chicago would shatter her plans, their plans, for a baby. Or at least any involvement in him being there during its upbringing. The company would want its pound of flesh.

Eventually Gill came back out of the kitchen, her dress was now completely open at the front down to her waist, and he could see that she'd purchased new underwear. Red, lacy and transparent. He was in a true dichotomy. He hated the fact that he could already feel the familiar stirrings in his trousers, but he also loved it too.

Dinner was delicious, but it shadowed in comparison to his view. Twice more she journeyed to the kitchen for more wine and both times she was a little more undressed when she returned. He had to admit that he loved this game.

'Dessert?' She asked, cocking her head to one side, giving him a knowing lopsided grin as she did.

John looked at that grin, it was the very same grin he'd fallen in love with all those years ago. As she picked up the plates she fluttered her long, dark eyelashes at him before turning on her heels, back into the kitchen. She was in there for a few moments, rattling the pots and plates. After a short while, she came back out. All she was wearing now was a small pair of black French knickers. Her naked breasts were pert and perfect in the dim red glow of the lamp and candles.

She took his breath away, even after all these years. Keeping her puppy-dog eyes on his, she knelt on her knees and crawled beneath the table.

John gulped. He felt her delicate hands at the buckle of his belt, he could feel them working at the bulge that had developed at the front of his trousers. He shifted to one-side as the bulge was getting rather uncomfortable, trapped inside its confinement. He didn't need to worry about that for too long, as her hands began to pull down on his zip allowing the angered beast to burst free. Then, instead of tiramisu, came the best part of the meal. As he felt the warm, wetness of her mouth taking him inside, all he could do was grip on the sides of the table. Once again, he was reminded that she was very good at this game.

They carried the meal on into the living room, then all the way up the stairs, culminating in the bedroom. While there he gave her, willingly, what she'd really wanted all night… a potential baby. As they both lay there basking in the afterglow of their fantastic, energetic, lovemaking she turned towards him. She propped her head up on her hand as she did. John couldn't help but caress her perfect, round breast, teasing the delicious nipple and areola with his forefinger and thumb.

Eventually she broke his reverie.

'You know I was at the fertility clinic today don't you?'

He stopped playing; he turned on his side and flicked the bedside lamp on. *This is where it begins*, he thought.

He turned back to Gill and smiled, trying his best for the smile to be a knowing, loving smile, but inside he felt cold and empty. 'You never gave me the chance to ask how it went.'

The Twelve

Present Day

5.

BACK IN THE bedroom, all alone again now. He was lying in almost the exact position he had been lying when this conversation had taken place.

He looked up at the ceiling and watched the reflection of a solitary car's headlights race across the smooth plasterboard, and sighed a low, sorrowful sigh.

'This is where it began!' He whispered into the darkness. 'The beginning of my end.'

One month earlier

6.

'YOU NEVER GAVE me the chance to ask how it went.'

Gill sat up, her animated face obviously excited at the conversation that was about to commence. 'Well, it went really well. They said that there's nothing wrong with us, either of us. Your sperm and my eggs are compatible and healthy. So, basically, they said to go home tonight and start making babies.' She smiled at him or rather, beamed.

'And that's what we just did?'

Her beautiful face fell a little at what he'd just said and she tilted her head a little. 'Well, yeah. You enjoyed it, didn't you?'

'Yeah, very much so, but I think you should've spoken to me beforehand. I feel a bit used now.'

This broke her.

'USED?' She shouted.

He instantly regretted his choice of words, and he knew now that the trouble he felt was coming like a distant thunder over a calm lake, was now here, and it was brewing up to be a storm. He turned away from her, wincing as he did.

Gill jumped out of the bed, totally naked, her pale skin was still flushed from her recent orgasm. Her face matched the flush, but the pink hue to her cheeks was nothing to do with ecstasy. She was angry right now, and every last bit of it was aimed at him.

'Don't you fucking turn away from *me*!' She roared. 'What do you mean by used?'

He closed his eyes and covered his face with his hand. He couldn't argue with her while she was still naked. She was totally gorgeous and he knew that he wouldn't be able to hold her eyes, no matter how angry he got. One flick of his gaze down her fantastic body and the argument would be lost, she would win, as usual. He got up slowly from the bed, grabbed his housecoat and stormed, silently out of the room.

He heard her coming up behind him like an articulated lorry baring down on him. He knew she would still be naked as she chased him down the hallway. Gill was a successful solicitor and she could, and would, always use any weapon she had in her arsenal to win an argument. To him, her nakedness might well have been a one hundred megaton bomb.

Still cringing about what he'd just said to her, he tried his best to withstand the hurricane blowing in the hallway. 'Listen, I'm sorry for using the word 'used'. It was the wrong turn of phrase. I've just had a strange day today, that's all,' he shouted from behind the closed bathroom door.

She crashed her way in to where he was stood with both hands on the sink, looking at himself in the mirror. Or more precisely, loathing himself in the mirror.

'Oh, so now you're sorry?' She screamed at him. She put her head in her hands and flicked her long hair back over her head. John couldn't help himself but marvel at how fantastic her body looked when she did it, she knew what she was doing, and it seemed to calm her down a little. John knew that it was merely a lull in Hurricane Gill. 'What's going on John? What's happening here exactly?' Her voice was calm and calculated, he didn't like it one bit.

When Gill was angry he thought that was when she was at her most alluring. She knew this and could turn it on and off with a notion, hence why she was successful in her field. But add to that that she was totally naked. John already knew that he was going to lose this argument, unless…

He turned towards her and attempted to close the bathroom door, pushing her out at the same time. He needed a clear head and no distractions right now.

Gill flew into a near rage at the shock of suddenly being pushed away. 'WHY ARE YOU AVOIDING ME?' She shouted, banging her fists on the closed door.

Alone now, John closed his eyes. He took in and held a deep breath. *It's because you're too fucking beautiful to argue with!* He thought, but said, 'I'm not avoiding you, I just don't want to start a f…'

'Family?' She finished for him.

He knew that she had a fast mind, and the speed of this quip had only served to prove that point.

'No, I was about to say that I don't want to start a fight. I've had a great day in work and a fantastic evening with you, I just don't want to spoil it,' he shouted through the door.

Gill went quiet. It was a long, pregnant pause. Despite himself he chuckled at the irony of that thought.

'You got the Chicago gig, didn't you?' She finally whispered. 'Yes, you did. You got the fucking Chicago gig, and now that you'll be a high flying first fucking team prick, you've forgotten all about your family obligations!' Her voice got louder, shriller as the sentence wore on.

He hadn't seen her this angry for… Well, he didn't think he'd seen her this angry, ever. 'Please calm down, just calm down. Go and put some clothes on, I'll be out in a minute and we can talk about this.'

The Twelve

It went quiet outside the door again; he flushed the toilet just so he didn't look like a complete coward ducking into the bathroom to avoid her. He opened the door, just a crack, and peered out. He felt like something out of a cartoon, the big hunter peeping through the door to see if the huge bear he'd been hunting was still there, hunting him. She was gone. Quietly relieved, he stepped out of the bathroom and made his way back towards the bedroom.

From the distance of the landing, he watched her get dressed. It was a guilty pleasure. When she was finished, she sat on the bed and began to comb her hair. She looked calm, so he walked in. She had her back to him, she knew he was there, but thought it best to ignore him.

'Gill, I never once said that I didn't want to start a family, it's just this opportunity, right now, it can make us.'

She turned around and looked at him; her eyes were red, not as red as her hair, but it was a close race. She wiped a falling tear from her cheek. This one, small action almost broke John's heart. She wasn't emotionally cold, far from it but she did fiercely guard her emotions. He could count on his hands the amount of times he had seen her cry.

'John, you're forty-two years old, I'm forty-one! Our clocks are ticking. We live really well, look at our house, our lives… our bank balances! Why do you need to pile the pressure on yourself and become a partner in a dead firm?'

'It is hardly dead, now is it Gill?'

'It is to me!'

He sat down on the bed next to her, he didn't attempt to put his arms around her, he knew that she wouldn't want that. 'It was you who got me into this promotion thing, you even bought me my suit.'

'A person can change, can't they?'

'Look, I know you're not happy, you haven't been since you gave up your job to concentrate on this baby malarkey.'

'I was happy once…' she replied.

'And you'll be happy again. The baby will come, you know it will, and if not, we always talked about adoption.

John was surprised then as she leant her head on his shoulder and began to sob.

He put his arm around her, to comfort and protect her.

'The trip isn't for another week; we can have all the baby making you want from now until then…'

This was a rather pleasing thought.

Still crying she curled herself up into a foetal position on the bed and closed her eyes.

John watched her fall asleep, his heart was broken and he was torn between his job, his future, and his family.

The next few days she was sulky and he was miserable. Miserable but excited too. The thought of Chicago and all the bells and whistles that came with it made him feel like a little kid at Christmas, but his elation was tinged with sadness, every time he thought of Gill. *She'll get over it…* he kept telling himself.

7.

THE DAY FINALLY came when he was leaving for Chicago.

Gill knew that he had an early flight, but had decided at two in the morning to take three sleeping tablets. She'd been complaining about noises coming from next door, that they had been keeping her awake. He didn't think it prudent to tell her that he never heard any noises, and that next door had been away for a week, and therefore, the house was empty.

In the early light the next morning as he was leaving, he took a quick look through the windows downstairs, but couldn't see any sign of life, but that was nothing out of the ordinary for five-thirty am.

As he wheeled his suitcase into the airport he called her mobile. It rang out onto her answer machine so he left a message. 'Gill, when you get this please remember that I love you, and I do want a family with you. I'll speak to you later OK?'

The airport lounge was a hive of excited travellers, all of them hustling and bustling here and there, getting their duty free and perfume. He smiled to himself, determined to have a good time.

8.

THE WEEK FLEW by almost in the wink of his eye. It had been fun, filled with meetings and parties, and he was feeling good about himself and his prospects at the company. Gill had sent him a few messages telling him that she loved him, that she was sorry for her mood, she couldn't wait for him to get home, that she'd had her purple dress cleaned and had been thinking quite a lot about lasagne just recently!

The few phone calls they had exchanged had only managed put him a little bit on edge. She'd mentioned, only in passing, but on more than one occasion, that the neighbours had been quiet all day, but had then started crashing about all night. She said she would've expected music if they had been having parties, but there hadn't been any. She likened it to someone trashing the house.

He *had* checked the house before he left, there hadn't been any sign of any disturbances that he could see, but then he'd only had peripheral access.

9.

JOHN WAS SAT at the bar in the hotel. He was sipping a long dark drink, and was lost in his own thoughts. Many of his colleagues were sitting around the bar area too, either alone or in small groups, all of them nursing their own drinks. The holiday vibe had fizzled out and everyone had started to look tired and jaded after the long flight, the long days, and the long parties. The subdued atmosphere made him feel a little homesick and, although it didn't show in his slumped gait, he was excited to be going back home. Feeling every day of his forty-two years, he decided to call it a night and slope off to bed.

It was the ungodly hour of nine pm in Chicago, he'd spoken to Gill just before she'd gone to bed, as it was now three am in London. He wanted to call her and tell her he loved her, but he also knew that she'd not be best pleased at being woken at that hour. He drained his drink, checked his phone for, what felt like, the hundred thousandth time, and then eased himself up from his chair.

'Guys, I'm off to bed,' he shouted to no-one in particular. He smiled inwardly as not one of them protested his leaving, but then he never really expected them to. He guessed that once one of them had made the commitment to leave, most were likely to follow.

'Take it easy John, early start in the morning eh? Breakfast for seven sharp, you good with that?' A large man shouted towards him in an American accent. He looked like he would be sat at the bar for the duration of the night.

'All over it Hank. I'm done in here anyway,' he replied, raising his hand in salute.

He pushed at the door towards the corridor, relishing the relief of escaping the depressing bar, when he felt his pocket vibrate. He rolled his eyes wondering who it could be calling him now, at this time.

He took the phone from his pocket and with the look of the weary, glanced at the screen. The beginnings of a panic began to rise in his chest. Why would Gill be ringing him now? His heart began to beat faster; he could feel blood rush into his ears.

'Hey baby, is everything OK?' He asked, trying his very best to sound excited to hear her, when in reality he was dreading what she had to say. He knew that something was wrong. All he could hear on other end were quiet, scared sobs.

With an unprecedented urgency, he began to speak down the phone. 'Gill, Gill... speak to me. What's wrong?' He was bent over, with his free hand in his other ear, trying to filter out all the other noises around him. He paced backwards and forwards before the elevators.

The next words she uttered shook his entire world to the core. They were something that he would have never ever expected to hear.

'There's someone in the house John!'

'WHAT?'

'... Someone... in the house. I've seen him!' Her voice was wavering, it sounded like she had the receiver pushed up close to her mouth.

He couldn't believe what he was hearing, he'd never, ever felt so useless in his entire life. He wanted to climb through the stupid screen of his phone and physically be near the woman he loved. He was in Chicago, four thousand miles away from her. She was

The Twelve

alone in a large house in England, and she came at him with this!

For a moment or two he was too stunned to say anything, he just stood outside the elevators with the phone at his ear. It wasn't that he didn't have anything to say, it was mostly because he didn't have the breath in his body to say it.

'Jesus Gill,' he managed to hiss down the phone. 'Have you rung the police? Can you ring Mick?'

'John... he's a child! I'm sure he's a fucking child. Just a boy!'

'What? Gill get out of the house right now.' He didn't even know he was shouting until a couple who were leaving the bar stopped and looked over towards him. 'Can you get out of the house? I'm ringing Mick right now, stay on the phone. Shit, I'll have to get someone else's phone. Hang on, stay there. Don't move from where you are.'

He sprinted back into the bar, pushing the door so hard that it banged on the wall, waking up the maudlin atmosphere inside, snapping everyone out of their reveries. As one, everyone turned to see who, or what, was making the racket.

Hank, the large man who had saluted him off to bed was the first to react.

'John? What's happening man? I thought you'd taken yourself off to bed.'

'There's someone in the house...' he panted. 'Someone. A burglar. Someone in there. With Gill... She's on her own.' He was speaking so fast that all his sentences were coming out as one, making him sound like he was talking another language.

'What? John, you're not making any sense. What's happening? You look as white as a sheet.'

He stared at the big man, with a totally blank expression on his face. He licked his lips, wetting them with what little moisture he had left in his mouth. 'I need your mobile, please give me your mobile.'

Hank fumbled in the inside pocket of his jacket; he didn't know what was happening but he knew his friend needed help, and he wasn't going to let him down. The whole room was watching with the same morbid interest that makes people slow down at traffic accidents, dwelling in the drama that was unfolding before them.

'Gill... Gill, are you still there? GILL...'

His eyes closed with relief when he heard her timid response.

'Yes, I'm still here,' she whispered down the line. Her voice sounded shaky, off balance.

'I've got a phone and I'm ringing Mick right now. I'm going to hand this phone to Hank, he'll talk to you while I talk to Mick. Have you got that?'

Without waiting for her answer, he handed the phone over to the big man and frantically dialled on the other one.

Hank looked lost and confused as he put the phone to his ear.

'Hi, I'm Hank, John's friend,' he said, feeling more than a little bit stupid.

John battered at the keypad of the phone, he waited in a cacophony of silence for the connection to click, and then experienced a full eternity before it began to ring. Eventually a groggy voice answered on the other end.

'Hello... Whoever this is better have a fucking good reason to be ringing at this hour?' Mick growled four thousand miles away.

'Mick... Mick, oh thank God you answered.'

'John?' Mick's tired voice asked on the other end of the phone. 'Do you know what time it is?'

The Twelve

'Mick, I'm still in Chicago. I've got Gill on my phone, there's someone in the house Mick, there's someone in there and she's alone.'

Mick's voice was awake and alert instantly. 'I'm on my way right now, I'll ring you when I'm there. Shit, give me... what, five minutes!'

Both parties hung up.

He snatched the phone back from Hank and shouted into it. 'Gill, Mick's on his way, he'll be five minutes' tops.'

There was the sound of Gill's sobs, and then, most alarmingly, a distant crash.

'GILL!!!' He was screaming now.

'John! I know who it is!' She whispered into the handset... and then the line went dead.

'Know who who is?' He shouted into a dead line. 'Know who *WHO* is?'

His sweaty fingers tried to call her back, twice. All he got was the engaged tone each time. He dialled Mick, it rang three times and was answered. 'I'm pulling into the street now,' he shouted down the phone. He sounded out of breath too.

'Hurry Mick she was screaming and her phone went dead. Don't bother with the key, just smash the fucking door in, worry about it later. Jesus, I feel so fucking useless!' His hand was clenched into a fist, so tight that his nails cut into his skin. He didn't even notice.

'The light's on in the bedroom. I can see someone walking about.'

'Break the door Mick, kick it in.'

'OK. I'll ring back in two ticks.' Mick hung up.

John found himself stood in the middle of the bar. He felt like the headline act at a sold-out rock concert, everyone in the room was looking at him. He stared down at his bloodied hand holding a mobile phone that was not ringing.

He tried Gill's number again, but it was still engaged.

'Shit, come on Mick!'

When he had time, at his leisure, to look back at the logs of his phone calls, he was always surprised to note that only three minutes elapsed between his unsuccessful call to Gill and Mick ringing him back. To John, he felt like he could have walked back to England in that time. Later, he would muse on the relativity of time.

The phone rang and John jumped, although he was anxiously waiting for the call, when it happened, he found that he didn't want it.

He clicked the button after just two rings. 'Mick, talk to me.'

'John, this is weird mate. I just told you I saw the light on and someone moving about yeah? Well, I'm in the house, I had your spare key. Gill is sound asleep in bed mate.'

He couldn't believe what he was hearing. He shook his head, not understanding what his brother-in-law was telling him. 'What?'

'I think she's taken something. I've tried to wake her up but she's not responding. She's fast asleep though. Other than that, everything's good, it's just fucking freezing in here, that's all.'

John's hand was covering his eyes; trying his best to comprehend the data he was receiving. 'Mick, are you telling me everything is OK? Gill's OK?' He spoke slowly, he wanted Mick to understand every word of the question he was asking him.

'John, it's the strangest thing. I'm telling you, I got to the top of your street and saw the bedroom light on. There was a shadow of someone walking about in the room. I thought it was Gill. I got in with my key. When I got inside, the house was in total darkness. You need to hear this John; I'm telling you that Gill is fast asleep. She must have left the air conditioning on full though, I can see my breath.'

'Oh, thank fuck. Oh, thank God. Is Laura with you?' He asked, calming down a little.

'Yeah, she is in the car, why?'

'Would you guys stay there tonight and ring me the minute Gill wakes up?'

'Listen man, no problem. I don't think Laura would leave her on her now anyway.'

'Mick, I really can't thank you enough mate'

'Maybe a big bottle of Kentucky Derby from customs would do the trick.' The sound of Mick's laughter, from so far away in London, was what calmed John down the most.

'You're on. Don't forget, ring me when she wakes up OK, no matter what time it is here. I'll have to go now though; I think I've had enough drama for one night.'

'You take it easy man, go and have yourself a large whiskey to calm yourself down. Everything is good on this end.' Mick hung up, leaving John stood in the centre of the bar still holding the two phones.

'She's fine.' He turned to everyone in the room and raised his head towards the ceiling. His shoulders slumped as he exhaled a long, slow breath. 'She'd taken some sleeping pills and must have had some sort of episode, a bad reaction to them, or something,' he explained. He was feeling a little silly at his reaction now, handing the phone back to Hank he looked a little sheepish. 'Thanks mate, I really appreciate it.'

Hank accepted his phone with a big American smile on his face. 'Hey, don't sweat it man. I'm just glad she's OK. Really.' He slapped John on the back.

'Thanks Hank,' he whispered as he slumped onto a stool at the bar. Hank indicated to the barman to pour John a whiskey, a large one.

10.

IT WAS FOUR am when Mick finally rang. John had been awake most of the night just staring at the ceiling of his room. He'd had a tight grip of his phone all night checking it every few minutes to see if he'd missed a call or received a text. He must have fallen asleep at some point as the theme from Star Wars jolted him up, out of the bed, in an instant.

'John, its Mick. She's up. She's a bit surprised to see all our ugly mugs in the house, but she's fine. Here you go.'

'John?'

The sound of her voice brought on waves of emotion. She sounded normal, if a little tired and confused. He silently thanked a deity, any deity, or even all of them, he didn't really care for that kind of thing, but he just wanted to make sure that someone was thanked that she was OK. Tears were welling up in his eyes.

'John, what's going on? Why are Laura and Mick here?'

'Oh Gill, you scared us all last night.'

'I'm getting a little scared here right now. What happened? What did I do?'

'You rang me at two in the morning; crying and whispering that there was someone in the house. Something about it being a boy, and that you knew him.'

He laughed, a strange little sound, as he replayed the events of last night through his head.

'Shit Gill, I nearly wet myself. I rang Mick to get around there as soon as he could. When he got there, you were fast asleep.'

'Oh John, I'm so sorry, I really am. There was so much noise coming from next door again, so I popped a couple of those pills. It must have been a dream or a hallucination, or something.'

'Well listen, I'm home the day after tomorrow, so get your lasagne recipe out and iron that purple dress, because I want to make babies with you.'

The silence from the other end of the phone was almost deafening. She was silent for so long that he thought that she had hung up.

'Gill?'

There was just a little sob.

'Gill, are you OK?'

'Yeah,' she said a little breathlessly. 'I'm sorry John. I just love you so much.'

He listened as she took in a big, shaky breath, held it for a small while, and then she was Gill again.

'Next door really are doing my head in. There must have been another party last night. I thought I saw someone in our garden too.' He could hear the confusion in her voice, she was double checking herself now, going over what might have been fact and what might have been hallucination.

He laughed. 'Don't start all that again!'

She laughed a little too. It was nice to hear her sounding normal again.

'Maybe I'm just getting a little lonely without you here to keep me safe.'

'Well, I'm back very soon, early in the morning the day after tomorrow. Do you think you can live without me till then?'

'Can you have lasagne first thing in the morning?' She asked with a cheeky giggle in her laugh.

'With you, I could eat lasagne all day, every day. Listen I've got to go now I've got an early start, so I'll speak to you in the morning, my morning, OK? Goodnight baby. I love you, you know?'

'I love you too!'

That was the last, two way conversation he ever had with his wife.

11.

THE NEXT DAY was his last in Chicago. It was a day of meetings, presentations and jollifications about the trip. All he could think about was getting back home to Gill, and her lasagne. He'd tried to call her on four separate occasions, and had received at least seven missed calls from her in return, but they kept on missing each other. They appeared to be playing mobile phone tennis.

A cocktail reception had been planned for that night, so when the working day was over he headed back to the hotel room, packed for the flight home and rang Gill at least another three times, getting the answer phone each time.

When he got out of the shower he'd had another two missed calls from her and two voicemails.

He sent her a text telling her that he was just on his way out, he knew it was late there in London, and that he wouldn't be taking his mobile with him, as the temptation to call her in the night would be too much. 'My future career hangs on the balance of just how many arses I can kiss tonight.'

He told her he loved her, changed into his tuxedo and then left the room.

As he closed the door, the light from his mobile phone screen, briefly lit the room in a dim green.

The name of the caller displayed on the screen was Laura.

12.

THE NIGHT WAS a good one. John got a little bit drunker than he'd expected to. The cocktails were flowing almost as fast as the stories.

When he eventually got back to his room he kicked his shoes into the corner before flopping, drunkenly onto the bed. Sleep overtook him in seconds.

He was far too gone to even think about checking his mobile phone.

13.

HE AWOKE TO a low key, but irritating buzzing sound. As he lifted his head off the pillow to investigate the sound, the room began to move around, all on its own.

He cursed himself for not ordering some pizza or kebab, or something, before coming to bed, they would have minimised the odds of him not having this bastard of a hangover right now.

The buzzing stopped and his head dropped back onto the pillow like a dead weight. He was asleep again in mere seconds.

The buzzing came again, and again, and again.

'Oh, for fucks sake!' He shouted out in annoyance. He almost fell off the bed when he realised that the buzzing noise was his mobile phone ringing. His head was dizzy and pounding, and there was a deep nausea rising in his stomach. He snatched at the buzzing phone the moment it rang off.

Like a man who had lost his glasses he regarded the phone through one eye, trying his best to focus on what he was seeing.

It was a missed call from Laura. At first, he couldn't fathom the information he was seeing on his mobile screen, but then a realisation dawned on him, and it turned his stomach worse than the alcohol in his system was already doing. With his eyes now wide open, he looked and noticed that he had voicemail too, a lot of them.

There was a strange sensation of his stomach dropping. It made his legs buckle, and he dropped the phone on the thick carpet, before bursting towards the toilet.

He barely made it before a stomach full of stale alcohol and bile exited from his mouth.

When he finished, he pushed his sweaty head against the cool porcelain of the toilet. He knew this was disgusting and unsanitary, but right now he didn't care. He felt like death warmed up.

The buzzing of his mobile phone started again.

His eyes darted out of the bathroom door and saw the small illuminated device lying on the carpet. It looked accusingly up at him, asking him a million questions; why did you drop me? Why don't you answer me?

He dragged himself up from the floor and stumbled into the main room. As he bent over to pick the phone up, the room began to swim around him again. With one shaky hand, he held onto the wall to aid his effort at standing up. After a few seconds, he'd managed to control the dizzy spell and he looked at his, now silent, mobile phone.

He sat down, reasoning with himself that, if he was sat down, then the hangover couldn't make him fall down. Fumbling for the button to unlock the screen the phone squirmed out of his grip and onto the floor next to him. The greasy film of sweat lining his hands was making it difficult to hold onto it, as he picked it back up a thought occurred to him in his still drunken state.

Gill…

He was having something akin to a premonition, as he wondered what could be happening with Gill now.

With his hangover all but forgotten, he pressed the #1 key for his international voicemail, it costs a fortune but right now that didn't matter.

The screen read:

YOU HAVE THIRTEEN NEW MESSAGES, MESSAGE ONE SENT YESTERDAY AT OH-SEVEN-THIRTY-THREE

He pressed the button to retrieve the message. He didn't want to, but was compelled to do so anyway. After a moment or two of silence, Laura's voice filled the otherwise silent room.

'John, its Laura, you need to ring me as soon as you get this... it's about Gill.'

He looked at his phone. Right at this moment he had never hated an inanimate object more than this mobile phone. His face filled with agony and dread.

Why did she have to say, 'it's about Gill'? Why, why, WHY? He tapped her name into his phone.

Sweat was pouring from him now and the stench of desperation and alcohol emanating from his pores was knocking him sick again.

It rang twice before it was picked up. It seemed like the person on the other end was expecting his call

'John!' He was a little relieved that it was Mick's voice who answered, he didn't think he could handle talking to Laura right now.

That's not his usual tone, he's usually happy! John's anxiety was reaching a peak.

'Mick, I got Laura's calls, she said it was about Gill, is she there? Can I speak to her?'

'Yeah mate, just one second.'

The relief of the past minute or so fell from his shoulders. When Laura had left the message, and said that it was about Gill, for some reason he'd feared the worst, but now he was about to speak to her. He felt a little more relieved.

'Hello John!'

It was Laura, the anxiety was back.

'Hi Laura, can I speak to Gill please?'

There was a silence on the other end of the line, it was filled with all kinds of horrors and evils, every bad thing he could think of in life, and death, came at him through that void.

'John. She's, she's dead! John, Gill's dead…'

John had a moment of perfect clarity right then. He dropped the phone and it landed on the hotel room floor with a thump. He looked all around him and he could see everything in the room, everything in the minutest details. He could see the stitching in the hotel bed sheets, the dust on the headboard. He could determine every scuff in the leather of his good shoes that were lying, discarded in the corner of the room.

Gill's dead!

Gill's *dead*!!!

He woke up maybe two minutes later lying on floor, his mobile phone lying next to his head.

Was that the worst dream ever?

He put his hands over his eyes and rubbed them until he was seeing stars and strange colours on the back of his eyelids. He had an aching head and his stomach was feeling a little more than queasy. *I must have hit the cocktails with some force last night,* he thought with remorse. Then he noticed his mobile phone on the floor next to him.

As if on cue, it rang.

It was Laura 'Hu… Hello?'

Reality crashed back into his life as he recalled the conversation he had with his sister-in-law, seconds before his white out.

'John, it's Laura again.' Her voice was shrill, on edge, it was like she had to speak to him, to relay this message to pass the grief onto him, like a one-hundred-metre relay member passing on the baton. 'Gill… she was, was, *erm*…' another waver in her voice, John could hear someone in the background mumble something to her in a deep, man's voice. '...murdered it seems, sometime through the night.' Laura broke down then and there was some scuffling on the other end of the line.

'John, it's Mick again. I'm so sorry mate... If she'd have come to stay with us last night like we asked. She didn't even want Laura to stay over, said she had to make some lasagne, whatever that meant...'

These words slapped John in the face, and he winced as he heard them. The lasagne had been for him. It was for him, and their special night together when he got home.

With a steel in his voice that he never really felt he answered. 'Mick, I'm packing my stuff now and leaving, I don't know when I can get a flight but it'll be today, in a few hours. I'll ring you from the airport.'

He paused for a moment and realised there was a question that he'd neglected to ask. One that he didn't want to know the answer to, but he also had to know at the same time.

'Mick, how... how?'

'It might be best asking these kinds of questions when you are back here man.

'Mick, tell me...'

'I, err...'

'JUST FUCKING TELL ME... PLEASE!' He shouted down the phone, instantly regretting it, these people were Gill's family, they were suffering just as much as he was right now. 'I'm sorry Mick, but my wife's dead and I need to know how it happened.'

There was another pause, John could almost hear Mick's brain ticking away, trying to figure out some sort of answer to this question, something to put his mind at ease.

'It's bad John.' Mick failed at the putting him at ease mission. 'Someone... someone must have broken in, although there's no sign of a forced entry, or burglary, or anything for that matter.'

'Mick!' John commanded.

'She's had her stomach torn out John! Is that what you wanted to hear? Does it make you feel any better, eh? Knowing that?' Mick spoke so fast down the phone, that John was having trouble interpreting what he was saying.

'Oh shit, mate. I'm sorry, I can't even begin to think what's going through your head over there… just, just get home eh… and safely yeah?'

John hung up the phone and looked around at the hotel room. He wondered exactly where to begin.

14.

JOHN'S FLIGHT HOME was a blur. He was 'debriefed' on the situation by the police while he was still severely jetlagged. He was ushered into a hotel room as he wasn't allowed into his house as it was currently a crime scene. He was numb.

He couldn't even get angry, his whole body, his whole life felt like he'd been hit with a mother-load of novocaine. He was devoid of feeling from head to toe.

He didn't want to stay in a characterless hotel room, he wanted to be with his family, with Gill's family. He moved in with Mick and Laura for the two days, until he was allowed back into his… or their home. He didn't really want to, but they made him feel so welcome. Nevertheless, he felt like he was in their way, hampering their grieving process. Gill was Laura's sister, and they had been close.

Work had been brilliant, so flexible. Giving him all the time that he needed off, all the space he needed to heal. They told him not to worry about his position, his job would be waiting for him when he decided that it was time to jump back on the horse. They sent flowers and cards. Some of them even visited.

And now here he was. Wide awake at three-fifteen every morning, sitting in his bed, drinking warmed milk and thinking about Gill.

It was all he could do during these wee small hours, to just sit and wonder, pondering on what must have happened, here in this house, in this room. On this bed!

Why haven't I thought about moving out, or at least changing rooms? He thought, the rising panic attack was not that far away. *My wife, the woman I loved more than anything, the mother to my future babies! She was killed right here…*

This single thought was enough to start the tears for tonight. Each night it was something else. Tonight, it was the loss of future babies.

After a short while the tears abated and the wanderings of his ruined, broken, fragmented mind began again. Gill. She had been disembowelled on this bed, and here he was sleeping on the thing!

He jumped out of the bed and pulled the covers off, he then pulled the mattress off before flipped the whole bed over. He kicked the side, realising too late that he had no shoes on. The pain shooting through his whole body caused him to scream out loud.

'WHO? WHO, MOTHERFUCKERS?'

Sat on the floor, cradling his foot he raised his head to the ceiling and seethed, before rolling over onto his side, burying his head into the carpet, and slowly crawling into a foetal position. Once there, the tears began again.

The Twelve

Present Day

15.

JOHN AWOKE THE next morning, sprawled out on the floor in his messed-up bedroom. At some point, in the few hours of actual sleep he had gotten, he must have climbed out of bed and set up camp down here.

With very little motivation, he gave a half-hearted attempt at tidying up the house, but gave up after his first job, putting the bedding back on the bed. He was just about to fix the covers, when the futile nature of the task hit him hard. *What's the point?* He thought, *I'm only going to get back in it in a few more hours.*

He gave up on the room and decided to take his chances with a shower.

The water cascading down from above felt like a blessing on his body. For maybe a nanosecond he was able to forget everything that had happened in the last few weeks and lose his thoughts in the steam and hot spray.

Eventually he dragged himself out of the shower feeling refreshed. He reached out for the towel he had positioned on the rail, but had to pause as Gill's hair brush caught his eye. It was just sat there, on the shelf. It had sat there, unused since… He didn't want to go there, but as he saw the strands of her auburn hair intertwined around the bristles, everything came back at once.

He sat down in the shower and cried like a baby.

Once he had regained a semblance of control, he got up, grabbed the towel, and making sure he never looked at the brush, dried himself off out on the landing.

It was all he could do now to wallow about in his own self-pity. He wondered and marvelled at how fucked up his life seemed right about now.

He dressed and styled his hair after a fashion, before slowly descending the stairs. He had woken up, filled with every intention of going outside the house, to leave this stinking mausoleum filled with Gill's ghost, and interact with normal, flesh and blood people.

His hand shook as he reached out for the latch to the front door, and then faltered.

He closed his eyes; his fingers gripped at the metal latch, the muscles in his jaw were flexing and relaxing, then flexing and relaxing again. It was beginning to hurt him. A sweat had built up on his forehead and palms. 'Come on John.' He hissed through bared teeth. 'You can do this.'

He watched, almost from the objective point of view of a casual, third party observer, as his fingers, white from the pressure he was exerting on the small knob, turned the latch and the door opened.

The wind and fresh air on his face felt alien to him as he moved towards the open space. He felt like a character in a film, like it wasn't him walking outside, but the protagonist in some unrealistic TV drama.

He knew he'd done it when he felt the wind blow through his freshly washed hair.

The shop on the corner of the road was to be his desired destination. He thought that maybe he should buy a newspaper. He'd been out of circulation for so long now, and he had a thirst to know what was going on with the rest of the world. He avoided the tabloid newspapers like the plague, scum papers he called them. It took him a little more time than he thought it might, searching for a newspaper with actual news in it.

The Twelve

He picked one up and regarded the headlines, something about Afghanistan. *Yeah, something a million miles away from me*, he thought with a little relief.

He purchased the newspaper and, feeling a little better about himself, decided to go for a walk in the park. He could sit down on a bench, feel the sun in his face, and read his paper.

Bliss, he thought.

The main headlines were regarding several Americans killed in a shooting in a shopping mall. 'Tragedy!' The paper called it. It gave him musc to think about his own tragedy, before moving onto another story.

Apparently, Italy needed something like a squillion Euros to be bailed out of their economic crisis… blah, blah, blah!

It was all boring. Two weeks ago, it would have been big news to him but since then he'd had a tad of a paradigm shift, and only the little things seemed important to him. Little things like how Gill died, who killed her, why was she killed.

Just the little things!

He put the paper down and regarded the day around him. The sun was shining and the birds were singing, there were children playing around the park areas.

All of this bored him too!

He turned his attentions back to the paper, burying his nose into the real news, back there on page six, where the smaller, more important stories were situated.

A headline there instantly caught his eye. It read: JUDGE FOUND DEAD IN HIS CHAMBERS.

Intrigued, he continued reading.

> Judge Robert Cobham, 42, was found dead early yesterday morning in his chambers. The gruesome discovery was made when cleaners

entered The Royal Courts of Justice, The Strand, London.

'Fuck…' he shouted, catching the attentions of a passing elderly couple, 'Robert!'
Ignoring the disgusted looks from the older couple, he folded the newspaper under his arm and walked rapidly out of the park, heading back towards his home.
Suddenly, the day seemed very, very dark.
As he closed the front door behind him he leant back and rested his head against it. 'This is the last thing I need,' he spoke, but it was directed to no-one.
He had never been much of a drinker, especially during the day, but today he felt like he needed it. He went directly to the drinks cabinet and poured himself a glass of scotch, a large one, and drank it. As the liquor blazed a trail into his stomach, he took the bottle and poured himself another. He thought about it a little, and then poured another one in the glass. When the fireball in his stomach had finally burnt itself out, he sat down in his armchair and re-opened the paper at page six.
It was definitely Robert, the picture proved it. It was the same pic that he'd seen when he read the news that an old friend had finally earned his wig. He re-read the article many times, attempting to absorb it all.

> Judge Robert Cobham had been working late in his chambers, alone when he was viciously attacked.
> The coroner's statement read that the fatal attack had occurred somewhere between the hours of three and four am. There has been no comment if there were any obvious motive for the attack, but believe that it must have been a

targeted attack as there was no sign of break in, and nothing had been taken from the chambers. Speculation that it may have been a 'revenge' attack is rife, as Judge Cobham had sentenced on an organised crime sting three years earlier, when twelve members of a family gang had been incarcerated for lengthy stretches.
Currently, the Judge had been deliberating over a tax fraud case involving big business.
All sources are stating that there are currently no official suspects, there is no evidence on the scene and there were no CCTV cameras working in the courts at the time of the incident.
This is a tragic ending for a Judge with a bright future. He was weeks away from inauguration into The Old Bailey, a rare honour that is only bestowed onto the best in their particular field.

'Shit man, is this what's happening in the world?' He mused. He closed the newspaper feeling the familiar sting of tears back in his eyes.

16.

A FEW DAYS later, John was in his local pub with Mick. Although he thought of it as a local, he had only ever been in it on three occasions that he could think of. Mick however, was on first name terms with the bar staff and a good number of the patrons. Over the weeks since Gill's death it had become a habit to get out for a drink most nights, only down the local, but at least he was out of the house.

Once the body had been released from the forensics and the coroner, Gill's funeral had passed without incident.

To John, it seemed to have passed him by altogether, without him having to do much of anything. Laura had kicked into organisation overdrive, she had contacted the funeral parlour and selected the coffin, she had arranged the cars, the church and all the flowers. All he had to do was pass over his credit card. She hadn't wanted it at first, but he insisted. He'd told her to spare no expense. Gill was worth it. He bought a new suit, got a haircut and a shave, and signed a lot of papers.

Several old, mutual friends had shown up and he'd been glad of their support, but he'd noticed a certain omission. At first, he couldn't put his finger on what it was, and it began to niggle him.

Then it came to him. When it did, he wondered why it had taken him so long to notice what it was. The realisation that no-one from their circle of friends from back in their university days had turned up, or even sent a card, had begun to stir certain memories, things that he hadn't thought about in years.

He wasn't that bothered that none of them were there, but he did think it was bad form. He remembered them all being so close, well close to Gill at least. He had a feeling that he had always kind of been on the fringe of the group. He wished that he remembered why they had all stopped meeting up at the end of that last year. But right now, he paid it no mind. Now he had a local, and he had Mick.

He knew that going to the pub most nights had been Laura's doing. She must have forced Mick out each night. He knew this because, although they *did* like each other and they were very civil to each other, they just had absolutely nothing in common.

At first the nights out had been rather strained affairs. John had been sullen and reserved, and prone to an emotional outburst now and then. Mick had been, sort of wishing that he was anywhere else, with anyone else, and was slightly embarrassed regarding the said, emotional outbursts.

But over the weeks they had grown close and formed rather an 'odd couple' feel.

'But Mick, this is the strangest thing I've ever known. I've had some time and done a bit of research into it. Right, first there was Patrick Mahone, he was a civil engineer working on a nuclear new build project. He was found dead in a caravan a few weeks ago. His stomach was ripped open, completely disembowelled. The press said it must have been wild dogs or something because his caravan was out in the open, although there's no evidence to back that claim up. They also thought that he might have died at least a day or so before he was found.' John was talking fast. His enthusiasm evident as he gripped at his pint and leaned forward towards his friend.

He stopped, paused in his thought.

Mick rolled his eyes, expecting another emotional outburst of tears and wails, but he was pleasantly surprised when John continued.

'Then Gill,' he continued, 'and now Robert. Look, this Judge found in his chambers.' He spread the crumpled newspaper on the table in front of Mick, knocking his pint, it was all Mick could do to stop it from toppling. He looked down towards the article John was pointing at.

'It's my bet that his stomach was ripped out too, I just bet you!'

'Oh, come on now, you're jumping to conclusions here. Anyway, what is the connection with all this shit?'

He leaned in, his slightly drunken face looking around the room as he did, Mick couldn't fathom what he was looking for, but as it is a contagious activity, he found himself looking around too.

'We were all in the same year at university Mick.' John whispered conspiratorially. 'We were all friends. I met Gill through these exact same people.'

Mick took a second to process the information he had just received, but he still came up a little lost in the conversation. 'OK, so that's a bit odd, but there is such a thing as coincidence you know?'

John shook his head and reached back for the newspaper on the table. *I'd love to live in your world,* he thought as he folded it away. *Everything so black and white, read The Sun and The Star, watch Sky News and Sky Sports, blissfully unaware of anything out of the scope of what the mass media wants you to think.* He felt a bit mean thinking all of this about his friend and brother-in-law, but as he thought about it, he realised that he was serious. He would *LOVE* to live in that world.

'So, we having another then?' Mick asked.

'Is that rhetorical?' John replied.

The Twelve

'Re what? Is that draft or out of a bottle?' Mick lifted his eyebrows and flashed him a wry smile of his own.

John couldn't help but laugh as his friend walked towards the bar. He nodded, he knew that Mick was one of the good guys. He had a genuine smile on his face now, it was probably the first honest one he'd pulled in weeks.

17.

ARRIVING BACK HOME John was a little worse for wear, he let himself in before turning to wave to Mick who lived just a few streets further down. He waved back, stumbled a little and then staggered on.

He was genuinely laughing as he stepped into the house. No sooner had he closed the front door than a wall of freezing cold air hit him. He shivered and grasped his hands together to get a bit of warm into them.

His breath was pluming in the air as he breathed, absently wondering why it was so cold inside as it was rather mild outside. He opened the fridge and took out a piece of cheese and some leftover cake from, sometime or other that he couldn't quite remember. Grabbing some dirty plates from the side of the sink, he wiped the crumbs off them onto the floor instead of into the full bin under the counter that had been their intended destination. Content with his feast he retired into living room. He placed the plate precariously on the arm of his chair, and then went back into the kitchen to grab himself a beer from the other fridge.

The cold was gripping. It felt like a snowy winter's day when he would rush out to play in the glorious white powder without putting gloves and a coat on first, before realising that snow was nothing like how it is depicted on TV. Totally freezing, wet and rather miserable. That was how he was feeling right now. As he walked past he happened to gaze, through one, half sober, eye at the thermometer on the wall. What he saw made him stop and really look at it. If it was working correctly and the reading was right, then it should have been a nice and toasty twenty-five degrees in here, it felt like it was about two or maybe even three degrees.

He tapped it with his beer bottle and looked again to see if that had made it work correctly. It hadn't.

'Ah fuck it. I'll look at it in the morning,' he slurred to himself as he opened his beer and gave himself, and the thermometer, a big 'Cheers!'

He took a long slug out of the brown beer bottle, hiccupped, and followed it with a loud belch.

'Fucking bastards...' he said out loud, taking a moment to marvel at the cold air steaming from his mouth. 'Bastards the lot of them,' he continued. 'Well, you know what? Fuck them, they missed out! Not one fucking bastard turned up.' He held his beer bottle in the air and looked up towards the ceiling. 'Well I loved you Gill, I was there. It's the people that are there in the end that count, isn't it? I don't care about university, you'll always be my Gill...'

He slumped down into his chair and put the cheese and the cake on his lap. He fumbled around underneath himself for the ever-elusive remote control. After a few seconds of fruitless searching he gave up, took another swig out of his bottle and then proceeded to take a large bite out of the cheese. *Food of the Gods...*

'...Even though I wasn't quite there at the end was I?' He asked, taking another, long swig out of the brown bottle.

He fell asleep in the chair, blissfully unaware when his beer slipped from his hand and spilled down the arm of the couch and all over his crotch. He didn't notice when the lump of cheese on the plate was knocked onto the floor and into a bowl of half eaten, almost solidified, beans from last week. The cake slipping off the arm of the chair and nestling between his legs, was not registered either.

But most of all, he didn't know that there was a silhouette stood, watching him in the doorway of the living room. A shadow that was dark, menacing and slight.

John never even flinched as the grey, cold, colourless hand reached out from the shadows and caressed his hair.

The Twelve

Redford University, South London.
20 years earlier.

18.

THEY HAD BEEN the popular ones in university. The one's who had been brought up with money and privileged backgrounds. All of them learning early that they could basically slope their way through university, spending daddy's money, and still walk away with top jobs all thanks to their 'family connections'.

All twelve of them. Well, eleven, until John turned up.

He didn't really fit in with their paradigm, and on hindsight, he could honestly say that he never really liked them either, any of them. Well, not all of them, there was only ever one of them that he could honestly say he loved.

Gill.

She was beautiful, gorgeous even, and she knew it. She had long auburn hair that she would wear free hanging most of the time. It had a natural loose curl to it and would bounce when she walked. Her face was a delight to behold. High cheekbones and a perfect, ski-slope nose with light freckles across it, in perfect opposition to her pale skin. Of all her features, it was her stunning, deep green eyes that stood out in any situation. She knew she was beautiful and she would always use it to the best of her abilities.

When John first met them, Gill was Carl Brookes' girlfriend.

Carl was a big man. His wide shoulders were heavily muscled and his thick arms were perfectly in scale to the rest of his body. If they had been in College in America, he would be referred to as a jock, but a clever one. He was studying Sports Science. Although he played rugby for the University, and played football, he dreamed of one day becoming a professional football manager.

John was a little intimidated by him.

Regardless of her behemoth of a boyfriend, John, the nerd, fell head over heels in love with Gill. It was pretty much love at first sight.

Chemistry class just wasn't doing it for him, and even to this day he never quite understood why he took that class in the first place. He submitted a request and was transferred into the Business Law class late on in the semester. Due to John's impeccable academic record, the head tutor was confident that he would be able to catch up on the few weeks he'd missed.

The lecture theatre was vast, almost the size of a stadium. John had daydreams of standing at the front, playing guitar and singing into a microphone. The fact that he was a lousy singer and he didn't know the difference between a G cord and an A, never deterred him from his fantasy. Today it was busy. There were a lot more students on this course than in chemistry, and to John's delight, there were also a lot more girls.   He was happy keeping himself to himself as he didn't really know anyone yet, so he sat towards the back of the room. He knew the theatre was empty for the next period, so he was planning on staying behind to play a little catch-up on his notes.

Lost in a world of business methodologies, he didn't even notice when a stunning green eyed and auburn haired beauty idled up to him, from out of nowhere, and introduced herself.

'Hi, I'm Gill and you know what? I think I'm going to partner up with you this semester!' She announced.

The Twelve

John looked up from his books, surprised a little at the intrusion, and instantly fell deep into the bright green pools that where her eyes. He could feel his face flush and knew that it was turning a bright red. He was always a terrible blusher.

'Ahem, eh.... OK,' he stuttered, instantly chastising himself for not thinking of something funnier to say.

The Goddess leaned in and whispered something to him that he would remember, verbatim, for the rest of his life.

'I'll sleep with you if you do all my homework, but I have to get at least a 2:1! Deal?'

She was smiling at him, his interest piquing at the 'sleeping with you' part,

His blush had reached a whole new record level. He thought that his skin just might end up peeling off his face if he continued to burn this bad. He felt a little swoony as, seemingly all the blood in his entire body had rushed to colour his face.

'I.... erm. OK. It's a deal.'

He couldn't believe he'd just exchanged witty banter with the hottest girl he'd seen since, well, since forever.

Gill began to laugh a genuine laugh, as she did she rifled her hand through his thick mop of hair. His skin tingled at her touch, but he had the feeling that to her it was like rewarding a brand-new puppy.

'I was just joking...' she said, breaking his heart.

She paused for a second or two and tilted her head, looking at him. He really didn't have a clue what to do in this situation, he was totally lost. 'But I don't know,' she said giving him the cutest lopsided grin he'd ever seen in his life. This grin was also something of hers he would take to his grave with him. 'With you, I might just consider it.'

She scuffed his head once more, *petting me,* he thought quite cynically, and then she walked off, down the stairs towards a gang of about ten others at the bottom of the lecture room.

He was in shock as he watched her go. 'Oh fuck, I'd consider it too,' he said, shaking his head.

Her tight backside wiggled seductively in the long figure hugging green woollen dress she was wearing. A pang of jealousy ripped through him as he watched her wrap her arms around the biggest male in the group, his heart broke for a second time as she planted a kiss on his cheek.

As the group walked away she turned up towards him in the seats, smiled and offered him a small wave.

The Twelve

Present day

19.

THE COUNTRY ROAD was dark, there were no street lights on these roads. The rain that had recently stopped, was threatening to pour down once again. This, along with how warm the weather had been today, made the surface rather slick.

The expensive white car was driving along this road far too fast for the conditions. The large man in the driver's seat was looking worried. His knuckles were white as he gripped the steering wheel taking another tight corner just a little too wide.

As he was driving, he was taking furtive glances into his rear-view mirror. It wasn't the dark road behind him he was looking at, it was the back seat. He caught a glimpse of his own eyes in the mirror and questioned himself for a moment on whether they were even his. They looked scared, crazed, wide open. His pupils were dilated, and the whites of them were a deep pink. They were the eyes of someone who was easily scared, he was not easily scared.

The car's tyres screamed as they rounded yet another tight bend, squealing against the wet asphalt. He was fighting a losing battle to keep a grip on the wet road.

Without any warning the power assist for the steering wheel went light, way too light. His eyes tore away from the rear-view mirror and now fixed onto the road ahead. He had always been taught to turn into a skid, but doing that now felt completely alien to him. He attempted to counter the skid, and only succeeded in making it worse.

'WHAT THE FUCK!!!!' He screamed as the white BMW turned a one-hundred-and-eighty degree turn on the narrow road, screeching to a halt facing the wrong way on the dark dual lane bypass.

He looked out of the window and saw nothing but dark wet trees outside. The car had skidded and had hit a shallow divot at the side of the road, bounced off the hedge running along the side of it and stalled. Fortunately, it was late, and these roads were seldom travelled at this hour.

Not yet acknowledging how lucky he was to still be alive, he lashed out a powerful strike from his big hands to the centre of the steering wheel. The horn blurred and the loud noise scared him a little.

With a shaking, cold hand he reached down, searching for the ignition key. He found it and turned it, pumping the accelerator as he did. The powerful German engine turned over first time. Revving heavily, he steered the car out of the ditch and corrected its position, pulling over into a layby.

As he mopped the sweat that had built up on his forehead with the back of his sleeve, he closed his eyes, taking a few seconds to compose himself. Once his heartbeat was back to something that resembled normal, he opened his eyes, fully intending to pull out of the layby and get home as fast as he could.

Not for the first time he caught a rank smell coming from somewhere within the car. The stink was like rotting meat. He had never actually been in one, but he guessed that it was what an abattoir smelt like, after it had been closed for five years. He pulled a handkerchief from the inside pocket of his jacket and held it to his nose. It was all he could do to block out the stench, and stop his stomach from turning.

The Twelve

He was shaking, rather badly. He didn't know if it was from his near accident, or from what had spooked him so bad in the back seat.

With the handkerchief still attached to his face he began to fiddle with the controls on the dashboard. Even though he knew it would make the stink even worse, he needed to get some heat into the main body of the car. It felt like the temperature had dropped maybe fifteen degrees. Steam was coming from his mouth through the handkerchief and his fingers. With his free hand, he reached into his other inside pocket and pulled out a small metal flask. Struggling to remove the lid, a large splash of the sweet, but strong smelling alcohol spilled out, all over his suit. Ignoring this, with a shaking hand, he raised the flask to his lips underneath the handkerchief, and took a large sip.

Why is it so cold? He thought as the fire from the drink blazed its trail down every tube leading into his belly. It offered temporary, but false warmth down there which he welcomed very much. He grabbed his coat from the passenger side seat and wrapped it over his large frame, pulling the collars up to his ears to combat the intense cold.

His breathing was laboured and large plumes of whiskey smelling steam were escaping from his mouth. He welcomed the smell, as it nearly, but not quite, masked the rotting meat stink. Once again, he looked at the controls on his dashboard and shook his head. The air con wasn't on; he just couldn't fathom why it was so cold.

Closing his eyes, he took several deep breaths, attempting to pull himself together. After a short while he checked both his wing mirrors, before indicating and pulling out of the layby.

Finally, he spared a glance into the rear-view mirror to see if the road was clear.

What he saw there chilled him to the bone. His knee jerk reaction caused him to slam on the brakes and the car skidded to a halt once again.

It was dark, its eyes were shining with a strange silver glow, and it looked... somehow familiar.

He blinked his eyes to rid himself of this hallucination, but when he looked back, the silhouette was still there. Feeling terrified, but rather silly at the same time, he turned to get a better look at what he thought was in the back seat. That was when the first sharp shooting pain ran up his left arm, leaving a tingling, numbing sensation in its wake. 'Oh shit!' He managed to wheeze as breath was suddenly in short supply in his chest.

'Who are you? How did you get into this car?' He gasped towards the thing in the back seat. 'Leave me the fuck alone. Get out! LEAVE ME ALONE!!!'

He didn't know if the cold in the car had become more intense, or if it was the knowledge of what was currently happening to him, making him think it was colder, but a shudder rippled through his large frame nevertheless.

Then the idling engine died with a splutter. Still gripping his arm, the driver turned back to face the road. Turning away from the unfathomable horror that was waiting for him in the back seat was difficult, but necessary. He grabbed at the dangling keys, trying desperately to start the engine up again. Nothing happened. His bulging eyes, wet with tears and sweat, regarded the illuminated dashboard before him, where the battery and the oil light was flashing red and green. The battery was as dead as a doornail.

The intense cold inside the car had caused ice veins to form on the insides of the windows. The driver turned once more to look in the back, as he did another pain whipped up his arm travelling rapidly towards his

The Twelve

neck. He took in a slow, shaky breath and allowed it to leave his body in fits and starts.

The figure was still there, and it was still looking at him with its strange, glowing eyes. 'What do you want with me?' He whispered, it was all he could managed as he hugged his stricken arm closer in to his pained chest.

A sound like a wild wind began to whip around inside the car. It began in the back seat and travelled back and forth. The rush of the wind and the blood pumping in his ears were the only things he could hear in the whole world.

That was until the wind began to whisper to him; they spoke one word. '*MUCH!*'

The big man was crying now, real tears ran down his cheeks. It was a strange sensation to him as he didn't think he'd cried since he was a baby. With a rising panic, brought about by the tears, the pains, and the fucking dead thing in the back seat, he began to rip at the handles in the doors, frantically trying to open them. He needed to escape the cold, the smell, the total madness; but mostly to escape the horrible shadow waiting for him.

The door wouldn't budge, he prodded the buttons for the electric windows, not remembering that there was no power, the engine had died taking all the electronics with it. *Everything except that fucking air conditioning*, he shouted in his head. It had gotten colder now, much colder.

The windows were opaque with thickening sheets of ice. His eyes regarded the fogged up rear view mirror and it took him a second or two to register that it was his own face looking back at him. His skin was deathly white and his eyes were petrified.

The eyes roamed away from his own pallor and dared another glance into the back seat.

To his dismay, the figure was still there. It was sitting as still as a garden statue, and was looking right at him. Even though he couldn't see its face, he instinctively knew that it was mocking him, playing with him, much like a cat plays with a mouse prior to getting bored and delivering the fatal blow.

The silvery eyes from the dark recesses of the dirty hooded top, stared up at him. A pang of recognition stirred within him, scaring him more than ever. The terror coursing through the big man's body was becoming far too much to bear for his weakening heart. A dull, sickly ache began to throb in his chest.

'I want much...' The ghostly vision spoke again, this time it didn't come from the wind, it came directly from the figure. 'I want what is mine...'

The whisper paused for a second before continuing.

'*Thiiiiiiirrrrrrrrteeeeeeeeeeeeen!!!*'

Although it was still a whisper, it was more akin to a shout in the big man's head. As the words floated through him, they seemed to stem the flow to his heart... as it gave way. The pain wrought new channels through his body as it intensified. His sweaty hands clutched at his chest.

His bowels opened in his trousers, it was a most unpleasant feeling and it added quite distinctly to the already extremely vicious smell within the car's interior.

'Is... Is this why you've been stalking me? All that... now I'm here, now I'm not shit!' He stammered, embarrassed that his voice was coming out as a whimper instead of the normally commanding tone he carried, and he was embarrassed by the wet uncomfortable feeling in his trousers. 'I... don't have... anything of yours. I... don't even know... who you are.'

Black rings had begun to form around the hollows of his eyes now, the eyes themselves had begun to gloss over.

The Twelve

'You do have something of mine, you carry it with you, and I want it back!' The scratchy whisper came like a portent of doom to him, heavy and ominous.

Slowly, the silhouette advanced. He took the time to notice that it didn't so much move, as it glided towards him, almost unearthly. A face formed in the shadow beneath the hooded top. It was only the hint of a face to begin with, shadows below the hood. But as it drew nearer the man began to make out the features, hair, eyes, nose, and something else, something resembling a mouth, but was more like a hole straight to hell.

Oh, my GOD, that mouth! He thought as another shot of red hot pain ripped through his chest and arms.

The driver's last ever word in this world echoed, unheard by another living soul, around the interior of his expensive car. He screamed it over and over and over...

'YOU... YOU... YOU... YOU?'

The car rocked, violently.

'YOU?'

A horrific, gurgling, incoherent shout was followed closely, by a terrifying scream of intense pain.

'Y...y...you?' The man's voice was weaker now, almost as if he had lost all hope, almost as if he was fading away. A flash of dark, thick fluid spattered across the windows on the inside of the car. As the fluid was warm, it began to melt the ice sheets that had formed on them. Another, shorter bout of violence rocked the car, and there was suddenly silence as it stood, perfectly still.

The clock on the dashboard turned to read three-fifteen am.

20.

JOHN AWOKE IN his living room. He was wet, sticky, hung-over, and hungry all at the same time. Something uncomfortable was digging into his back. He reached around, rummaging behind him, eventually pulling out the bottle of beer from between him and chair. With blurred eyes he gazed at it, then he looked at the stale cake that was squashed into his clothes, and the dried-up cheese sitting in the mouldy sauce of the week-old beans on the floor next to him. It was at this precise moment that the futility of his existence came crashing down around him. That the nausea caused by his dehydration, excessive alcohol, and poor choice of late night snacks, began to rise.

He only just made it to the bathroom before he was sick.

Sat on the floor, his thoughts turned to just how clean the filthy looking and foul smelling porcelain bowl that he had his face pressed against, really was.

'Is this it? This must be it. Rock bottom. I need to sort myself out, this is disgusting. I need to pick myself up and run with the ball again,' he whispered as his face cooled against the yellowing bowl.

An hour and a half later, and after much procrastination, he was showered and stood in his hallway with his phone to his ear.

'Hi, yes this is John Rydell... Yes, John... Oh thanks for your kind words... Yeah it has been, it really has. Well I'm ringing to let you know that I think it's time I came back to work... Yeah, I've been on special leave...

The Twelve

No... no, I think it's the right time... I was thinking maybe Monday? Yes, this Monday coming... Ah, oh right... Sorry. I've been so out of it for a bit. Bank Holiday eh? Yeah, well let's make it Tuesday then... Yeah, I'll bring them with me... Line Manager, check... Great... yeah, I honestly do think it's time... Thank you, eh Julie... goodbye, bye now!'

With the stress of the HR Department phone call done, pangs of hunger began to rip through his stomach. He made his way into the kitchen and caught himself whistling a little tune. This made him smile. Well, almost.

He made himself a bowl of instant noodles, then, after cleaning up the mess from last night, on and around his chair, he sat down and turned on the television.

Daytime TV was no real inspiration, it was an unending spiral of negativity and desperation. So, he continued flicking through the multitude of channels filled with similar rubbish on his subscription package before, finally catching a channel with the news.

As he slurped down the last of the noodles in the bowl it heralded the end of the news program he was watching. It finished on a funny story about a cat that had made its way onto a football pitch, gotten hit by the ball, and deflected it into the back of the net... 'Purr-fect goal!' The newscaster quipped.

The national news then turned into the local news for his area.

A serious looking, middle-aged man came onto his screen with a graphic of the London area behind him. He smiled a grim smile towards the camera before launching himself into the local news.

'The body of a man, discovered in his car this morning on the Edmonton Bypass has been identified as that of Carl Brookes. Mr Brookes was the manager of first division football side Leyton Orient. He was discovered in the early hours of this morning by a local farmer...'

A picture of a large white BMW car parked haphazardly on a country road, the car was surrounded by yellow police tape, replaced the London graphic.

'The police have not released any details of how the man died, or if they have ruled out foul play.'

The news then moved onto other things…

John was as still as a statue, the noodles that he had been slurping from the bowl had begun to fall over his face as he regarded the TV screen, his mouth agape in shock.

'Carl Brookes… Manager of Leyton Orient?' He asked the TV screen. 'Is that him?'

Putting down the bowl of noodles and wiping the residue from his mouth, he reached for his mobile phone. It was only when he tried to grab the damned thing that he realised his hands, and his whole body was shaking. He punched in Mick's number and it was answered on the fourth ring. 'Mick, I… Oh, Sorry Laura, is Mick there? I really need to speak to him… Thanks.'

He waited for a few moments as the phone was passed over to Mick.

'Hello…' Mick sounded almost cheery on the other end of the line.

'Mick, have you seen the news? Carl Brookes is dead!'

'Who?'

'Carl Brookes, the manager of Leyton Orient.'

'Oh, right. That's, erm, tragic isn't it.'

'Mick, he was another one that Gill and I went to university with. Gill used to go out with him before we hooked up. This is what I was telling you about last night. I'm not being paranoid Mick, it's just *too* much of a coincidence.'

Mick was silent for a few seconds. John could hear something playing on the TV in the background, it was the only indication that the line hadn't dropped.

The Twelve

Eventually he spoke up. 'Hmm, maybe there is something there after all. But what could it be? Why would anyone want to kill off your friends?''

'I don't know man.'

'Think we should meet up later and talk about it?'

'OK, yeah, that sounds like a plan. What time were you thinking?'

They made their plans to meet up in the local pub before saying their goodbyes. As John hung up he felt cold, almost instantly cold. The temperature in the room must have dropped at least ten degrees. As he exhaled he could see his breath before him, again. He remembered doing the same thing last night when he got home from the pub.

Shivering, he stood up and looked out of the window onto the street. The people walking past the house were wearing loose summer clothing. The sun was out and it looked like a gloriously beautiful summer day, but inside his house the light had almost gone, casting gloom throughout the room.

A bang from upstairs made him jump, it sounded like something had fallen off a wall.

With his heart thumping in his throat, he turned around sharpish and looked towards the stairs. He made his way, gingerly, out of the kitchen towards the stairwell, his hackles were up, and if the goose-bumps on his arms hadn't been caused by the temperature drop, then they would have been caused by the feeling of dread that suddenly enveloped him. The stairway was, for some unexplained reason, for the time of day and the number of windows around them, very dark. As he approached he glanced up towards where the noise had come from, he found himself holding his breath but didn't know why.

'Hello?' He shouted up into the gloom.

There was no answer.

He put his hand on the banister and began a tentative ascent. The darkness on the landing was closing in on him, it felt like all the daylight was being sucked out of the house, turning it into night, smothering all the joy out of the day.

And the cold! The stairs were even colder than the living room.

His heart was beating ten times faster than normal; he could feel the rhythmic pulse in his ears as he got to the top of the stairs. Every instinct in him screamed to give this endeavour up. It was the script to every single horror movie he had ever seen. He was heading towards the danger, towards the axe-wielding, murdering mutant hiding in his bedroom, as opposed to getting as far away from it as he could.

He was scared, but he couldn't put his finger on what of, exactly. All he could think of were the deaths of his three friends, and, of course, his wife.

In this house. He finished for himself, rather wishing that he hadn't.

There was another noise, this time he was confident that it come from his bedroom. *Our bedroom*, he corrected himself.

There was somebody in there, he could hear them routing around inside. His fear was abating as anger began to take over.

'Hello! Hello! Is there anyone there?'

There was still no answer.

Even though he was terrified beyond belief, his anger had built up, instilling in him at least a small amount of courage. He half shouted, half whispered, 'Look if there's someone there, I'm unarmed, there's very little of value in the house, so please just leave and we'll say no more about it. Deal?'

The Twelve

The adrenaline coursing through his body, mixed with the cold, the fear, and the anger, was making him shake almost uncontrollably.

'WHOEVER YOU ARE, GET THE FUCK OUT OF MY HOUSE!!!'

Later, when he reflected about what he was just about to do, he couldn't believe that it was him. He had never been a confrontational person, but the unexpected rage that was building up inside propelled him forwards, into the room to blindly confront whoever was there.

To his relief and surprise, the room was empty. Empty except for the stink.

The smell was overpowering and it caused him to back out of the room, holding his nose, trying to stop the threatening vomit from making an appearance. Then, as instantly as it appeared, it disappeared.

Confused, he made his way over to the bed searching all around the room for the source of the noises and the smell. He reached out his hand and touched the bedcovers. It was so cold in the room that the duvet crackled under his touch.

There was a movement in his peripheral vision, it was something dark and big. He whirled around, fuelled by pure adrenalin. In his mind's eye he saw a youth, an intruder coming at him, maybe with a knife, a large dirty, blood stained knife. Perhaps even the very same knife that killed Gill.

There was nobody there.

There was *something* there though.

On the floor, before the wardrobe, lying on its front was a metal picture frame. He bent over and picked it up, a sharp intake of breath and a wince ensued as the cold metal of the frame bit into the skin on his fingers. He nearly dropped it as it was so cold, and in his juggling, he flipped the frame over. What he saw gave him a small jolt of surprise.

It was a group photo. All the old gang from university were on it. A bolt of nostalgia ripped through him as the memory of when this photo was taken, suddenly came back to him.

It was the last week of their fresher year. All twelve of them were present.

Gill was centre of the picture with her arms wrapped around Carl Brookes and Brenda Osman. John was off to the left standing next to Patrick Mahone and Lynda Witherspoon (they all called her Lynda Withawhy, as she always announced herself as Lynda, with a y). All the others were there too. Ben Lomax, Debbie Baines, Tony Corliss, Nicky McEvoy and Jenny Weaver…

Good times, he thought as he sat down on the crunchy bed to study the old photo.

An unprecedented rage built up inside him, and he readied himself to throw the picture frame onto the floor or against the wall and forget all about it, when something caught his eye, making him look a little closer at the actual photograph.

It was a grainy colour group shot, some of them were pulling funny faces, and others were just looking straight into the camera. But four out of The Twelve faces on the picture were blurred out.

His eyes were automatically drawn to Gill. He could tell that she was pulling a goofy face, but her features were mostly blurred, they were all out of focus. Carl was next to her looking right into the shot, John could tell he was smiling, but he couldn't see it properly. He looked for Robert's face and saw that his too was blurred out, as was the fourth, Patrick Mahone's. All of this was far too much of a coincidence for it to *be* a coincidence.

As if he was suddenly repulsed by holding the frame, he threw it onto the bed, rubbing his hands together as if to get the feel, or the filth of the frame off

The Twelve

him. He quickly made his way back downstairs. All fear of an intruder, burglar or murderer, completely forgotten.

Absently noticing that the house had become somewhat warmer again, he decided that he needed to get out, to go for a walk or to the pub, anything to distance himself from that photograph.

Redford University, South London
20 years earlier

21.

JOHN WAS SAT in a boring business economics lecture; he'd been off ill the week before so, once again he had a fair bit of catching up to do if he wasn't going to fall behind too far. The first year was coming to an end, and even though the marks for this year didn't really count towards the final grade, he didn't want any tardiness leaking into his study. The lecture was wrapping up and the very poor showing of students who'd even bothered to turn up were all looking bored out of their heads. John had planned to stay behind after the class hoping to catch up on his missed notes.

That was when he noticed that Gill Castle had turned up for this lecture. Even though he hadn't seen her for a while, she had never been far from his thoughts. He felt like he did back at school every time Nicola Johnston had walked past, with the same adolescent squirm in the pit of his stomach. She was sat with the big guy she was dating, John assumed he was her boyfriend. There were a couple of others sat with them too.

Oh, you lucky bastard, he thought, shaking his head as he rummaged through his bag with an absent mind. He noted that none of the group had even made one note during the whole lecture; they never even had their books out.

'So, next week we'll be looking at 'preferences for risk', why our economy thrives on risk, and who takes the fall when the risks go bad…' The lecturer at the front

The Twelve

of the hall was addressing the class, concluding his lesson, fighting the good fight, but ultimately losing.

Everyone was already packing their bags in preparation to leave. Everyone except John.

As the attendees began to file out Gill and Carl spotted him in the thinned-out crowd. He noticed, but pretended not to see them. Out of the corner of his eye he watched them wave goodbye to their other friends and then make their way over towards him. Both had huge grins on their faces as if they were sharing a joke, or a secret.

'John, isn't it?' The big lad offered his huge, shovel of a hand out to him, John accepted and was rewarded with the most powerful handshake, and painful hand crush he'd ever experienced.

'I heard a rumour that you want to sleep with my girlfriend.' He said this as he looked John straight in the face. His own face still smiling that same smile.

John felt his skin burn crimson and adrenaline build up in his body, this person intimidated him, and he thought that he knew it too.

'I…. erm… I…' he began to stutter as he tried to think of something of a fitting reply. His eyes flittered over towards Gill for some help, but she was fixing him with a stern stare from her gorgeous green eyes.

The big man, finally laughed out loud and slapped John on the shoulder so hard that he was physically moved about six inches to the left.

'Don't worry about it, everyone wants to sleep with her, even the girls,' he quipped.

Gill was laughing now as she looked over at him; she tipped him a sly wink and an almost secret smile.

He felt his face bloom once again.

'Anyway, I'm Carl, Carl Brookes. I'm studying sports science but I have to take electives, so lucky me, economics is one of them. The problem I've got is that I haven't got a fucking clue what they're talking about. I don't know what I'm going to do my coursework on and the course is almost over. I was wondering if you could help me with that. You know, just get me on the right track. I'd pay you…'

'I don't know about that Carl, I'm scraping by this course as it is,' he lied.

'I'll show you some naked photos of Gill here.'

'OK, I'll do it!' John, replied almost instantly, laughing at his own joke, but he could feel himself blushing again as he glanced over at Gill again.

Both Carl and Gill roared with laughter. 'I didn't think it would be *that* easy…' Carl scoffed.

Gill shook her head but was still smiling. 'You boys are all the same.' She turned her attention to John. 'Hey, listen, a few of us are going to the Cooler for lunch. You fancy coming and meeting some of the gang?' She asked him. 'Think of it as a liquid lunch'

The smile she offered him was too enticing to refuse and he wondered, absently, just how much blood could rush to a person's head before it blew, as he set off on another blushing safari.

'Eh… yeah OK then, that sounds great. What time?'

'About half past one.' Carl replied kissing Gill on the forehead. 'Baby, I got to run, I'll see you two in the Cooler, yeah?'

'Yeah…' they both replied in unison.

'Great!'

Carl hurried off to an unknown and un-offered destination leaving John and Gill alone in the lecture theatre. John was feeling uncomfortable alone with such a gorgeous girl. He looked at her, she was twirling her hair and looking away from him. He knew that he needed to say something, but he'd never ever been any good in situations like this before.

'So, am I really going to get to see naked pictures of you?'

Inside he was cringing, fuming with himself. His innards were all folding in on themselves. He felt stupid beyond belief and like the biggest pervert and letch that Redford University had ever produced. He could not believe what had just come out of his mouth.

She looked at him and laughed out loud, maybe it was shock, or maybe she was laughing at how pathetic and desperate he sounded. But nothing could have prepared him for what happened next. She hooked her arm in his, and flashed him a cheeky, sexy smile.

'Maybe...! Who knows, you might even get to see the real thing!' She leaned in and gave him a little kiss on his cheek. 'See you in the Cooler.'

He needed to sit down. The pure volume of blood that rushed to his head at that precise moment, was enough to cause an imminent haemorrhage.

'Eh... yeah, half one,' he stammered.

She turned away from him and opened the door to the lecture theatre. Just before she stepped out, she turned back and gave him a little wave and a smile, breaking his already fragile heart.

He sat down at his seat with a flop, and attempted to continue to study. It was a futile attempt, and he knew it. He was done studying for the day, his mind and indeed his loins, were now pondering exclusively on other things, or more precisely one other thing.

Packing up his books he made his way across the campus to the Cooler bar, stopping first at a cash machine as he did. He couldn't get the idea of Gill offering to let him see the real thing out of his head. Was she toying with him, to get him to do hers and Carl's coursework for them, or did she genuinely like him? Either way, Carl was huge and intimidating, so he thought it better to just keep his mouth firmly shut and see how this all panned out.

The Cooler was the name of the student union bar on campus. It was dark and a little dank inside, but that was how they liked it in there. He'd frequented it a few times before with some friends from his computer sciences classes. He ordered himself a plate of sausages, mash and gravy. If it was going to be a liquid lunch, then he thought it would be prudent to get something of substance inside him before the drinking began.

Carrying his tray of food he found a table to sit at. As he did, he heard a familiar voice from behind him talking loudly, and obnoxiously into an expensive mobile phone.

'Yeah, number twelve... Sorted. Yup, bit of a geek type... Clever though... I'm going to get him to do some coursework for me... Hah, yeah might as well get something useful out of him. I think he's hooked on Gill, so ditto about her as well eh?' The loud voice laughed out loud at this last point.

John sat down with his back to whoever it was. As he did, he casually turned around to see who the owner of the voice was. Carl was sat at a table the in the corner of the room, the large and clunky looking mobile phone to his ear, he was making sure that everyone in the room could see the fact that he owned one of the expensive new-fangled devices. John didn't think he'd noticed that he was there, and by the nature of the conversation, he assumed that it was about him. *Number twelve?* He thought. *What the fuck does that mean?*

'Hang on, Tony... I'm here with Debbie now... Hah, yeah well, you know Debbie!'

John looked around the gloomily lit bar, there were several other people dotted around the room, but he couldn't see anyone else in there who could have been with him.

'Oh, yeah!' Carl suddenly shouted out loud. 'Oh, FUCK yeah!!!' He shouted again, banging loudly and

The Twelve

heavily on the table. After a few seconds, he spoke again sounding a little out of breath. 'I'm sorry Tony; you didn't need to hear that then.'

Why not, everyone else in here did. John thought as he turned back around towards his lunch.

'Sorry man, I'm finished here now, here she comes... or was that me?' He laughed out loud again.

John turned back around towards Carl's table and saw something he never expected to see, ever.

A small, petite girl crawled out from under the table. She had short blonde hair in a bob cut, and a very pretty, almost beautiful face. She was smiling and wiping her mouth as she got out from underneath the table and sat next to Carl. John couldn't believe what he'd just seen. The girl then leaned into Carl and gave him a kiss on his cheek.

'See you in about an hour,' she said and then walked off, passing John's table as she did. She was still wiping her mouth.

'Oh yeah... Fuck man, she knows how to use her mouth that one. Anyways, getting back to number twelve...' Carl continued on the phone.

Suddenly, John didn't have much of an appetite for his sausage and mash, and he certainly didn't want to meet up with these people later either. He was no prude, not by a long shot, but what he had just witnessed knocked him sick. With a disgusted look on his face he pushed the thick sausage and white creamy mash away from him and stood up to leave, trying to make himself as inconspicuous as he could.

He made it out towards the main door of the bar before Gill banged into him coming in the opposite direction. Her smile beamed as she saw him.

'Going somewhere? Or just eager to see me again?' She smirked, a genuinely fantastic smile was aimed right at him.

'I was… eh, just going to get some money,' he lied.

'Did you see anyone else in there?' She asked, looking over his shoulder into the darkened room.

'I… erm…'

Just then the small girl, Debbie, appeared in the foyer. 'Gill,' she called as she walked over, 'I'm just going to get changed, spilled something over my top. Carl's inside waiting for you. Who's this?' She asked looking John up and down, while exaggeratedly wiping at a stain on the front of her top.

'Oh, sorry Debs, this is John. He's meeting with us later.'

John found himself staring at the stain on her top, he was hoping beyond hope that she wouldn't want to hug him and give him a kiss. He didn't think he would be able to do that.

'Well, hello John. Now, I know that they're fantastic but you don't have to stare at my tits all the time you know!' She said with a mocking grin on her face.

'What? I, erm… I wasn't, I was, eh…'

'Is he always like this?' She asked, turning to Gill and jokingly pointing at him.

Gill shrugged and laughed. 'It seems so.'

'Well, I've got to go and change this top, I'll see you guys in bit.' She pointed at John again while directing her next question to Gill. 'Number twelve, right?'

'Looks that way.'

Debbie looked him up and down once again with an approving grin. He felt uncomfortable in her gaze, like he was a piece of meat on her plate. 'Nice.' She smiled and walked off, still rubbing at the stain on her top.

Gill looked at him. 'Are you coming in or what?'

'Yeah. I, I think I've got enough money on me anyways.'

The Twelve

As they walked in together Carl saw them and stood up. John instantly looked at his crotch and noticed that his fly was half undone. *What the hell am I getting myself into here?* He thought.

Carl took his hand with another one of those crushing grips, his huge hand enveloping John's small one easily. He did his utmost not to give away the fact that he was reeling in pain. 'You just missed Debbie, she left about two minutes ago,' he said glancing over their shoulders towards the exit.

I can't believe he can be so nonchalant about what was just happening, and in public too. 'No, we saw her; she had a spill on her top, she said that she needed to go home and change.'

Carl smiled a coy smile and shrugged his shoulders theatrically.

Gill rolled her eyes and laughed out loud. 'Oh, for fucks sake Carl. You didn't? In here? You pair of dirty bastards!'

'Hang on a minute!' John held up his hands, his face filled with wonder and confusion. 'I was just in here and I saw…'

'Debbie, sucking me off?' Carl finished for him.

'Well, yeah… what's going on here? I thought you two…' He pointed between Carl and Gill.

'Well we are and we aren't.' Gill replied, 'More aren't than are, since I met you.'

She said this as if it was an aside comment, something that didn't really mean anything to her, but John felt himself blush yet again.

He looked at her like he had just stepped out of the old wooden house in Oz, and was suddenly surrounded by colourful munchkins. His brain couldn't quite comprehend that this, fantastic, gorgeous girl was saying this... About HIM!!!

He was gushing inside, he could hear a chorus of angels singing, but he knew that he was in dangerous territory stepping in-between this Samson of a man, and his Delilah, so he decided to let the comment go,

'Aren't you angry with Debbie?' He asked, still not understanding the dynamic at play here.

'Nah, she does that to everyone, and Carl here has never been one to decline a blow job. Anyway, we need someone with her skills.'

At this point a group of others, who John kind of recognised as the people he'd seen Gill and Carl with a few times, began to file into the Cooler and make their way over to where they were standing.

'Ah, everyone's here I see...' Carl said, a huge smile breaking on his face.

All except Debbie, John thought with a smile. He wanted Debbie to come back as the more time she was there the more time he'd have with Gill.

She returned a few minutes later wearing a different top. John hoped that she'd swilled her mouth out before coming back too, and this thought brought a smile to his lips.

'What are you laughing at?' Gill asked with a playful smile and nudge.

He regarded her with a sly look, and a sly smile of his own. 'I'll tell you later.'

'You're on!' She whispered to him, and he felt his heart sing. An odd sensation for him.

They all sat chatting around a large table. He was introduced to all the new members, the name 'Number Twelve' was bandied around quite a bit. He was getting a little confused about it all and was longing for a moment alone with Gill so he could ask her what it all meant, and what she meant by her previous comment.

Carl was over at the bar handing his credit card over to the barman. 'Right, in order to use my dad's card

The Twelve

for the first round, everyone has to shout out their number. I'll begin… ONE!!!'

A man who John hadn't been introduced to stood up and shouted 'TWO!' Gill was three, Debbie turned out to be eight, the guy Carl was talking to on the phone earlier, Tony, was eleven…

He was the only one not to shout out a number. When everyone was done they all turned and looked at him expectantly. Feeling more than a little self-conscious, he stood up and shouted 'Twelve!'

As he did, the whole group cheered and applauded as one, and as if on cue, the barman struggled over with a huge metal tray with at least forty shots on it.

'Shots for The Twelve. Let's drink and welcome our newest member, bringing the circle to completion. 'The Twelve.' Carl shouted accepting the tray from the barman.

The shots continued all night. Carl's dad's credit card must have taken a massive hit. John had the impression that this kind of thing happened quite often. He vaguely, remembered a drunken group photograph being taken outside the bar in the daylight. But what he did remember, and would never forget, was that it was the first night that he had a long, lingering kiss, with Gill.

Present Day

22.

BACK IN JOHN'S modern day hell, he was sat on the couch alone in his house and feeling all alone in his world. Gill was gone, and he had to face the reality of that every single day for the rest of his life. An ice-cold cup of tea was stood next him on the coffee table and the remains of a sandwich, God only knew what type, was nestled between his legs.

It had also gotten dark outside. He stood up, ignoring the screaming from his muscles and creaking of his knee-caps, and shook the sandwich off his legs onto the plate that he had assumed was its original location. He picked up the cold tea cup and carried both items into the kitchen.

His spirits were low.

On entering the kitchen, he noticed something hanging on the wall by the door, he had never noticed anything hanging there prior to today, and he was damned sure that he hadn't been doing some extra-somnambulistic DIY activities.

His mind fogged over and he felt a little dizzy as he noticed that it was the very same picture that he'd had in his hands upstairs in the bedroom. Panic washed over him as he dumped the dishes and reached out at the frame. As he touched it he yelled in pain as the intense cold of the metal, once again seared the skin on his fingers, temporarily fusing them to the frame.

The Twelve

He did his best to let go of it, having to shake it out of his grip a couple of time before it dropped onto the kitchen floor.

Blowing on his fingers to warm them from their shock, his eyes rested on the picture staring up at him. There was something about it that caught his eye. He bent down to pick it up, scrutinising the blurred-out faces. Previously, four of them were out of focus, but now there were five.

He couldn't be sure if it was the same picture as before. It looked like the same frame, it was the same pose, the same location and it featured all the same people, but his brain screamed at him that it couldn't be. John had a clear recollection of throwing it back onto the bed, upstairs, last night. So, it couldn't be hanging here on the kitchen wall. Also on that one Debbie's face wasn't blurred as it was on this one, not as much as the other four, including Gill's, but blurred just the same.

Still holding the cold frame, he ran upstairs to the bedroom. His head was throbbing, the pulse was in complete rhythmic timing to the rapid beating of his heart. When he got to the top of the stairs, he had to stop for a second or two as he was seeing colours before his eyes. *I need to get some exercise,* he thought abstractly.

He entered the bedroom and looked onto the bed. There was no picture!

A quick search around the floor and the surrounding area proved fruitless; there was no other picture in the room. He was holding the original, albeit slightly altered, picture from last night.

Debbie's face was changing, it was going out of focus, exactly like the others, the ones who were dead.

A sinking feeling hit him in the pit of his stomach. He had never realised that a mere thought could make him feel physically sick, until right then. *If Debbie's face has been rubbed out, and the others that have been rubbed out are dead, does that mean? OH SHIT!!!*

He ran back downstairs into the back room that acted as his office, and fired up his computer. He opened his contacts application and pressed D on the keyboard. A short scan of the list and there were no entries for Debbie.

He pressed B for Baines.

Scan, scan, and scan.

Baines, Debbie. Relief surged through him that the number was there, he only hoped that it was a current number as it had been several years since they had been in touch.

He rooted into his pocket for his mobile phone, but it wasn't there. He tried to remember the last time he'd used it, and couldn't. The thing could have been anywhere.

He rushed into the living room and looked on the single chair, thankfully, it was there poking out of the cushion that had so recently been promoted to his bed. With a sigh of relief, he pressed the button to wake it up, but the phone screen stayed dark. As he pressed the power button to turn it back on he realised that the battery must have died on it. He cursed it, and himself as he was always forgetting to put the thing on charge.

He grabbed a pen from the messy sideboard and made his way back into the office. He scribbled down the number on a scrap of envelope, it was an unopened bill by the look of it, and then commenced to search for his phone charger.

~~~

About twenty-five miles away across town, Debbie Baines was putting the final touches to her immaculate make-up as she was getting ready for an evening out on the town.

~~~

John ran back up his stairs, he had an idea that the charger was in the bedroom.

~~~

Debbie was looking fantastic, her hair was perfect, her make-up was on point, but it was all an, almost perfect, illusion. Underneath the layers of foundation and blush, her face told a different story. The cold scared eyes and the lines of worry held their own secrets.

Standing in the hallway downstairs, she was cradling the receiver of the house phone in her hand, her voice sounded a lot more than just a little scared as she spoke into the receiver. 'Yes please, a taxi for Baines. Two Elden Drive. Five minutes? Thanks, I'll be on the step.'

~~~

John was in a near panic, he was frantically searching for his elusive phone charger. He had pulled out the contents from all the drawers and cupboards in the bedroom. 'Fuck, fuck, fuck... I promise... I promise, please let me find this charger, and I promise I'll tidy up tomorrow.' he prayed to whatever God, or patron saint ruled the finding of phone chargers in emergencies.

~~~

Debbie placed the receiver back onto the cradle of the phone, terminating the conversation she was having with the taxi firm, and cast a furtive glance over her shoulder towards the door of the kitchen. She squinted her eyes, as if she was trying to see something that was proving difficult to see. A crash rang out from somewhere in the house and she jumped up throwing open the front door and rushing outside, into the front garden. As she slammed the house door closed behind her, she leaned back on it and breathed a long sigh of relief.

~~~

'Aha! Got you, you bastard.' John shouted as he ran to the plug socket, plugged the white charger in and began to charge his phone. He quickly turned it on, becoming rapidly impatient with the inordinate amount of time it took to boot, and then, when it was finally ready, he dialled the number written on the envelope that was still in his hand.

As Debbie was leaning against her front door, something crashed against it; whatever that something was, it had only missed her by mere seconds.
From a distance, she looked like a beautiful, happy, thirtyish lady, the colloquialism these days would have been MILF, but on closer inspection it was obvious that she was not happy at all, in fact it looked like she had been crying, a lot. The nervousness in her face spread to her red, erratic and wild looking eyes. She stood on the door step, hugging herself to combat against the cold that was eating into her, although it was a warm and balmy August evening, the cold had chilled her from inside the house.
A familiar noise cut through the new-found silence in the house behind the door, it was her mobile phone ringing. 'Fuck,' she muttered while rooting through her purse, looking for her phone even though she could hear it ringing from inside. 'Oh fuck!' She was sobbing again now, her waterproof mascara working overtime to stop her from getting 'panda eyes'. 'Why, why, why? Why the fuck is this happening to me?'

'Pick up, pick up, pick up, pick up!' John was shouting into his phone as it rang out. 'Come on, PICK THE FUCKING PHONE UP!!!'
'You have reached the voicemail of De...' John hung up before the voicemail fully kicked in. He dialled again. It rang out again. Three times he did it, all to no

avail. On the third attempt, he left a message. 'This is a message for Debbie... Debs Baines. This is John Rydell, from university. Erm... I, erm... Well, I was wondering if there was any chance of us meeting up. I've got something kind of urgent I need to tell you; can you give me call on this number when you get this message? Please, we really need to talk.'

As John was relaying his number, Debbie's taxi turned up. The BEEP BEEP BEEP tone, informing her that she had a text message rang as she walked down the path towards her waiting taxi.

'Oh well,' she sighed, trying to crack a smile. 'I'm not going back in there to answer that.'

'Are you OK love?' The driver asked her as she got into the back of the taxi.

'I will be when I get away from this fucking place, can you take me to the Leisure Lounge in Soho?'

The driver was happy with this fare, it was over the other side of London, and would cover most of his daily settle. 'OK treacle... Soho it is.'

John was sat in his bedroom with his phone still in his hands; he was looking both depressed and distraught. The million times that he'd nervously rubbed his hands through his hair had caused it to become a greasy mess, and his eyes were red. Tracks of tears were beginning to form on his cheeks where the tears that were welling up in his eyes, fell.

A strange noise filtered up from downstairs, making him turn to look out at the darkness of the landing beyond the bedroom door. Once again, his heart felt like it was stuck in his throat, fighting with his tonsils to escape his body.

He had read many times in the past about people, who, when they were afraid, or really looking for something, could decipher words and voices or even visions from everyday noises and pictures. Like children making pictures out of clouds. Right at this moment he was having one of those experiences. The strange sound coming from beyond the door sounded like a voice. And the voice sounded like it was talking directly to him, but only one word was decipherable.

It sounded like Thirteen!

That didn't make any sense to him at all.

23.

DEBBIE MANAGED TO make it to the Leisure Lounge with as minimal conversation as she could. The taxi driver, bless him, kept asking if she was OK. She nodded and smiled and laughed politely at all the right places. When she paid him, she told him to keep the change, he was more than happy with the sizable tip, and he drove away into the night a happy man.

She unlocked the shutters and doors to let herself in and disarmed the alarm system.

The place was large and dark, and after everything she had endured the last few days, it was also intimidating. With haste, she turned on the lights and looked around at her club. It wouldn't be open for at least another week, but she just loved being here and taking it all in. Since the decor was mostly finished and all the fittings in place, she felt it was becoming more and more like the club she wanted it to be.

'Six more days…' she said, her own voice scaring her a little in the silence. 'Six more days and I'll have brought my little dream to fruition.'

24.

FIVE DAYS EARLIER Debbie had come home to a strange smell in her house. She didn't know it then, but that was the beginning of the strangeness that was to plague her for the next week.

It was a sickly-sweet smell, akin to rotten meat. She had never, really, been one for home domesticity, but the smell was so bad that she donned an apron, some rubber gloves and she scoured the kitchen from top to bottom, looking everywhere for the source of the smell.

Initially she had thought that a sausage, a piece of steak or maybe some chicken had fallen down the back of the fridge and began to rot. She took it upon herself to pull out the fridge-freezer to look, holding a cloth over her nose to block out the lingering stink.

She clicked the torch app on her phone and shone it into the dark recess behind the utilities, angling the light to get into all the nooks and crannies. She found nothing obvious that could be causing the smell.

She removed the cloth from her nose to see if she could locate whatever it was with her nose, but as quickly as it had come, it had gone. There wasn't a trace of the bad smell anywhere. She knew that she wasn't going mad, the smell had definitely been there.

Shrugging it off, she pushed the fridge freezer back into its place and breathed a deep sigh. All the work and the long hours that she had been putting into the club lately was taking its toll on her, she was exhausted both mentally and physically. She decided that she would pour herself a drink and at least try to relax.

The Twelve

Taking an expensive bottle of red wine out of her cupboard, she uncorked it and grabbed a large glass. She turned the TV on and poured the drink while simultaneously flopping onto her couch and kicking her shoes off, wiggling her toes in relief of their freedom.

Thick, semi-coagulated blood glopped from the neck of the bottle into her glass.

The strange weight of the thick liquid falling into her glass made her turn away from the reality TV show to look and see what was wrong. The scream she emitted came from the top of her lungs as she dropped the gore filled container. As it shattered over her beige carpet as she jumped up from the couch to look at the extent of the mess. She was expecting to see some horrific, gory spillage, but all that was there was smashed glass and red wine sinking into her deep pile shag.

She had to look twice, to make sure the stain was only red wine. It was!

Fuming, but also more than a little freaked out, she went back into the kitchen to give the cleaning solutions a second outing that night. As she opened the cupboard door a wave of the same stench hit her and she was forced aback, falling on her backside as she did. Holding back a gag with her hand over her face and pinching her nose at the same time, she dared a peep inside, dreading seeing what could possibly be causing such a smell.

A swarm of flies burst from the dark recess of the cupboard, she screeched as she waved them away with dawning horror.

Once she had recovered from the flies she activated the torch app on her phone once again and peered, tentatively inside. In the gloom of the cupboard, towards the back, was a large mound of what she could only surmise, was offal. It looked like raw liver, intestines, faeces and general gore.

She screamed again and scrambled backwards on her behind, using her hands to propel her away from the hideous sight.

Nausea was rising in her stomach and she was convinced that she was going to vomit. *Get a grip of yourself Debbie. How would all that shit get under there?* Still covering her face to defend against the smell, she braved another look inside, bracing herself for what she would see. But all there was inside was a jumble of rags lying in a heap.

'Oh, my God.' She cursed to herself. 'I'm working far too hard. Fuck the drink and the carpet, I need to go to bed.'

Shaking like a leaf and still half in shock, she made her way to her bedroom, shedding her clothes as she did. Naked except for a small black thong, she flicked out the light and crawled into her comfortable bed.

In her exhaustive state, she didn't notice the dark, hooded figure lurking in the shadows, sitting in her occasional chair in the corner of the room. She missed the soundless way the figure had gotten up and leaned over to stroke her hair. All she did was emit an incoherent mumble as the ghostly figure stroked her cheek. She didn't even see the silver eyes open within the darkness where the figure's face should have been underneath his dirty hood.

The figure allowed its white, dead looking hand to roam up the length of Debbie's small but perfectly shaped body, scratching lightly, almost playfully on her olive skin. Wherever it touched, goose-bumps rose and she gave another, unsettled squirm. It continued to explore until it came to her stomach. There, its hand stopped, hovering for a small while as if it was divining for water.

Seemingly satisfied at something, the figure stretched its dirty, too white fingers, before removing its cold dead hand. Then it disappeared back to wherever it had come from.

Debbie opened one eye, dreamily, and looked around the room. She'd just had a strange dream. It brought back, not memories per se, but strange feelings about her days in university.

With a small, slightly troubled smile on her face, she fell back asleep.

25.

THE NEXT MORNING Debbie woke up feeling terrible. She'd had a troubled night's sleep, fuelled with nightmares and stupid falling down holes in her sleep moments. 'Urgh, please don't be coming down with something. Not now,' she mumbled to herself as she crawled out of bed and stumbled into the bathroom.

Sitting down on the toilet she cast her mind back to what had happened last night. Chuckling to herself, she stood up and flushed. 'All work and no play Debs.'

She reached her hands in through the shower curtain to turn the shower on, and the spray of water felt nice on her arm. Looking forward to the same warm spray covering her entire body, she turned to look into the mirror. She didn't want to wash her hair and have the bother of drying it, not today, so she grabbed a bobble and began to gather it all together to put it up at the back.

What she saw in her reflection caused her to scream!

Her face was covered in deep, red scratches. They looked random at first, but once her initial shock had died down, she noticed something worse about them. They formed a word on her forehead.

The word was 'WHORE'.

Instantly her thoughts heralded back to the strange dream she'd had last night.

She had dreamt that she had been making love, no scrap that, she knew the difference between making love and fucking, and the way that they had been going about it, she could say with some confidence, that she had been fucking some random guy. Another, complete stranger had been watching them. She had been aware that this someone had been watching her, and she had been enjoying the feeling.

The person, who by now she thought she knew somehow, had tried to join in. Normally this wouldn't have been a problem as she enjoyed that kind of thing, but the new person began to hurt her. He had been... scratching her.

Knowing that there was no way she could have scratched a word into herself, she leaned closer into the mirror for a better look. There was no doubt that the scratches formed that word, and the strange thing was, it had been written in reverse. If she'd done this in her sleep, surly her reflection now would have been spelt the right way around, plus the letters would have been uneven, not neat and tidy like they were.

They didn't look deep enough to leave a scar, but the word, it was undeniably there.

She ran out of the bathroom, and down the stairs. She wanted to look in the large mirror in the hallway, where she could get up close and inspect them with some clarity, away from the steam of the bathroom. Dreading what she was going to see, she looked into the mirror.

There was nothing there.

Her face had no scratches on it at all. Not quite believing what she was seeing, she leant in close to inspect her forehead, tracing her fingers over the skin to feel for bumps or cuts. There was nothing there but smooth skin.

She was stumped! She had definitely seen the word 'WHORE' scratched into her forehead. All she could do was stare into the mirror in disbelief.

Not knowing if she had still been dreaming, she made her way back upstairs. Her hands shaking as she grasped the banister.

In her confusion, and even in her near naked state, she hadn't noticed that the temperature had dropped by more than a couple of degrees.

26.

LATER THAT DAY she was sat at her desk in her, almost complete office, in work when she received a phone call on her mobile phone. She casually picked it up and looked at the screen at the caller ID, it read 'HOME'.

Weird, who'd be calling from home?

'Hello… Hello, who's this? Mum, mum is that you?'

She was hoping it was her mum because she was the only other person she knew of who had a spare key.

'Mum, Mum are you there?'

There were audible movements on the other end of the line, it sounded like someone was rubbing the receiver against clothing, creating a horrible sounding crackle. This scared her; it meant that there was someone there.

Then came a sound like heavy breathing. Like a breathy voice filtering through the receiver of her phone. It sounded like a long drawn out word, before the line went dead.

'Thiiiiiiiiiiiirteeeeeeeeeen.'

Debbie shuddered as she felt a chill rip through her, turning her skin into a landscape of goose-bumps. She could feel a chill in the air too, which was odd considering the heating in her office was on, even though she shouldn't have needed it in the middle of summer.

Who was that? She thought, as a pang of panic began to rise in her stomach. Her mind was cast back to the strange dream she'd had and, what she was now thinking of as, her episode, this morning. Another thought came to her, the one regarding the wine and the offal in the kitchen.

She suddenly had an urge to go home just to see if there really was anyone there, but she wasn't going back there alone. Not after all the strange things that had been happening.

She looked at the work roster that was on her desk, she wanted someone that she could rely on to come back with her. It turned out that Jack the electrician was the only other person working in her club right now, all the others were on different assignments.

She got up out of her chair and straightened her dress before walking out in the worksite that would eventually become her club.

'Jack, are you about? Could you come in here a moment, please?' She shouted into the large, empty room.

A young man in his early to mid-twenties poked his head around her door. 'Hi Debs, what are you after?'

Debbie smiled at him. He was a good-looking lad, the thought of going back to her house with him could be quite the diversion she needed.

'I need to go back home for a while, I've left my other bag and there are some papers in there that I need. The only thing is...' She looked at him, biting her lip. 'I need you to come with me. Could you do that?'

Jack's face lit up like a child's on Christmas morning. He'd heard of Debbie's reputation as a man eater with the habit of sometimes taking home the help for some 'extras', and today it seemed, it was his turn. 'Eh... yeah, I'm sure I can do that. What time were you thinking?'

Debbie smiled at him again, the real reason why she was going home temporarily forgotten. 'Right away,' she said with a twinkle in her eye.

The Twelve

It was a short car ride back to her house, travelled in an awkward silence. Jack was too nervous to conduct much conversation, and Debbie was more than a bit apprehensive about what they'd find in her house. Her mind kept taking her back to her dream, and the hallucination of the scratches on her face.

When they arrived, she turned towards Jack, smiled, and slid her hand between his legs caressing his crotch. 'Are you coming in?' She asked him, a salacious smile creeping across her face.

Jack didn't need to be asked twice. He had unbuckled his seatbelt and was out of the car in a flash.

As she walked to her front door, she had to stifle a smile as she watched him struggling to conceal the erection in his work trousers. She was proud in the knowledge that she still had that power over men, no matter what age she was, or they were.

'Come on then,' she whispered while inserting her key into the lock, turning her head slightly to watch him make his way up her path. She pushed the front door open, and then turned to enter.

The moment she stepped over the mantel and into the house she was overwhelmed with the same thick, rotting meat stench as last night. Only this time it seemed worse, fresher somehow, in a bad way, so bad that it set off her gagging reflex. She put a hand up over her mouth attempting to stem any vomit she might have expelled.

'Oh, Jesus Christ, don't go in there,' she shouted back at Jack as she rapidly stepped out of the house. 'That stench is awful!'

'What smell?' He asked looking at her a little confused as he passed her and stepped into the hallway. 'I can't smell anything, well, nothing bad anyway.'

'Are you joking?' She asked fighting off another gagging spell, this time she felt the saliva building in her mouth as a precursor to throwing up.

Jack shrugged his shoulders and shook his head. 'It is a little musty, that's all.' He turned to look at her, and raised his eyebrows, live lust twinkling in his eyes. 'So, what happens now? Do we go upstairs or stay here in the hall? I don't really mind either.' Confidence had grown in him now that she had made her intentions clear. 'I'm so fucking horny for you,' he re-iterated this by grabbing his crotch while Debbie was still stood outside, watching.

She rolled her eyes and removed her hands from her face, testing the air as she did. The smell had gone now, but it was still lingering a little in her nose.

Jack turned and walked into the house, she was just about to follow him inside when his shout from further inside, stopped her dead in her tracks.

'Oh fuck, oh shit… man that's so fucked up.'

Jack rushed back out of the gloom of the hallway, he was pointing towards the kitchen. His face was ashen and it was his turn now to hold his hand to his mouth, attempting to control a gag.

Debbie was rubbing her nose trying her best to rid herself of the smell that, apparently, only she could smell. She stepped inside after him wondering what the hell could be going on now. Jack was stood against the hallway wall; his hand was over his mouth as his eyes watched her.

'Don't go in there,' he whispered as she approached. He was shaking his head and his face was grey.

The sight that greeted her in the kitchen caused her to finally lose control of the gagging reflex that had been threatening, and she vomited all over the floor. Jack was backing out of the hallway, heading towards the front door.

The epicentre of the carnage in her kitchen focused on the large blender on her counter, the one she used to make fresh smoothies for work. She couldn't remember the last time she had used it, and when she did use it, she usually put it away after washing it out. Today it was out on the counter, and she must have left the lid off it when she'd used it last.

And, uncharacteristically, left it plugged in.

It looked like a cat; she didn't even own a cat! It must have gotten into the kitchen and fallen into the blender, somehow activating it.

Drying blood, meat, gore and shredded bone completely covered the kitchen.

It had sprayed up the walls, the ceiling and all over the worktops. Some of the bones and the fully intact head were still inside the jug. The poor thing's glassy, wide eyes were still open and they seemed to be looking right at her. Accusing her of something.

Jack had made it to the front door. 'I'll just wait for you in the car,' he announced as he exited the house.

Debbie had stopped vomiting but she was now physically shaking. She sat down on the only clean high stool in the kitchen and looked all around her, wondering how on Earth a cat could have gotten into her kitchen, never mind activating the blender.

As her eyes swooped across the bloody room, she noticed the telephone, the one in the hallway that she'd just passed. The one whoever made the call to her mobile must have used. The receiver had not been put down properly, and there was something resembling blood all over it. This was strange as the carnage in the kitchen hadn't affected the hallway at all.

Slowly, she edged down the hallway towards it. As she got closer she could see that it was blood.

It looked like it had been wiped over the phone on purpose, it looked like something had been scrawled in the receiver.

Like the number 13, she thought tilting her head to see it better.

'What the fuck is happening here?' She said out loud, jumping a little at her own voice. Backing away from the telephone, she slowly made her way out of the house to join Jack.

She offered him one hundred and fifty pounds' cash to clean up the kitchen for her, and invited him to stay the night, she was far too spooked to stay in there alone tonight. He gratefully accepted both.

Apart from some deep cleaning of her kitchen, followed by pretty rugged, and rather satisfying sex the rest of the day was uneventful.

They both drifted off to sleep around half-past ten, both worn out by the events of the day and the third helping of carnalities. As she drifted, she couldn't help but think about the number thirteen…

27.

'Thiiiiiiiiiiirteeeeeeeeeen.'

Debbie shot bolt upright in the bed. Had she been dreaming, or did that word just filter up to her through the house? She wiped her forehead removing the freezing cold sweat that had built-up onto her arm.

Jack was still lying next to her, gently snoring, he didn't ever stir at her sudden activity.

Her heart was pounding in her chest, and her nakedness was responding to the severe chill in the air.

She slipped out of the bed and grabbed her housecoat wrapping it around her to combat the cold. She looked at the clock on the bedside table, it was ten minutes past three in the morning.

Without even thinking about the events of the past two days, she made her way downstairs to the kitchen to grab a drink. She had a thirst akin to a hangover. This normally happened after a heavy night with company.

She flicked on the lights and marvelled at her nipples. The cold had tightened them up into small, hard buds that stood out against the silk material of her nightgown. She shuddered at the cold and wrapped her arms around herself in a vain attempt to shut it out.

The metal of the tap on the sink was freezing to the touch, almost to the point of burning, and the glass that was next to the draining board had a thin sheen of ice frosting on the surface. As she picked it up she left melting fingerprints in the frost.

She filled the glass and took a long, deep drink from it, relishing the feeling of the cold liquid travelling along all her tubes, until it reached her stomach. She refilled it and turned around to go back upstairs. As she did, something darted from the corner of her eye, something dark and large. It rushed from her peripheral vision only to disappear back into the shadows of the kitchen.

Taking a sharp intake of breath, she slammed the glass down on the counter and spun around to see what it was. She was hoping, beyond hope that it was nothing, just her oversensitive imagination. *Maybe it was the ghost of that cat!* She thought, trying to make light of the situation, but only succeeding in scaring herself more in the process.

She had never realised how big her kitchen was until that moment, until she gauged how far she would have to travel to get out of the freezing cold room and back into the dimly lit hallway, back to Jack and the relative safety of her bedroom.

She jumped again as a dark figure once again darted out of her peripheral vision. This time she knew that it wasn't her imagination. She saw it more clearly, and it was bigger than last time, much bigger. It was more like a small person in a hooded top, than the ghost of a cat.

That was enough for her. Leaving her glass of water, she sprinted out of the kitchen and upstairs taking them at least three at a time.

'Jack… Jack, wake up. WAKE THE FUCK UP WILL YOU!' She shouted, in a whisper.

Jack opened he eyes, he was tired, but once he saw Debbie leaning over him, her nipples poking through her open robe, he was fully awake in an instant. He flashed her a wide smile. 'Hey baby. You want to go again?'

'No I don't want to fucking go again. I think there's someone in the house. I don't know, maybe a kid in a hoodie or something. He might have been the one who did that fucking cat.' She knew she was clutching at straws with this statement, but she was feeling a little lost and more than a little bit vulnerable.

Jack was up like a flash, showing off all his male bravado. He pulled on his trousers and looked at her. 'You stay here and I'll go and sort the little bastard out.'

This left Debbie all alone in her bedroom, giving her time to reflect on her current situation. *I hope he catches the little shit. More so, as then he can fuck off home and I can fire him in the morning, than anything else.*

'Good luck,' she whispered to him, flashing a small, insincere smile. She closed the door behind him and listened intently, following every creak of each step he took as he crept along the landing towards the stairs.

Then there was a short period of intense silence, where she guessed he was either still on the stairs or down in the kitchen. The cold was striking, but she was sweating now, despite only wearing a thin, silk dressing gown.

She had heard the phrase used many times in films and books, mostly in parody of a situation, but right now, the silence that was coming from the rest of the house, really was deafening.

'WHAT THE FUCK?'

The fury and the fear in the shout made Debbie's heart skip a beat and then double in time as if to make up for it. Her wild, terrified eyes scanned around the bedroom. She didn't know what she was looking for, or even if she was looking for anything, but her eyes rested on the clock on her bed-side cabinet. It read fifteen minutes past three.

'WHO THE FUCK ARE YOU?' Another shout came from outside the bedroom door.

A tear slipped down Debbie's cheek and she pulled her thin robe tighter against her body, more of a significant protection against what was happening elsewhere, than to combat the freezing air that was now seeping into her room.

'Thiiiiiiiiiiiirteeeeeeeeeen!'

It was a whispered reply to Jack's shout, and it floated up the stairs, into her room and into her ears.

'FUCK THIS SHIT!' Was the last shout she heard from Jack before the front door opened and then slammed closed.

Her eyes opened wide as she realised what had just happened. She dashed over to the window and pulled the curtains apart and was just in time to see him running off down the street in nothing but his trousers.

Confused and scared, she looked back towards her bedroom door.

'Thiiiiiiiiiiiirteeeeeeeeeen!!!'

More scared than she had ever been in her entire life, and angry too, she called on every bit of courage she could muster and shouted, 'Hello… Is there anybody down there?'

Grimacing with the cold, and the rather stupid idea she was having about leaving the bedroom, she grasped the metal door handle. Wincing in pain, she wrenched her hand away from it, shaking and looking to see if there had been any damage. The handle had been so cold that it had burnt an imprint of the slight pattern around its circular circumference into the smooth skin of her palm.

She wrapped her hand in the silk of the dressing gown, knowing that it wasn't going to offer her that much protection, but maybe enough to get the door open. It did.

Looking down the dark landing, she could decipher nothing through the gloom. A wall of freezing cold air hit her before rushing right through her. She would have sworn an affidavit right there and then that the cold had been directed at her. It ripped through her clothing, her skin and muscle, chilling her body, literally to the bone.

Wishing that she had taken the time to put more layers on, but warmed and spurred on by pure adrenalin, she began to creep her way along the dark landing towards the stairs. The thought of switching on the lights was abhorrent to her now; she felt a kind of comfort in the dark. She didn't want to even think about what was down there, never mind see it.

'Hello... Hello!' She shouted. Her words croaking in her dry mouth.

There was a loud crash from the kitchen that made her jump and a little involuntary scream escaped from her mouth. It was quickly followed by another crash and the smashing of glass. She turned on her heels and ran back up the stairs, into the sanctuary of her bedroom.

She slammed the door closed and threw all her weight behind it, barricading herself into the room, away from whatever, or whoever was currently destroying her kitchen.

Panting heavily, she watched her cold misty breath plume and then dissipate before her face.

The noises stopped, there were no more whispers, the only sound she could hear was the rapid rushing of blood through her ears. Another minute of shaky breaths ensued, before she put her ear to the door. She couldn't hear anything now, this allowed her to hope that whatever was out there had given up for the night. She climbed onto her bed and wrapped herself up tight in the duvet.

As she lay there, silently, tears began to well up in her eyes. Eventually they became too heavy to hold and they began their intended journey down her cheeks, moistening her pillow.

Against all the odds, she fell asleep.

As she did a dark figure looked in at her through the open curtains of the second-floor window. It was the silhouette of a young boy, wearing a hood.

28.

DEBBIE AWOKE EARLY the next morning, opening just one eye, checking to see that she was still alive. She popped her head out of the duvet and regarded her room, everything seemed in order. Her screaming bladder ordered her out of the confines of her bed, and forced her beyond the boundaries of her sleeping quarters. She felt much braver than she did last night, and marvelled at how much scarier things seemed at night.

She opened her bedroom door and peered around it, taking in the landing with one swoop, there was nothing there. Tentatively she made her way towards the stairs, the fact that she was tip-toeing like a child on Christmas Eve night amused her, but not enough to distract her from why she was tip-toeing. At the top of the stairs she stopped and listened for any noises coming from anywhere within the house. There was nothing. Only the sounds of the cars passing in the street outside.

Continuing to tip-toe, she made her way into the bathroom, before she continued her safari downstairs. The floor of the kitchen was littered with the remnants of smashed cups and glasses in the kitchen, but nothing else of note. Nothing that she could attest to making the other noises she had heard, the whispers. *Maybe Jack just wanted to get away from me, and smashed those glasses himself,* she thought with a smile. *Well the little shit will be long gone before todays over, that's for sure.*

Feeling a little better, that there was no-one in the house, she ran back up the stairs and put on a pair of carpet slippers, before going back into the kitchen and pouring water into the kettle. She leaned back on the counter and sighed, taking in her surroundings. Anger was building in her now. 'Oh yeah, his ass will be fired quicker than I can flick one of his shitty installed light switches,' she spat as she opened the cupboard to remove one of the few remaining cups.

Her mind wandered back to him running off down the street in just his trousers and she managed to chuckle a little. 'Pussy!' She laughed.

The rest of the morning was particularly uneventful, although she did get a little jittery while she was in the shower and couldn't see anything other than the mist through the glass door, but the fear was ultimately in her head.

She arrived in work feeling a little fresher than she did the day before, ready to do some damage to Jack's career. Before she could, she noticed that there was another electrician working on the wiring this morning. With a confused look on her face she approached the older man. 'Hi, I'm Debbie, the owner. Can I ask who you are, and what's happened to Jack?'

The older man took his screwdriver out of his mouth and placed it on the counter next to him, before wiping his hands on his work trousers. He held it out for her to shake. 'Alright love, I'm Kenny. Jack rang me this morning and asked me to cover for him, apparently, he's taken a job abroad, got offered it out of the blue last night… lucky bastard. So, you're the owner, are you?' She accepted his outstretched hand, reluctantly.

Feeling more than a little flustered she dismissed him with a wave of her hand. 'I'm sorry for being so abrupt, I just need to get a coffee and get to work.'

Kenny watched her as she walked away into her office. He smiled and shook his head while checking out her rear. 'Jack, you lucky bastard,' he mumbled before getting back to work.

29.

THE NEXT FEW days and nights were quiet, so quiet that she almost forgot about the escapade with the dead cat and the 'chicken shit' electrician. She was getting herself dressed and ready, because the club was officially opening in two days and she was hosting the launch party in the restaurant opposite it tonight. It was a thank-you for everyone who'd had a hand in the club's development.

She always enjoyed her reflection, and tonight was no different. She could see that she was starting to look the part as she applied her make up, but then she knew that she was building on a solid foundation. She looked good for her age, and she gave herself a little wink and a giggle.

A crash from somewhere below her caused her to jump and her pulse instantly shot up to almost double as the adrenaline began to pump through her system. Her heart dipped into her stomach, and goose-bumps shot up her arms.

The temperature in the room had dropped by quite a few degrees.

She put down her lipstick and stood up, slowly. She began to iron out the creases in her figure hugging dress with hands that were shaking rather badly. She was doing anything to try to ignore the rising fear within her.

There was another crash... and then another.

Shit... she thought grabbing her purse, *I'm late. I need to ring a taxi and get out of here, right now.*

In a semi-panicked state, she grabbed everything she needed from her room and stuffed it all into her handbag, then she picked up her mobile phone and made her way out and along the landing. As she left her room, the door slammed violently behind her.

'Thiiiiiiiiiiiirteeeeeeeeeen!!!' The whisper floated over the air.

She tried to run downstairs, it was difficult in the heels she had on, but she did her best. Another crash came from behind her bedroom door. She made it to the bottom of the stairs; and in tears, she dumped her bag and phone on the occasional table next to the house phone. She picked up the receiver and dialled a taxi, before escaping from the madness of her house, onto the step to await the taxi's arrival.

She thought she could survive one night without her mobile phone!

30.

ONE SILENT TAXI ride later and all the weird stuff happening at home was almost forgotten. She found herself sat in her complete, clean and rather luxurious office in her very own nightclub; The Leisure Lounge. Or at least it will be the night after tomorrow after the grand opening. Tonight, was all about celebrating new beginnings.

She pulled open the bottom draw of her desk and removed a bottle of very old, very expensive whisky. She poured two large glasses, both were for her. One was to calm her nerves regarding tonight's party, and the other was to try to forget all her spooky woes back at home.

She sniffed the sumptuous aroma radiating from the crystal tumbler, and sat back in her expensive, leather chair. The years and months of planning and dealing with contractors and solicitors were finally paying off. Tonight, she would sit back and smell the sweet smell of success.

She downed one of the glasses as if it was a shot, the fire in her belly did wonders for her bravado. She looked around her office and smiled, raising the other glass in a toast as she did. A toast for herself. The issues at home were drifting away on the euphoric cloud she was now settling in on. *Oh well, hopefully I won't be going home tonight anyway*, she smiled again, thinking about the young investment banker she'd had her eye on.

The second glass she savoured, sipping it, enjoying the light-headedness it gave her. She didn't want to get drunk before the party, so she put the bottle away, and smartened herself up in the mirror. She gave her club one last look before she walked over to the restaurant, beaming with pride.

As she left, she was unaware of a dark shadow in the reflection of the mirror. A thin figure in a black hooded top with shining, silver eyes that followed her as she left the club.

The Twelve

31.

THE NIGHT WAS a roaring success; everyone was there from the builders through to all the top investors. The only notable absence was that of Jack, the young electrician. But Debbie didn't care much about that, as tonight was all about her and her dream... The Leisure Lounge.

The young investment banker she'd had her eye on was indeed there, and he in turn, did indeed have at least one eye on Debbie's shapely assets. In fact, he'd had his hands all over them most of the night too.

By two-thirty am, most of the guests had staggered off home after having made the most of the free bar and the excellent food. There were just a few stragglers clinging on, making all kinds of excuses to not go home to their nagging spouses.

Debbie and Trevor, her young investment banker, were in a booth, both were very drunk, very horny and making a complete spectacle of themselves, but in turn, neither of them cared.

The owner of the restaurant made his way over with an apologetic smile on his face. His business had had a fantastic night, but now, alas he had to kick out tonight's generous meal ticket. He approached the booth with his hands held out before him, wringing out a dirty looking apron as he did.

Debbie looked up at him from where she'd previously had her head buried into Trevor's lap. Her hair was a mess and most of her make-up had been transferred onto Trevor's, vacantly smiling, face.

'Ms Baines, it's now nearly 3am. I have a wife and children to support. I must go now or my wife will accuse me of having an affair with the head cook... Of which I am by the way, he's a lovely boy of 23, but what she doesn't know won't kill her... I really must kick you out now, OK?'

Debbie sat up from her prolapsed position in the booth, wiped her mouth and offered him a drunken smile. Her dress had been misplaced at the front revealing her lacy red bra. She blinked at him trying to focus her vision to see who it was who was throwing them out.

'Oh, I'm sorry, Matteo!' She slurred drunkenly. 'It's OK, I completely understand.'

She got unsteadily to her feet and dragged the deliriously happy looking Trevor, who was busy fixing the fly of his trousers, up with her. He fixed his tie, and looked all around him, as if he didn't have a clue where he was.

'It's just that, erm... Trev here doesn't want to go home to his wife just yet. He wants to stay here with me... Don't you?' She draped herself all over the hapless looking Trevor, who looked at her with another vacant grin on his face.

Trevor, looking like some kind of mannequin doll, just nodded his head in agreement, not quite understanding what he'd just agreed to. His face was covered in Debbie's lipstick, as was most of the collar of his white shirt.

'I'm sorry Ms Baines, but I do have to close... I thank you for your business and continued support, but...'

With some effort, she fished her keys out of her bag. Smiling, she staggered a little away from the booth and gave Matteo a big kiss on his lips.

The Twelve

It was a kiss that Matteo could have done without, especially after having just witnessed where her lips had been.

'Tell your wife, I'm so grateful! Oh, and congratulations on the head cook by the way…' she winked, '…he's gorgeous.' She tipped Matteo another, exaggerated wink and grabbed onto Trevor's waiting arm.

She dragged him, dazed and confused, out of the restaurant and across the road towards her shuttered up club.

The night was warm, so the only rush she had to get inside was purely carnal. She struggled to open the front door as the key just didn't want to go into the lock. She turned towards Trevor gave him a drunken smile and put her finger to her lips. 'Shhhh,' she whispered, stifling a giggle. 'We'll be in in a minute.' Trevor staggered forwards a little grabbing her boobs as she was bent over. 'Hey… you just wait till we get inside eh?' She laughed shrugging him off, but with a sexy look, well, as sexy as she could do at two-forty-five in the morning with at least two bottles of expensive rosé wine, and God only knew how many cocktails, inside her.

Finally, she got the door open and the two of them almost fell inside. The first thing they both noticed was the intense cold; it was freezing inside. 'Jesus, I'll go and put some heating on,' she slurred as she dragged herself away from her man of the moment. 'You just go and make yourself comfortable.'

A few minutes later she returned from the kitchen having finally located the heating and working out how to turn it on. Although the room was still freezing cold, she was warm with excitement thinking of how hot it was about to get. Trevor was laid out in one of the booths in the main body of the club, naughty thoughts ran through her head as she slipped off her tight, figure hugging, red dress.

'Don't you worry mister. I'll have you warmed up in no time at all,' she whispered with a salacious grin.

Looking and feeling fantastic in her red lacy underwear, she made her way over to where Trevor was waiting for her. The bra pushing up her petite firm boobs and the red lacy French knickers extenuating her fantastic figure, were not helping her to stave off the cold of the room. Her skin was covered in goose-bumps and her nipples were so tight they were beginning to sting.

That was when she noticed the smell. It was the same rotten meat smell she had noticed in her house. It wasn't as strong as it had been, but it was here none the less.

Trying to ignore it, she dimmed the lights and approached the couch. All she wanted to do was to get naked, and get Trevor naked too. One; because that's what she did, she was a very over sexed lady, and two; because she wanted, desperately to feel the warmth of another body next to her. The cold in the room was becoming unbearable.

Trevor, you're about to get the fuck of your life, she thought. *No way you're going to want to go back to that stuck up prig of a wife.*

She slipped onto the couch next to him and began to kiss his neck and work the buttons of his shirt undone.

He didn't kiss her back. In fact, he didn't do much of anything at all.

Frustrated, she pulled back from him with an angry jolt and poked him in the ribs. *If he's fallen asleep, I swear I'll...*

'Hey you, wake the fuck up. You're about to hit the sexual jackpot here!' She whispered, loudly at him.

Feeling anger and frustration building up inside her, she pushed at him. It wasn't a particularly heavy push, but he fell off the couch under the power of it, nonetheless.

As he fell, the rotten meat smell came back in waves. This time it was putrid. The thick, sticky stench overpowered her, hitting her stomach and mixing very badly with the hors d'oeuvres and the copious amount of alcohol she'd consumed that night.

Her mouth watered up and she could taste bile, as she turned her head and threw up, trying her best not do it all over the sleeping Trevor's suit.

Shit, is this my new thing? Vomiting over my dates? She thought between heaves.

As she put her hand on the seat before her, to lean over and see if she had vomited on the hapless Trevor, it landed in a sticky, dark pool that she hadn't noticed before. It was wet and cold. She lifted her hand up to her face, but couldn't instantly identify the dark liquid covering it. What she did notice was that it was everywhere, and on further investigation, she found that it was coming from Trevor.

It was blood. Thick, dark blood.

Instantly she was sober. She didn't want to, but felt like she was compelled to reach her shaking hands down to him and open his jacket.

His body was cold, wet and sticky. Her hand continued down the front of his shirt, hoping upon hope that she would feel some warmth, maybe a heartbeat, or any reaction to her touch.

Reaching lower, down towards his stomach her hand found a wet, sticky hole.

She leaned over to look, but the sight she was greeted with made her heave once more. She turned her head and vomited again, this time it was all over herself and the couch.

His white shirt was stained dark towards his stomach, it had been masked by his jacket. A hole had been torn by whatever, or whoever, had done this and even in the dim light of the club, she could see right into his chest. His internal organs and his ribcage were exposed and a strange steam was rising from the hole like a smoke machine at a disco. Thick, dark blood was haemorrhaging from the hole too, and the pumping was beginning to slow as his organs, and heart, were winding down like a clockwork toy, allowing death to seep into his body.

She sat up and wiped her mouth attempting to rid the vomit from her own cold face. She looked down at the vacant face looking back up at her. All Trevor's handsomeness was gone, it had been replaced by cold, dead eyes that stared at her and lips that were already turning blue.

A scream was building up inside of her, she could feel it, but could not do anything about it. She tried to let it out, her mouth opened and she built herself up to it, still, no sound was forthcoming.

In a state of utter panic and now completely sober she scrambled up off the couch, careful not to stand in any of the blood or vomit and not to touch Trevor's dead body.

All she wanted to do now was to get the hell out of this club. She eyed her crumpled dress on the floor not ten foot away from all this horror. It looked like an oasis of calm, of normality. It was a relic from another age, before everything changed and she began vomiting on her dead boyfriend.

The blood and vomit all over her naked skin was making her stomach churn every time she looked at it. Closing her eyes and stifling a sob she attempted to rub it off her hands and body, but only succeeded in smearing it deeper into her skin. It was like trying to get oil off her hands, it just wouldn't go.

The Twelve

Teetering over the dead body, she bent over it, trying to retrieve her dress.

A series of truly horrific sounding cracks ensued. She had no idea where they could have come from, until one of Trevor's cold, dead hands reached out and grabbed her leg.

This time she had no problems letting the scream out. The sound was horrendous, guttural and almost primal. The effort her stressed out body put into emitting the scream made her lose control of other, more basic bodily functions. Her bladder opened freely and the feel of the warm liquid trickling down her freezing cold leg caused her a strange, itchy sensation. Terrified, she had to look down because it felt slow and thick, like it was blood. Her relief that it wasn't blood, was overshadowed by the horror of the situation.

Trevor's corpse had a cold vice like grip on her leg, so tight it was cutting the blood circulation to her foot and, even through her panic she could feel the pins and needles begin. She wondered if this was what it was like to be paralysed with fear.

'Please let me go, please let me go... Please let me go,' she whispered underneath her breath, as the strong fingers of the corpse below her tightened with another series of sharp cracks. Instinct caused her to look down at her leg, and she instantly regretted it.

Trevor's head slowly rotated towards her. The noise of the cracks from the already stiffening bones in his neck were somehow worse than the sight of the reanimated corpse' skin stretching over tendons, as it revolved. It moved like it was a rubbish special effect in a stupid science fiction film.

She hated science fiction.

Her vision blurred with tears of fear and panic, and her head began to spin. The horror story unfolding below her was threatening her very breath, making her feel woozy. Fainting was the last thing in the world she wanted to do right now. A strange compulsion drove her to look at his face, the face that she had been kissing a few moments earlier, although right now it felt like years ago. His, now purple, lips had been caressing her ears and neck, and she had been longing for them to caress somewhere else too, somewhere a lot more intimate. That thought alone made her want to run, to bolt, get out of her club and just keep on running and running and running. Never looking back, never coming back; hard work and months of her life or not, she was done with this place.

She expected to see Trevor's glazed eyes staring up at her, with maybe a maniacal rictus grin cutting across the pallor of his face. Nothing could have prepared her for the sight that did hit her as she regarded her supernatural captor.

The face was blacked out, hiding under a dirty hooded top. All she could make out were silvery, glowing eyes from somewhere deep within the abyss. The horrendous smell was back, worse than ever, and she thought she was going to vomit again.

Without releasing her from its grip, the vision before her slowly began to remove its hooded top. Her eyes were fixated on what was unfolding before her.

As the hood slipped, the thing's face was slowly revealed to her. At first, she couldn't tell if it was male or female, or even if it had a gender. The lighting in the room was dim, but she could see that its skin was grey, with a strange tint to it, making it look like something that had been dead, for a long time.

Then she noticed its mouth, or what purported to be a mouth.

Puffed, ripped, swollen and wet skin clung to the open wound at the bottom of its face. Thick black semi-coagulated blood dripped from the mess. Debbie wished that she couldn't, but she could see teeth inside it. They were few and far between, crooked and in awful condition, but they were there.

Her eyes widened, as some deep, hidden, repressed memories hit her from the blue, or more likely from the dark. She shook her head, frantically denying the presence of this spectre. 'No… No… Not you. How could it be you? How could you be here? You're… dead!!!'

The figure held her with its silvery eyes, and his hideous mouth spread wide in an attempt to smile.

The pale skin on its face then began to rapidly age right before her eyes. Deep wrinkles appeared as it began to discolour, turning a deep, ugly green. A thick, vicious slice of skin on its neck began to spill more of the foul smelling, thick blood.

Its eyes narrowed and it attempted another smile for her, this time she could hear the ripping of its skin as the ruin of its mouth tore wider.

Even though the white, decaying head had been badly shaven, taking with it most of its sexual identity, she understood that this thing was male. He spoke to her.

'Thiiiiiiiiiiiirteeeeeeeeeen.'

She fell, fainting flat out at this ghastly, unearthly sight.

She was only out for maybe a few seconds before flickering her eyes open again, looking up at the ceiling of the club. Almost, for a few blessed seconds, she believed that she had been experiencing a bad dream, a vivid nightmare, but a nightmare just the same. Reality came back at her with a slap, as she realised that she was lying in a pool of blood and vomit and the whole, nasty reality came crashing back around her.

She looked up and the sight that greeted her caused her to start screaming again.

The clock on her wall read three-fifteen am.

The ghost, or shadow, or vision… whatever it was, was stood over her, looking at her, seeing her. Real malevolence radiated from his silvery, dead eyes.

Trevor was lying next to her, dead, discarded now by this thing that had used him somehow.

The spectral boy loomed over her, she could see the thick drool dripping from the ruin of his jaw, dripping down onto her naked leg, every drop filled her with dread and revulsion. The skin from his hands had stripped away, transforming the fingers into long sharp boned claws. They wiggled as he advanced on her.

'You have something of mine, and I want it back,' he hissed, it seemed impossible that the legible voice could pass from the maw of its mouth.

Debbie couldn't move, she was completely powerless to stop this ghoul advancing on her.

The rotting meat smell was coming off this ghost in waves, it turned her stomach to think that this thing had been in her house, in her kitchen, in her shower, probably in her bed.

Thick rotten skin dripped from his face and the from the deep cuts in his scalp, as he bent closer towards her. It mingled in with the dark jelly of blood as it dripped in long slow, wet strands from his face, onto the skin of her naked stomach. She closed her eyes, because the act of looking at this thing was driving her brain into a frenzy. It was as if she couldn't quite comprehend what she was seeing.

Her stomach was burning, she thought it was from where the skin and blood was dripping on her, but it took a moment and a quick look for her to realise that it wasn't the concoction that was burning. The sharp intense pain down below was caused where the cold, bony fingers of the spectre had pierced, deep into her skin.

She witnessed the same steam rising from her open wound that had risen from Trevor's, before a

The Twelve

plethora of colours overtook her vision as the skeletal hands delved deeper inside her. She had never encountered a level of raw, unadulterated pain as she did right now. The hand, now red with her blood, extracted itself from her stomach. She wasn't sure if she had screamed or not, and to be honest she didn't really care, as the full contents of her stomach spilled out from the tear the hand had caused, and slowly slopped down all over her body. She just had time to observe her murderer look at something in his skeletal hand, before the lights in the night club that she would never see open, brightened, right before dimming again, as she died on the floor, in a pool of her own innards and vomit.

~~~

A few moments earlier, outside on the street, a late-night couple were walking home from having drinks in the town centre. Both were a little bit tipsy as they walked arm in arm.

On passing the Leisure Lounge a blood curdling scream ripped from deep inside the building.

'Oh, my God, Alan did you hear that?' The girl asked her partner.

Alan's face looked shocked and scared. 'Yeah, I did. Do you think we should call the police?' He asked, unsure of how to proceed.

Another scream, a woman's scream, this time longer and more agonising than the last, culminated in a wet, bubbly crescendo.

32.

CHIEF DETECTIVE ADDISON made his way to work in his small, gloomy office in the police station. He was a big man, but wasn't fat. It was obvious that he'd been fit in his youth, but as he was now touching his late-fifties, it had mostly turned to bulk.

When he arrived, he entered and removed his coat with a resigned sigh. As he was a senior detective one of the younger detectives came into his office with a hot steaming cup of tea.

'Oh, you're a life saver you are Michelle. Thank you,' he said with a smile, as he received the cup from the pretty, younger woman. 'So, what delights do we have today then?' He was trying his best to sound chirpy.

'It's been a busy night sir, there were several fights, a couple involving knives and one domestic, four muggings, two burglaries…' She paused for a second, more for dramatic effect than anything else. '…and this,' she finally concluded.

She dropped a file onto his desk just as he sat down.

'What is it?'

'It's a double murder sir. In a club in Soho.'

Addison sighed and rolled his eyes. 'Another one?'

'This one isn't gang related sir, well, at least it doesn't seem it on the surface. A business woman and a banker. We think she owned the club and he might have been her date, a married one.'

'Married eh? Well, we have our first suspect then. Has anyone contacted the wife?'

'Yes sir, she's very distressed, but she was at home with the children all night, her telephone records verify that. She made quite a number of long calls. The MO doesn't quite fit a crime of passion.'

This piqued Addison's interest. 'How so?'

'Well, it's the manner of the killing sir. It seems that the banker has been killed rather quickly, there was a large hole in his abdomen, death would have been painful, but mercifully swift. The female however, she's been completely disembowelled.'

Addison's face creased at the word disembowelled.

'Her stomach and internal organs have been ripped from her, death would have been painful and prolonged sir.'

'Do we have anything to go on?'

'SOC are there now, have been since about six this morning. Nothing to report back yet. Next of kin are being located now, and we have her address.'

'Is Andy back in yet?'

'No sir, Detective King is still off on sick.'

He sighed and his large shoulders slumped a little. 'Shit, I'll have to take this one alone then. Thanks Michelle, if you don't mind, I'd like to get into the bones of this report right away.'

Michelle lifted her eyebrows and smiled at him before exiting the room. She turned around and looked at the big man. 'Her mother allowed us into her home, we have her mobile phone sir. And guess what?'

Addison was in no mood for guessing games. He closed his eyes and sighed again. 'What?' he asked.

'There wasn't a lock on it. We have a voicemail sir.'

Part 2

Present Day

33.

JOHN AWOKE THE next morning, relieved that he was waking up in his bed and not in a chair in the living room. He'd taken four of Gill's sleeping pills the night before, just to make sure he'd make it through the night for once, and now he was feeling equal parts refreshed and groggy.

His whole body was screaming at him not to, but eventually he dragged himself out of bed. While still in a bit of a fog he checked his mobile, and as he did, in near perfect timing, it began to ring.

Hoping it was Debbie returning his call, he looked at it and was a little disappointed as the screen read, UNKNOWN CALLER.

Feeling rather apathetic, he tossed the phone onto the bed and sat there, staring into space. Allowing the phone to ring off. He then got up and made his way to the bathroom to get a shower. The phone chirped twice, notifying him that he had received a text message. If it was an unknown caller, and then a text message right after, it usually meant some spam, rubbish phone call. He ignored it and stepped into the roasting hot, delicious shower.

The water coupled with the soapy suds all over his body made him tingle, he thought that, quite possibly, this might have been the best he'd felt since Gill's death. He put his head under the water, opened his mouth and let all his problems, momentarily, wash away. For the first time in a long time, he felt at peace.

He stayed in there for at least half an hour. He noticed that his skin was beginning to wrinkle so he decided it was time to get out and dry himself off. His phone chirped twice again. Wrapping his towel around his waist, he walked back into the bedroom and picked it up as he was towelling off his hair.

The message read:

'YOU HAVE ONE NEW VOICEMAIL... PLEASE PRESS #1 TO RETRIEVE YOUR MESSAGE.'

This brought back bad memories of Chicago.

He looked at the screen and hesitated for a short while. *Well, I suppose I'll need to hear at least one real human voice today,* he thought as he complied and pressed #1 into his phone.

An electronic voice chirped at him. 'You have ONE new voicemail left TODAY at zero nine thirty-five... to play this message please press one.'

He pressed one.

'Message ONE... BEEP.'

'Erm... Hello... This is a message for Mr John Rydell. My name is Detective Addison of the London Met. I need for you to call me back on this number 01268101888, it's a matter of some urgency, that's 01268101888, thank you.'

'To hear this message again press...'

John hung up on the voicemail.

He sat down heavily on the bed, the modicum of peace he'd felt a few moments ago was now hanging by a thread. He looked at the phone again and scowled at it as if it was a close friend who had let him down, seriously. Twice!

What would a detective in the Met want with me? Could it be a break in Gill's case?

With butterflies fluttering away, deep down in his stomach, he picked the phone back up and listened to the voicemail message again. This time he made a note of the number on a small pad and pen that was on his, or more precisely, Gill's dressing table.

He punched the numbers into the phone and it answered on the third ring.

'London Metropolitan Police force, how may I direct your call?' The officious sounding voice on the other end asked.

At least it's a human voice and not some stupid recording, he thought. 'Hi, my name is John Rydell. I've just had a message to contact a Detective Addison on this number.'

'If you could hold the line for a moment, while I connect you to Detective Addison's office.'

There was a barely audible 'click' and John was sent to the deepest darkest limbo of somewhere called 'ON HOLD'. There was no music to listen to, just two very ordinary bleeps every few seconds.

He visualized falling through an endless abyss, the monotony of the blackness broken only every few seconds with two small red BEEP BEEPs flashing past him. Time moved differently in the land of 'ON HOLD'.

'Mr Rydell, thank you so much for calling back.'

The suddenness of the voice on the other end snapped him out of his reverie. 'It's... erm, it's no problem. Can I ask what this is all about?'

'You'll have to excuse me for my bluntness, I don't like to beat around the bush, but I'm afraid it's a bit of bad news.'

No shit! I only ever seem to get bad news these days.

'Did you leave a voicemail message on Ms Debbie Baines' mobile phone last night, around eight thirty?'

John's hackles were instantly up and he was suddenly feeling rather testy. He knew that if the detective was being that precise regarding the time, then he already knew the answer.

'Yeah... we're old university friends. I've had a few issues lately and was wondering if we could have had a bit of a get together.' Panic began to rise in his throat as he thought hard about what he left in that voicemail message. He didn't like where this conversation was going.

'Mr Rydell, can I ask where you were last night?'

'Can I ask why?' He asked, instantly on the defensive.

'Of course you may, but if you do I might need you to answer my questions here at the station. For now, I'm more than happy to conduct this over the telephone.'

John noted the smugness in this man's voice. He had a good idea that the man on the other end of this line loved his job, and the power that went with it.

'Oh right, well, I was here, at home, all night.'

'Alone?'

'As it happens, yes I was. My wife was recently...'

'All night you say? Home alone? You never left the house at all?'

'Yes... I...'

'Mr Rydell, Ms Baines was murdered last night. Her and a young man, at her club, The Leisure Lounge. Have you heard of it?'

John sat down, shocked... no, not shocked, he was dumbfounded. He suddenly felt cold again. Cold and lost.

'Have you heard of it Mr Rydell?'

'No.'

'So, you've never been there?'

'No. I…'

'Are you certain of that Mr Rydell?'

'Yes, I'm sure, I've never heard of it. Look, I'm sorry, but am I being accused of something here?'

'No Mr Rydell, what I'm trying to do is to eliminate you from my initial inquiries, and maybe create a timeline of events. A frenzied, violent attack has taken place in the early hours of this morning, you happen to ring one of the victim's hours before she dies, asking to meet up. You tell her you 'have something urgent you need to show her.' Can I ask what that was Mr Rydell?'

The realisation of what the Detective had just told him was beginning to sink in, and John was shaking as he pondered the question. His vision was beginning to tunnel as he looked over to the floor where he first saw the picture. 'It was just, erm a… just an old photograph, but… but a good one. It was of us all together!'

'Mr Rydell, I'm sorry to do this, but I'm going to have to ask you to bring this photograph into the station. I'd very much like to see it. Can you get here tomorrow morning? Cairo Street Station. Just ask for me any time after nine thirty. I would urge you to clear your schedule Mr Rydell.'

What schedule? He thought, *all I had pencilled in was a full morning of moping about followed by an afternoon of wallowing in self-pity.*

'Yeah… I can make it for just after nine thirty. Can I ask a question Detective?'

'Of course, you can, I'll do my best to answer, but I can't guarantee it.'

'How did she die?'

There was a period of silence on the other end of the phone. Then Addison cleared his throat and spoke. 'I'll see you tomorrow morning Mr Rydell, don't forget that photograph, will you? Good day sir.' Addison hung up on his end.

John was left sitting on his bed holding his mobile phone to his ear. He was already lost in his own thoughts.

Redford University, South London
19 years earlier

34.

JOHN AND GILL'S relationship blossomed over the next year.

They became almost inseparable. John's social status had had increased with the association with the 'cool kids' and more specifically with his relationship with Gill.

University life still had its own stresses and strains, as the workload that they had to undertake tripled, but there was always time to socialise.

If there was one thing that he could say about The Twelve, it was that they knew how to enjoy themselves.

John was lying in his bed in his untidy flat, Gill was lay next to him, both were naked and there were post coital cigarettes glowing in the ashtray resting on the creased bedsheets between them. Sheens of sweat covering their skin from the physical exertions they had just finished putting each other through.

'I've got a question that's been bugging me for a while now!' He spoke, breaking the silence between them, while still staring dreamily up towards the yellowing plastered ceiling. He took a long drag on his cigarette.

'Fire away big boy.' She turned, resting on her elbow and flashed him the lopsided grin that he was already falling, deeply in love with.

'All this twelve shit everyone goes on about all the time. What exactly is it all about?'

The Twelve

'Ah!' She chuckled a playful little laugh while turning onto her back. John couldn't keep his eyes off the movement of her naked breasts as she did. She knew this, and loved the power they had over him. 'Well, last year Carl sent me off on this mission to make sure we recruited the right person as our number twelve. It was deemed that that person was you.'

He took another drag at his cigarette before her answer finally sunk into his head. He sat up in the bed and stared at her in disbelief. 'What?' He asked, surprised at himself at how quick to anger she had gotten him.

Gill cracked up laughing. 'You big dick. I got you there, didn't I? Jesus you're so easy to wind up.'

She sat up and extinguished her cigarette in the, already crowded ashtray. Once more John found himself marvelling at the shine of her beautifully pale skin, and how pink and gorgeous her nipples were in the sunlight streaming through the curtains. *Jesus, I should be a poet,* he thought with a smirk.

She caught him looking at her, grabbed her pillow and hit him with it, right in the face, laughing as she did.

'Eyes up here soldier,' she playfully scolded him, pointing two finger towards her own eyes.

John pulled a hurt face, before leaning over and kissing one of them. 'Sorry, you know I can't help myself.'

She flashed yet another lopsided grin before continuing. 'I suppose it's time you found out what it's all about anyway. Considering that it's all going to be ramping up this year. The Twelve is something that Carl dreamed up, well him and Robert. They claim that if you can get twelve people together, willingly of their own free will, and if they all share a common cause, perform a trial or a personal sacrifice or something like that, then due to the…' she made quotation marks with her fingers and pulled an exaggerated face, '…mystical properties of the number, they'll all get to make one wish. I think it's a kind of occultist thing. Robert's really into that. Debbie likes to think that she is, but it's probably only because of the sexual element involved. That girl is a slut.'

The was no malice in her insult of Debbie, what John had gotten to know about her, she probably wore the word as a badge of honour.

She pulled the pillow back from John and tucked it back underneath her head, she leaned over him to grab another cigarette from the bedside table. John revelled in the feeling of her nakedness against his own skin.

'Carl's really into the sex bit too. I don't think that he really believes in the entire occult scary stuff, but Robert, fuck! He thinks he's some kind of high priest or something.'

John's interest was piqued now. 'What exactly are the sex bits all about? Do I, or *we* have to do anything?'

'How about I show you?' Gill gave him her trademark lopsided grin and pulled the covers up over her head. Grinning, John dived in after her.

After a few minutes of very enjoyable fumbling and intense, mind blowing sex, they were back lying on the bed, looking up at the ceiling again. He couldn't believe his luck.

'So, come on, tell me about these sex bits.'

Gill sat up again, her skin the brightest object in the dust mote filled sunlight gleaming through the window. She leaned over onto her elbow again and looked at him, her face deadly serious for once. She flicked her long auburn hair over one side of her face and fixed her eyes, sternly on his.

'OK, but before I do, we need to establish that we're just having fun here, yeah?'

'Yeah…' John shrugged, intrigued. He decided that keeping the feelings that were growing towards her to himself for the time being, was probably the best idea for now.

'And you are not my official...' she made quotes with her fingers again, '...boyfriend.'

He nodded in confirmation. 'Well, erm, yeah OK then.'

'Well then. When we meet, we'll all be naked. Apparently, we all must give up our earthly bodies to this master, whatever his name is. Once the master has had his fill we all have to copulate within a pentagram or something or other. No messing about either, full on, hard core sex. That's where Debbie comes in, even though everyone will have to do it with another member, two participants must do it with *everyone* in The Twelve. Those two are Debbie and Carl.'

'What? They have to have sex in front of everyone?'

'No, you knob! You're not listening. They have to do it at the same time as everyone. Carl says there has to be a sacrifice too.'

John sat up a little more in the bed, he was looking at Gill as if she had just told him that he'd have to kill his own mother. 'What? A sacrifice? Like we're going to have to kill something?'

Gill flashed him another lopsided grin. 'No... I think it's something like the giving up of your body to the master, in a sexual way, that kind of thing.'

His face was still furrowed in disgust but there was also a hint of delight in there too. He hated the idea of Gill having sex with anyone else. He wasn't naïve enough to think that her and Carl hadn't done it in the past, but the idea of them doing it in front of him. On the flip side of that thought, he kind of liked the idea of having sex with Debs, or someone else in the group.

'And you're OK with this?'

She ignored the question, deciding instead to take another long drag on her cigarette.

'So, how did he pick The Twelve?' He asked trying to steer the conversation away from the sex bits.

'Well, we all just kind of come together. Carl and Robert knew each other prior to university. Debbie was going out with Patrick from the first week of fresher's, and the others, well we all just sort of drifted together, like me and you did.' She gave him a small kiss on the nose before flicking the covers away from her and climbing out of the bed.

He frowned. 'Where're you going?' He leaned on his back to get a better view of her nakedness.

'Where we are going, you mean. Don't you remember? It's Brenda's party in the hall tonight, it's not every day you reach twenty-one, is it?'

35.

THE PARTY WAS fantastic. The hall was full, filled with all their friends and acquaintances from their classes at university.

The atmosphere was electric. Brenda's dad was well off and had laid on the free bar. 'This must be costing him a fortune,' Debbie shouted over the boom of the music. 'Imagine putting your credit card behind the bar at a student party!' Everyone laughed including Carl whose father had put his credit card behind the bar most nights.

They were sat in the centre of the room, all of them on two large tables pulled together to make one. The twelve of them, together again, like they seemed to be most of the time these days. Carl, Debbie and Robert were sat together towards the top of the table. Debbie was chewing on Robert's ear and it looked like he didn't really mind. John was next to Patrick and Brenda, but he couldn't keep his eyes off Gill on the other side of the table. Not in a jealous way, even after their conversation that afternoon, but he just couldn't help marvelling at how damned gorgeous she was.

She was sat at the bottom of the table with Nicky McEvoy. Nicky was a small dark haired girl, pleasant enough on the eyes, but seemed quite reserved. She was holding hands with Ben Lomax.

Everyone was having a good time and everyone was drunk. The only strange thing about the night that John noticed was, when any other people who were outside of their circle of twelve came to the table, either to wish Brenda a happy birthday or to just chat with friends from their classes, they were either dismissed or ushered away. Sometimes it was politely, other times not so much.

He'd been talking to a guy he knew quite well from his computer science elective; his name was Kevin and he was most definitely not one of The Twelve. 'So, what did you think of those mid-terms?' Kevin shouted over the sounds of the music, he was holding a mostly full glass of lager in his hand while leaning in with one hand in his ear, trying to listen to John speak.

'Ah, piece of piss mate, nothing to them... I just get my head down and breeze them.' John was bragging a bit, but since joining The Twelve he'd become quite popular, both with the boys and the girls. In the back of his mind he was almost disappointed because since he'd met, and became associated with Gill, more and more of the female student body had been attracted to him. Every time he was tempted, all he needed to do was think about Gill, and the other women just didn't compare.

'Yeah...' Kevin said almost nonchalantly as he was looking out over the dance floor, towards the table where the rest of the group were sat. He realised rather quickly that Kevin hadn't really came over to talk to him, the guy couldn't keep his eyes off Jenny.

Jenny was one of The Twelve. The girl was physically beautiful. She was majoring in sports science with Carl, but leaning towards the physiotherapy side of things. She was also a regular little 'gym bunny'. Her long blond hair was usually tied back in a tight pony-tail, but not tonight. Tonight, she wore it flowing, and there was a natural looking wave to it, giving her face volume.

'Look at that,' Kevin sighed as she walked past. She offered John a cute knowing smile, and he tipped his glass up to her in response. She ignored Kevin completely.

She was the type of girl who looked good in anything she wore, but tonight, in the orange cropped top and short cheerleader style skirt, she had the attention of most of the male patronage in the club, whether they were accompanied or not.

'Jesus, man, she is FIT!!!' Kevin continued, more to himself than to John.

John watched her go past and he had to agree with his friend. She was indeed a beautiful girl.

Kevin turned to him, suddenly animated with an idea. 'Hey John, do you think you could hook me up with that Jenny bird? She is gorgeous.'

John shrugged, it was no skin off his nose, he was happy with Gill and couldn't see himself with anyone else for the rest of his life. 'I don't see why not. I'll see what I can do.'

'Jenny... Hey Jenny.' He caught her attention with his shout. 'Come here a minute, would you?'

She was all smiles as she made her way over to where John and Kevin were stood. 'Hey John, you having a good time?' As she asked this it was obvious that Kevin wasn't even on her radar.

'Yeah, excellent party. Hey, I'd like you to meet my good friend Kevin here.' John replied motioning towards him with his beer in his hand.

She looked at him and beamed a wide, enthusiastic smile.

'Hi Kevin, you enjoying the party?' She asked.

'Yeah, this DJ is great. Listen, I was won...'

'Well, if the DJ's that good, then why don't you fuck off back over to the dance floor and enjoy him then?' She said, still smiling that dazzling smile of hers.

Kevin recoiled as if he had been slapped, which in a way, John supposed he had.

Jenny flashed John a warm smile, winked at him and then walked back the way she'd came, but not before stopping and kissing John on the cheek with a small, but lingering kiss.

He was shocked, and embarrassed about what had just occurred. He couldn't believe what had just happened. His wide eyes didn't even register her kiss, and with his mouth still agape, he watched her walk back to her seat at the table.

When he could speak, all he could manage was an attempt at an apology.

Kevin had rebounded from this knock-back a lot better than John had, and was nodding as he watched Jenny walk off.

'Kev, mate, I'm so sorry!'

'Ah, don't worry about it man, it's not the first knock back I've had tonight. Listen, I think she's right, I'll just fuck off back over here and enjoy the DJ. I'll see you in computers on Monday, yeah?'

He chinked John's glass and walked off back towards the dance floor. John tracked his movements as he put his pint down by the big speakers on the other side of the room, before skulking out of the exit.

John was livid. He turned back towards the group intending to challenge Jenny for her rudeness, but before he could say anything, he was accosted by Carl and Robert, Ben and Patrick were stood behind them. 'John, can we have a quick word mate?' Robert asked, making it sound like it wasn't a request.

He looked at the four lads before him, confusion and intimidation where the two words that flashed through his consciousness. 'Yeah, of course.'

Carl put his arm around him and led him away from the group, towards a small dark recess in the club. 'Let's just go over here where it's a bit quieter eh?' He guided the bewildered John away from the crowd, and the other three followed. He looked to see were Gill was, and

The Twelve

saw her still sat at the table, looking this way, watching what was happening. A look of slight concern on her face.

Robert took John by the elbow and turned him to face him. 'John...' he began, speaking to him like a teacher speaking to a class of naïve schoolchildren, '...you need to get your head around the fact that you're a part of The Twelve. You're better than anyone else in here. You *will* achieve greatness in your life, and that greatness will be due solely to us.'

'You can be their friend, John,' Carl continued. 'You can talk to them, drink with them, maybe even fuck a few of them, but we're The Twelve and we don't need them, or anyone else. Six guys, six girls, it's the eternal number man. It won't be long now and everything will become clear to you.'

'Come clear for what?' John asked.

'You'll see,' Carl replied, patting him, condescendingly, on the shoulder.

John didn't feel too much like partying after that conversation, but he thought his absence would look too suspicious, and after all, he wondered if he would have gotten with, and still been with Gill if not for this little group. Completely sober now, he went to the bar and ordered himself two large vodka and cokes. He wondered, not for the first time, what the hell he had gotten himself into.

36.

TWO DAYS LATER, it was Monday morning. John's Sunday had been spent alone, mostly revising, and trying to keep his distance from any of The Twelve, including Gill. That had been difficult. When she had called his flat, he feigned a bad hangover and told her that he needed to go back to bed, they had had several superficial conversations over the course of the day, but the truth was that he was more than a little sickened by what he'd witnessed, and he needed time to process that.

Absence, as they say, makes the heart grow fonder, and he was already ready to cave from his abstinence. He was missing Gill too much to stay away from them all completely.

He was sat in the lecture room for the early morning computer science class, and was studiously going over some of his notes before the lecture began.

He looked up, just as Kevin entered the theatre. His head was down and he was removing his bag strap, slowly and carefully from over his head.

'Kev… Kevin, over here mate.' John shouted to him.

Kevin turned to face him.

John was stunned at what he saw.

As Kevin raised his hand to acknowledge him, he winced and grabbed at his shoulder with his other hand. His face was a mess. He looked like he'd been horrifically outmatched in a boxing ring. His nose was swollen with a white plaster over the bridge, it was supporting two

The Twelve

puffed-up and purple eyes, and there was a butterfly stitch over one of his eyebrows.

He smiled at John, as much as his bruised bottom lip would allow, before turning away and sitting on the far end of the theatre. Several other students watched him as he limped over to his seat.

John couldn't believe what he was seeing. Angry and infuriated he got up from his seat and chased his friend down, calling after him.

As Kevin turned around to face him, John saw that his wounds were even worse on closer inspection. His eyes were red and rheumy, his bottom lip was swollen as it was healing from a deep cut.

'Jesus, what the fuck happened to you man? I only saw you Saturday night?'

'Oh, sorry John. I didn't want you to worry about it.' His voice had a small lisp to it as it was obvious it was hurting him to talk. 'I was in a little world of my own then. Fuck, well, I got off not long after getting the old heave-ho from your fit mate.'

John shook his head, still deeply embarrassed about that situation. 'Kev man, I'm so sorry about that, it was rude and out of order and I must say a little bit out of character of her. I think she was just a bit drunk you know.'

Kevin put some effort into raising his hand to stop him from talking. 'It's fine man. Anyway, as I was saying, I got outside and had to get some money from the machine to get home, that's when I was jumped. Bastards got thirty pounds and my CD Walkman.'

There was a distinctive, thin white cable protruding out of Kevin's top; it was the cable of a CD Walkman, the same cable that was calling Kevin a liar right there and then.

He noticed John looking at the cable and tried to discreetly hide it away.

Ignoring this, John continued. 'Did you call the police?'

'Nah, I just went to A&E and got myself patched up, it's no biggie, I'm fine.'

Not entirely believing this elaborate story, John continued. 'Listen, I still want to apologise for Jenny, man it was just...'

Kevin tried to smile, it was once again obvious that this hurt him too much as he put his hand up to the cut in the lip, he licked it to see if there was any blood. There wasn't. 'Listen, don't worry about it,' the smile continued to look painful, but his puffy eyes held a little bit of lightness. 'It turns out I got her number anyway.'

John looked confused. 'You did? Oh... right then, well happy days!'

'Yeah, it is. Listen I got to run, I'm cutting this class today, I've got somewhere to be, but I'll catch you later.' He turned and limped off, struggling to put his bag back over his shoulder, he stopped and turned towards John. 'Can you do me a favour?'

John looked at him. In truth he felt a little bit sorry for this lad. He'd never seen him hanging around, or having conversations with anyone other than him. He also felt kind of responsible for what had, or hadn't, happened after the Cooler on Saturday.

'Yeah, sure. Name it.'

'Get me the notes for the class, would you?'

John smiled. 'Yeah, no worries, go on, get to where you're going man, and take it easy when you get there. No more fights, OK?'

Kevin gave him some thumbs before limping off out of the lecture theatre.

He watched him go, confused as to what had happened on Saturday night. Nothing sat right with him about it. The strange talk that he'd had with Carl and Robert right after the pretty awful knock back Jenny had

The Twelve

instilled on Kevin, and then him turning up, beaten to a pulp but conveniently in possession of Jenny's phone number.

He walked back to his seat and was pleasantly surprised to see Gill sitting in the seat next to his, he hadn't seen her come in. His heart began to flutter as she flashed him a lopsided smile.

'Hey stranger.'

'Hey you,' he replied.

'I've missed you. You know I could have cured that little hangover of yours,' she said as he sat down next to her and gave her a kiss. Her hand slid down secretly towards his crotch and gave him a saucy little squeeze.

'You could? So now you tell me, after me lying on my deathbed for two full days,' he lied.

'Yeah, well… maybe a little space makes things even…' she squeezed his crotch again for emphasis, '…better!'

John was looking around the theatre, no-one was paying them any attention.

'Listen, I'm not hanging around any computer classes, it smells like a meat pie in here,' she announced looking around at the other students. 'I just came to tell you that I've missed you and that I've kind of got us hooked into a foursome tonight with Nicky and Ben.' She grimaced a little as if waiting for his approval.

He rolled his eyes, but smiled anyway. Nicky was OK, but he thought Ben was a little bit intense with his in-depth knowledge of video nasties. He did want to spend some time with Gill though.

'Back to mine afterwards… I baked some lasagne over the weekend, I've still got some left.'

He was broken right there and then, he couldn't resist her lasagne.

37.

'I'M REALLY LOOKING forward to the meeting; at least we'll get an idea of what all this involves,' Ben said as the waitress brought their meals over to their table.

John was feeling awkward, he hadn't had much contact with this couple before this meal, apart from being in the same room as them a few times, but Gill seemed perfectly at ease.

'I think Ben's just excited about seeing Carl's arse,' Nicky giggled.

Although he didn't really know them, John was starting to warm to them. They had quite a funny side, when previously he had thought of them as a little 'stuck up'.

Gill was laughing as she took a swig of her large glass of rosé wine. 'Believe me Ben, you're not missing anything. When I think back about all those blackheads!' She pulled a face while swigging another gulp from her wine glass. 'I think Johnny Boy here's more interested in Debbie and Jenny.'

John blushed a bright red. *I really need to control these blushes,* he thought while laughing out loud.

'See!' She shouted, teasing and pointing at him. 'Look how red he's gone.'

She reached over and tickled his ribs, everyone at the table laughed and drained their drinks.

The night had been a success.

The Twelve

When the meal was finished and the bills had been paid, they made their goodbyes and the two couples went their separate ways.

John and Gill walked down the canal walkway towards her flat. She slipped her arm within his arm linking him, and they walked, silently, for a small while. He liked it when she did that.

He was a little drunk, but he still needed answers, and now seemed as good a time as any to get some. 'Gill, what's happening? What exactly are The Twelve doing? I've tried to ask Carl a few times but he just swerves the question. Why has there got to be twelve?'

'Do you like my lasagne?' Gill asked from left field.

'Eh... yeah, you know it's one of my favourites, but you're skirting my...'

She turned towards him quite unexpectedly and kissed him full on the mouth.

They'd kissed any number of times before, they'd even had mad, passionate sex, he'd done things with Gill that he never, ever thought he'd do with a woman as good looking as her, but there was something about this kiss. Something deeper.

'I'm glad you like it.' She whispered, a little breathlessly.

She smiled at him. For the first time in their relationship he saw her looking vulnerable, open even.

'It's my all-time favourite thing to cook. Let's go home right now and enjoy the best lasagne you'll ever taste, and tomorrow we can talk, OK?'

With that she led him off towards her house.

When they got inside she dragged him straight upstairs. He never got to eat his lasagne that night.

38.

JOHN WAS LYING naked in Gill's bed smoking one of her cigarettes. She'd gone downstairs to get them a can of lager each. As she came back into the room holding two cold tins; John moved over to make room for her in the bed.

She placed one can next to him and the other she opened and put on her bedside cabinet, and then she climbed into the bed and cuddled right into him.

He loved how the feel of her cold skin against his warm skin brought him out in goose-bumps, it also gave him a ping of arousal down below.

'Did you enjoy that?' She asked with the lopsided grin that now he'd fallen head over heels in love with.

He pulled an exaggerated non-committal face. 'It was alright like… I've had better.'

She laughed and jumped on top of him and began to tickle his ribs again, giggling even more when he fought back, tickling her.

After a few nice moments of pretend, naked wrestling they both flopped down onto the bed, sighing as they did.

He sat up, cracked open his lager and looked at her. Her beautiful pale skin had red welts in it now where he'd been tickling her. He sat there for a few moments, just staring. *She's almost a different person when she's not around the others*, he thought.

'Hey weirdo… take a photograph why don't you, it'll last longer,' she kidded him.

The Twelve

'Gill, I need to know what's happening here. Both with us and with The Twelve.'

'Oh, the first part's really easy,' she replied smiling. 'We're falling in love.' She gave him a bright smile and then manoeuvred her hand down inside the blankets. John gasped, and involuntarily jerked forwards, spilling a little of his lager onto the bed sheets, as it reached its destination.

It took him a few seconds to recover. 'You know what I mean, what's the script with The Twelve?' He asked this as he wiped the spilled beer from the bed.

Her hand grasped his semi-erection tighter, causing him to squirm again, in a delicious way.

She sighed a little and then let go of his manhood. 'OK. We're all going to find out exactly what the details are when we meet.'

'Everyone keeps going on about this meeting,' he interrupted. 'When's it supposed to be?'

'Within the next couple of weeks apparently, after the end of year party.'

'So, what are we going to be doing at this meeting? Is it all the sexy stuff you mentioned? I mean, other than that, what's really the point?'

Gill turned all serious on him. 'The point of The Twelve is to achieve greatness, for all of us. All friends together.'

John laughed, as he did he realised he sounded a little more than condescending. 'How is a sex meeting going to get us all to achieve greatness?'

She sat up herself and reached over for her can of lager. 'It's an occult thing. The sacrifice of our bodies. That's what the sex is all about. The sacrifice, along with some old incantations Carl and Robert know, that's what'll bring about our greatness.'

John took a swig of his lager; he wasn't looking at her now. 'Well, I hope I'm not selling my soul to the Devil, just for quick shag with you and Debbie.'

A flicker of anger flashed across Gill's face, it was only there for a fraction of a second before she turned and smiled at him. Her hand was creeping back underneath the covers. 'I'm hoping it's not quick,' she said raising her eyebrows, while she did her best to raise something else too.

John laughed again. 'Jesus, I never thought of that. What if I can't, you know, rise to the occasion?' He meant this to come out sounding like a joke, but, as he heard the words come out of his mouth, it became a real and deep paranoia.

Gill ignored his little quip and continued to massage his already hard cock again. 'Then, apparently, something or other happens and we're able to make one wish,' she continued. 'It can't be something like 'I want one million pounds' it should be something along the lines of 'I want to be a successful lawyer or doctor' or something like that. Then, within twenty years it'll all come true apparently. I don't know if I am one-hundred percent sure about it, but nothing ventured, nothing gained eh?'

'Twenty years, Jesus that's forever, what do we do until then?'

He grabbed her and rolled her over on the duvet, and climbed on top of her. His erection was strong and ready for her. She reached down and grabbed his shaft; she stroked down and then began to cup his balls. As she did her piercing green eyes were looking deeply, lovingly and passionately, into his blue ones.

'I've got a few ideas,' she said raising her eyebrows and flashing him her gorgeous lopsided grin.

Present day

39.

A WORRIED LOOKING John was sat in the police station waiting room, he'd brought all the correct ID and paraphernalia with him, and he was also custodian of the photograph, the same photograph that he couldn't bring himself to look at anymore.

He'd noticed that morning that two other faces had now begun to blur, Nicky McEvoy's and Ben Lomax's. It seemed that each time he looked at it someone else would be... disappearing.

Debbie was now completely gone, along with Gill, Patrick, Carl and Robert, and here he was, alive and well sitting in a bland reception room in a bland police station.

'Mr Rydell,' a rather bland looking receptionist, fitting in with the décor, called his name and he looked up towards her. 'Detective Addison will see you now.' She led him into the back of the station, and indicated towards a door.

A rather gravelly voice behind it shouted after she knocked. 'Come in.'

He entered the room and was greeted with a big man wearing spectacles, a mop of unruly hair and a tweed jacket. The face completely suited his voice.

'Mr Rydell, thank you so much for coming in. Please take a seat.' The detective stood and indicated the seat opposite him at the small wooden table in the centre of the room. 'Please, allow me to apologise for my abruptness on the telephone yesterday, but you must understand the pressures we work under here when we need to determine if we have a murder case on our hands. In this case, we're still working on that, and I had to talk to you, just to cover every base so to speak.'

'Thanks Detective, I do appreciate that. I'm under a bit of stress myself, I recently lost my wife to a ...'

'So, I understand, Mr Rydell,' he interrupted opening the file and looking at the sheets of paper inside. He adjusted his glasses as he continued. 'She was home alone I believe; you were in...' he leafed a couple more of the pages, 'erm, Chicago?'

'Yeah, I was on business. I see you've done your homework,' John said with a humourless smile.

Addison nodded as he looked across the table at him, and closing the file. He could feel the policeman stare, probing about in his head as he did. 'Indeed I have Mr Rydell. I have to in this line of work.'

There was a moment of intimidating silence between them then, John felt most uncomfortable.

'Did you bring the photo I requested?' The detective asked, eventually breaking the silence.

Already we're into the dark areas, I'd hate to be guilty and have to face this guy, John thought.

'I'm sure you're aware that there are some coincidences here Mr Rydell. I don't know if you've been brought up to date on this case, but Ms Baines was killed in much the same manner as your unfortunate wife.' He opened his files again and took a quick look. 'Gill.' He concluded.

All John could do was nod; he felt the blood rush through his ears again.

'Coincidence and inconsistencies, Mr Rydell, and I think this picture you have in your possession, may create more questions than it answers.' He paused for a few moments studying John's reactions.

The Twelve

'May I?' He finally broke the silence again and offered out his hand towards John. Indicating that he wanted the picture.

John rummaged in his inside pocket until he found the small envelope he'd put it in, mainly to stop it being damaged, but also to stop himself from having to look at it again.

'I need you to know that prior to the day before yesterday I'd never even seen this photo, I never even knew it existed.' Feeling like a guilty party, John handed the photo over to the detective.

'I'm willing to guess, that the people behind these blurred faces are, your wife, Debbie Baines, Carl Brookes, Robert Cobham, and Patrick Mahone. I've no idea who these other two people are,' he stated, pointing the pen he was holding towards the blurred images of Ben and Nicky.

'You'd be right, Detective. The other two people are Ben Lomax and Nicky McEvoy, although I don't know if that's still her surname. I haven't seen them in quite a while. I'm a little bit concerned, as when their...'

He wasn't given the chance to complete his sentence. 'I'm going to need this photograph, Mr Rydell, and I'm also going to need you to stay local, at least until we can eliminate you from all of our enquiries.' Addison began to shuffle the file before them, before picking up the photograph from the table, giving it a cursory glance before slipping it back into the envelope.

'I'm free to go?'

The detective looked at him and cocked his head, inquisitively. 'Unless you have any other business, then yes Mr Rydell, you're free to go.'

John stood and held out his hand towards the big detective. Addison looked at it as if it was something alien to him, before tentatively taking the hand in his and shaking it.

John left the room alone. He felt dirty somehow, as if he had been violated or raped or something. He left the station with a cold shudder, only wanting to get home as fast as he could, and get a shower to wash this filthy feeling away.

As he journeyed home on the train all he could think about was the photograph. It *was* pretty damning. This thought led him to another regarding his old friends.

I'll have to contact Ben and Nicky somehow, warn them that something terrible might be coming their way. His ponderings carried him all the way to his front door.

An odd sound come from inside as he stepped over the mantle into the house. He stopped and listened again, holding his breath and trying to filter out everything else around him.

It was silent once again.

Shaking his head, he continued, gingerly, into the hallway. The first thing that hit him was the stink. A thick, vile stench slamming into him as he entered the house. Gagging somewhat, he proceeded inside. He wrapped his jacket over his nose and mouth to filter out the smell before moving further inside. The filter didn't work, and he fancied that he could almost taste the foul smell.

The second thing he noticed was that the reoccurring, freezing cold was back. Again, he fancied that he would be able to see his own breath before him if he didn't have the jacket wrapped around his face.

As a test, he stepped back outside the front door onto his path, it was like walking through a curtain of warm air. The instant he was outside he warmed up.

He stepped in, freezing, he stepped out, warm.

This is madness, he thought.

He re-entered the house, determined to find out where the smell was coming from, and to find out the cause of the intense cold.

The Twelve

He knocked the living room door open with his hip, one hand was guarding his nose while the other was rubbing his arm in a vain attempt to keep warm.

Something by the television screen caught his eye instantly, something that hadn't been there before he'd left for the police station this morning. Adrenaline coursed through his body as he stared at it in disbelief.

The bones in his neck creaked as he snapped his head around the room attempting to locate the obvious intruder who had placed it there.

There were no signs of a break in, everything else was normal, nothing was out of place, anywhere, with the exception for the one, small, impossible object next to his TV. It shouldn't have been there, but it was, and he was looking right at it.

'Hello… Hello,' he shouted around the house, feeling a little silly. 'Listen, if there's anyone in here, please just leave. Just take what the fuck you want, I don't care anymore, but leave me alone.'

He scanned the room again, this time looking for any other small, subtle changes, but nothing had been disturbed, everything looked as he would have expected it to look.

He forced himself to look towards the TV again. The object was still there, it mocked him, hurting his brain. Nothing had been taken, but it seemed something had been given!

His hands were shaking rather badly. He didn't want to touch it, twice his fingers had fallen for its trick, but he knew that he had to touch it, he had to pick up the impossible object, if only to inform his brain that it was there, and not a figment of his warped imagination.

He reached out towards it. His fingers exploring its boundaries, testing it to see if it was safe to touch. He still couldn't believe that it was there, in his living room. He braved the touch, and although very cold, this time it didn't bite. He ran his hands over it, trying to gauge if it was real or not. It most definitely felt and looked real.

He put the photograph, the exact same photograph, in the exact same frame that he'd just left with Detective Addison in the police station, back down onto the TV unit. He blew on his hands trying his best to get blood flowing back into them due to the cold in the room and from holding the cold, metal photograph frame.

Dazed, he shuffled out of the room shaking his head. 'I've had too long a day.' he said aloud to, he hoped, no-one as he made his way upstairs towards the bedroom.

He flopped onto the bed and wrapped the covers tightly around himself. He was asleep almost instantly, even though it was barely past noon.

Downstairs in the living room the picture on the TV stand began to alter. Ice fingers crept over the metal of the frame, licking at the glass. The blurring of the images of Ben Lomax and Nicky McEvoy was complete and the image of Brenda Osman was just beginning.

40.

THE POLICE ARRIVED at Mr and Mrs Lomax's residence; it was not the first time they had been called to this wealthy address in Chessington. The Lomax's were a very nice couple, well off, respected members of the community. But their children seemed to be uncontrollable, or one of them at least.

William Lomax was a tearaway; he had been from a young age. If there was trouble in the street or the surrounding areas, the police would put a bet on that William was either at the centre of it, or at the very least in the peripherals.

This time the police feared the worst.

PC Chamberlain was first responder on the scene. He had received the call when he came on duty at midnight for the graveyard shift, so called as this was the shift were all the weirdos, psychos and zombies came alive to run riot in the streets of London. 616 Vulcan Avenue. An address most policemen around this area knew only too well. Benjamin and Nicola, Mr and Mrs Lomax, were the parents of William.

When this particular call came in and it was passed to PC Chamberlain, he promptly put it towards the back of his priority list. It was Friday night in Chessington, twelve miles away from Central London, the busiest night of the week. All the young 'chavs' from the sleepy part of the village would be out, running amok in the pubs and bars. The location also attracted many office type people who would rather pay a lot less for their drinks while they were out than in the downtown west-end bars.

So, a call from an address in sleepy Vulcan Avenue, a sprawling green area of the town, relating to the fact that the residents of number 616 were fighting again, could they please send someone to investigate, was bottom of the list domestic disturbance stuff.

As it turned out, there wouldn't have been anything he could have done anyway, even if he had turned up at five past midnight.

The Twelve

41.

AT TEN PM in 616 Vulcan Avenue Ben Lomax was upstairs in his study. He was doing what he did best, something he loved and was passionate about, he was cramming. There had been a rudimentary change in the university curriculum, where he was a senior lecturer. It was evident that they wanted more computer based practicals in physics these days. He could never keep up with all the new-fangled technology. But if he was to have any hope of becoming the front runner for the Dean of Learning in the university, then he had better roll with the changes. With that interview looming in four days, he thought it prudent to get to grips with the ins and outs of it all. It had been hard at first, a whole new world of terminology and syntax, but once he had gotten his head around the fundamentals, he was finding it all rather fun.

Nicola Lomax, his wife, was downstairs in her study; she was learning lines for her part in the long running radio soap opera she was the main star in, 'if you could actually star in a radio soap opera,' her husband would tease her.

What she knew, and no-one else did was that they were killing her character off in a bizarre, gardening related tragedy. She had been offered a lead part in a new television based situation comedy. It was a newly commissioned sitcom, based around the adventures of a group of bored wives of men who spend all their time in their inner-city gardens. It was called 'And the Plot Thickens'. She was so excited, it meant the real fame, that she had craved and longed for, was now within her grasp.

Their oldest son William didn't live with them anymore, well at least not officially. He'd moved address about twelve times in the last two years, but they'd wake any number of times to find him sleeping on the couch in the front room. He usually stayed for two or three days, getting all he could from them, including free bed and board, before leaving again, usually taking any money and any number of valuables he could find, with him.

Mark was their second child; he lived away in university and was shaping up to be a good kid. He worked hard to receive excellent grades in school, picked himself up a fantastic part time job while studying. He had a rather attractive, intelligent girlfriend and a group of nice friends. Basically, he was a million miles removed from his wayward brother.

But their pride and joy was fast asleep in her room.

Carla was five, she had been their last hope for saving their marriage, and it seemed to have worked a treat. She was a beautiful little thing, loving, attentive and best of all fast asleep in her room; that was usually their cue to have a little drink.

But not tonight!

Tonight, was different.

Over the last few days their nice, little cosy life had been turned a little upside down.

They had been experiencing strange events, both in their home and in their workplaces. Vile smells, mysterious cold snaps, feelings like they are being watched. There had even been instances of strange shadows darting out of view from their peripheral vision. These bizarre events had been unsettling for them, as they had been happening to them individually, never together. They had both dismissed them as tiredness or nothing more than coincidence, and had both failed to mention them to each other.

The Twelve

Tonight, was different. It was probably due to their hard schedule, the upcoming changes in their lives, and just general tiredness, but there was an edge about them both. They couldn't be in the same room as each other without a stupid squabble breaking out. They thought that a little time apart, in different rooms would do them the world of good.

At about ten pm, from his study just a little further down the landing, Ben heard his daughter get out of bed and walk out of her room. This was a strange occurrence as she was normally a deep sleeper, once she began to snore and twitch, that was her for the night.

Worried that she might be a little sick, he swivelled on his chair and listened to determine what direction she went. After a few seconds, he got up from his desk and went onto the landing to investigate.

As he opened the door he jumped back, grabbing at his chest as he did. Carla was in the doorway, rubbing her eyes, holding her brand-new teddy bear and looking up at him. Her hair was all messed up and her eyes were red, not from crying but from being rudely awoken from a deep sleep.

'Hey baby, what's the matter?' He panted as breath slowly seeped back into his body. He was rubbing his arms over his sleeves to warm his skin from the sudden temperature drop in the house that he had only just noticed.

He picked her up and gave her a big daddy hug.

'Where is mummy?' She asked in her sleepy, whiny voice.

'Downstairs baby face, do you want me to take you down?'

'Yes, please daddy. I *really* don't like that man!'

Ben's face fell. Although he loved ghost stories, and was a fiend for gore films and ghost hunts in his youth, there was something different about a little girl telling you that she had seen a strange man. A shiver ran through him, when she didn't smile and laugh it off.

'What man?' He asked glancing back towards her room. Her ajar door looked cold and distant along the landing in the dull glow of her nightlight.

'The man I told you about the other day daddy. Were you not listening to me?'

'Of course, I was baby. I'll tell you what, let's go and see mummy and you can tell us both all about it eh?'

'Can't you just go in and tell him to go away Daddy? I don't like him, he hides his face.'

Ben half smiled at his daughter, this wasn't something that he wanted to play with right now. He had studying to do, that had nothing to do with men who hid their faces in little girl's rooms.

'Let's go and see mummy, I'll make you some hot milk and jam on toast, OK?'

She broke out into a big smile and hugged him around his neck. As she did, he noticed that her skin was freezing cold, and that they were both blowing clouds of breath with each word. He glanced back at the room. As he did a strange noise, like a wind whipped around him, but it sounded more like a whisper.

'Thiiiiiiiiiiirteeeeeeeeeen.'

The hairs on the back on his neck stood up at the sound and he carried Carla down the stairs, maybe a little bit faster than was safe.

~~~

A few nights earlier, around about the time when Ben had started to notice the smells and the cold snaps; Carla had come to their bedroom complaining that a strange man was looking at her from the corner of the room. She claimed that he'd pulled a funny face at her, even though he didn't have a proper mouth, and then he'd gone away again, through the wall.

The Twelve

They'd both laughed this off a childish nightmare. 'Too much television before bedtime,' they'd both agreed.

They had then carried her into her room and checked it all out anyway. Mainly for Carla's sake, but to be perfectly honest, for their own peace of mind too. They made a game of it, checking the outside of the house too, letting Carla know that they were leaving no stone unturned.

To both of their relief, they had found nothing.

Individually, they found it a little disturbing that Carla's strange dream had come during their own bouts of undisclosed strangeness, but they racked it up to silly coincidence.

~~~

'Mummy, Carla's had another nightmare.' Ben announced as he carried his little girl into his wife's study.

'Oh no,' she cried. 'Come here my beautiful little girl.'

Nicky took the headphones off her head and opened her arms out wide for Ben and Carla to both come in for a cuddle. 'Do you want to tell mummy and daddy what scared you?'

'It was the man again mummy, he was in my room! I don't like him and I wish he'd just leave me alone. He stinks! He did speak to me this time though.' The little girl was enjoying the centre stage of attention she was getting from her parents, and was ready to tell everything. 'What does the number thirteen mean mummy?'

Nicola pulled a face and shook her head. 'Nothing honey,' she answered glancing over at Ben with a quizzical look. 'Some people think that it brings bad luck, that's all. Why do you ask?'

She pulled an annoyed face, clearly enjoying herself. 'It's what the man kept whispering to me.' She screwed her face up and held her fingers out, making them into claws. 'Thiiiiiiiiiiirteeeeeeeeeen!!!' She whispered in a creepy voice that sent another rash of goose-bumps up her father's spine. 'Just like that.'

Both parents looked at each other. Ben shook his head, raising his eyebrows towards his wife. She shrugged her shoulders, neither of them had any idea what the little girl was talking about. They both feigned empathy towards her.

'Tell daddy what this man looks like.' Ben put Carla down on her mother's lap and sat next to them on the big chair to the side. *I bet Will's got something to do with this,* he thought. *If he has, then he's not going to get away with it this time.*

Carla was beginning to get into the swing of her show now; her audience were in thrall.

'Well, he's little bit smaller than you daddy, and I think he's younger than you too. But don't worry, you're not creepy like him.' She flung her arms around him giving him a massive hug.

'That's OK honey, when did he start to come?'

'He usually comes right after the yucky smell does. He smells really bad. It's like someone has done a big poop and not flushed.' She ducked her head towards her parents then, worried that she'd said a bad word and wondering if she was going to be in trouble.

When she saw that she wasn't, she continued. 'After the smell, well then it always gets really, cold, freezing cold, like it is now, but worse. I have to wrap my blankets around me extra tight to keep the cold out. It's usually when my clock has a three at the start.'

She had the full attention of both parents right now, especially after the comments regarding the smell and the cold. Nicky was starting to get scared. 'Does this man, does he… touch you?' She was gingerly broaching the subject that she knew Ben would want to explore too. They both shared a look, it was something that neither of them were ready to talk about to a five-year-old. Both silently praying for an answer in the negative.

The little girl gave them such a dirty look, like she thought she was talking to two of the most stupid people on the planet. 'No! He can't touch me, but he can walk through walls.' She giggled a little then turned her attention to her mother's computer screen. 'Is the cartoon channel still on?'

Both of them felt slightly relieved. Ben hated himself for thinking that maybe William had been touching his sister, but nothing could surprise him about that boy anymore. Nicky even laughed a little at Carla's total switch away from her creepy story.

'Imaginary friend!' Nicky mouthed silently to Ben. 'She'll be fine. Go back to your books.'

He smiled, kissed the top of Carla's head and walked out of the room.

As he got halfway up the stairs he was hit by the rank smell again, and the intense cold. *What could be causing that?* He thought. He flashed back to Carla's story and shivered a little as he continued to climb. Nearing the top of the stairs he had to stop as he overheard something Carla was saying to her mother.

'Oh mummy, I forgot to tell you that the man also asked me to tell you that he would be seeing you soon, you and daddy. So, you'll be able to see him for yourselves then, won't you?' Carla was not looking at her mother now as the cartoons had her full attention.

Her little face turned deadly serious and she broke her attention to the TV to look at her mother, she was sporting the biggest, saddest eyes that Nicky had ever seen. Amidst the jittery fear, she was feeling regarding what her daughter had just told her, it still broke her heart to see her little face like that.

'What is it honey?'

Tears began to well up in her eyes and her bottom lip began to tremble. 'He's not going to be my new brother, is he? I don't think I'd like him as a brother.'

The Twelve

42.

WELL AFTER MIDNIGHT, much later than he usually worked, Ben stretched and reached over to turn off his computer. *I'm never going to get to grips with that thing*, he thought with a dismal shake of his head. As he left the study, the thick, cloying stench of rotten meat hit him again. It was so bad that it almost felt... physical! He held his nose, hoping that just this small a gesture would be able to block out the rankness of the house. *I'll have to get someone in*, he thought. *If it's a dead cat or something stuck in the chimney flue then I don't want to have to deal with that.*

'Nicky...' he half shouted, half whispered down the stairs. 'Nicky... are you still awake?'

There was no answer.

He continued downstairs and entered into the living room, noticing as he did, that the television was still on. Some kind of strange cartoon was playing and he stopped to watch it a little. A sponge, with arms and legs and wearing a pair of lederhosen, was talking to some bizarre, phallic looking pink creature. He shook his head and tutted. *Things have really changed since Tom and Jerry,* he thought as he moved to turn the TV off.

On removing his hand from his nose, he noticed that the smell was worse down here than it was upstairs, if that was even possible.

He thought about Carla's imaginary friend, and it chilled him, a shudder wracked through his body. The cold was back now too, only this time much worse than before. His arms, beneath his t-shirt were a sea of goose-bumps and every hair on them were stood to attention.

His nipples were so tight that they were stinging where they rubbed on the fabric of his clothing.

He turned to regard the room, and saw the damnedest thing.

Nicky was sat on the couch, stock still; her eyes were wide open and staring out at him. Her face looked… wrong somehow, less like Nicky. She looked older, and she looked petrified.

Carla was in her arms sleeping soundly.

'Nicky, what's wrong?' He asked, genuinely worried.

'Thiiiiiiiiiiiirteeeeeeeeeen!!!' Came a whisper, almost as loud as a shout, from somewhere behind him.

'Remember… thiiiiiiiiiiiirteeeeeeeeeen?'

Ben swallowed and clenched his fists. He didn't want to even consider what could have made that sound. It brought back details of every video nasty that he had laughed through during his youth. His imagination brought forth images of clowns and spiders and masked mad-men.

Using every last force of his will, he turned around, very slowly. He didn't want to, but he was a slave to his curiosity, and it was telling him that he needed to follow the sound of the eerie whisper.

What he saw was worse than any special effect, mostly because this wasn't a film, this was real, and it was happening to him, not some scantily clad college kids in America. It caused him to, let loose the loudest, most spine-chilling scream he'd ever emitted in his whole forty-two years. It was this exact scream that prompted their closest neighbours to call the police.

He could feel all control ebbing away from his bodily functions, and his bladder opened of its own accord. A small amount of urine leaked from him, staining the front of his trousers, as he fought a raging internal struggle to regain control. He wasn't one hundred per cent sure if he was hallucinating, or not. He had come to the rational conclusion that he couldn't be as Nicky was seeing this horror too.

The only difference between them, was that she didn't seem to be able to move, whilst he could.

Sat in the large armchair to the side of the television was a man, or it could have been a boy, Ben couldn't determine due to the dark hooded top he wore. The hood was pulled up, intentionally hiding his face.

There was an aura of complete and utter malice about him. Ben had found the source of the smell of rotten meat and faeces after all, it radiated from this boy, as did the intense cold.

Plumes of steamed breath emanated from the dark hood as the thing beneath it, breathed. The temperature in the room continued to drop. The horror of this figure in his living room, of it watching him, of it appearing from nowhere, was enhanced by the one rational thought left in Ben's head. He thought that he knew this apparition, somehow.

'Are…. Are you the boy from Carla's room?' It was the only question he could bring himself to ask.

As if on cue, the ghost began to remove his hood, his silver eyes glowing brighter in the darkness underneath. The sight that Ben beheld was far worse than the smell and the cold combined.

The impossible thing revealed itself and he saw that it was, indeed a boy. His head had been badly shaved bald, there were huge and deep divots of flesh sliced away, revealing red and raw meat beneath. The skin around his glowing eyes looked bruised and beaten, maybe even rotten.

Everything about the boy's face below the twisted, broken stump that was his nose was almost non-existent. In the location where his mouth should have been, there was only a deformed, puffed out mess. The hole was far too wide for his face and it looked like it had been crudely ripped.

Thick, black, blood dripped from the maw and trickled down the hooded top, adding to the dirt and grime that had already collected on it. In the crease of the boy's neck, Ben could see a flap of dirty skin that had been peeled back. The flap was so deep that he could see raw flesh and blood bubbling within, possibly even bone too. The shape and look of the wound indicated that he had had his throat cut, very deeply, allowing Ben to see more of the raw meat beneath the surface.

The boy's flesh that wasn't bruised and bloody was grey and ashen. There was every indication that this ghoul had, sometime in the past, succumbed to foul play, and if that were the case, then this figure before him, even if he did look real, would be a... 'Ghost!' Ben blurted out loud.

He removed his gaze from the abomination, he'd seen far too much.

A wicked and malevolent smile tore across the boy's face, as it did more of the disgusting black jam began to pour from the ruin of his mouth and from the neck wound. Globules of dirty, old blood dribbled down his hooded top. His horrific semi-smile continued to rip the deformed gums within. The dark vileness continued to spew forth from his mouth.

The boy did have teeth however. Ben didn't really want to, but he couldn't help but consider the boy's obscure mouth. He noticed that the ghost's top and bottom line of front teeth from incisor to incisor were mostly missing, all that remained were a few ragged, black and green, rotted stumps. They looked like they had been roughly slotted back into the gum.

Fear and disgust had frozen Ben to the spot, but somehow, he managed to turn around to look towards his

The Twelve

wife. She was still sat in the same position holding Carla, who in turn was still fast asleep.

'Who are you? What do you want?' Ben stuttered as he continued his gaze towards Nicky and Carla. He would have looked at anything to not have to peer upon the ghastly vision in the chair.

'Much...' came the whispered reply. 'Gaze at me... look upon me...' The latter was not a request.

Both Nicky and Ben's heads turned involuntary to look upon the ghost at its insistence.

'Do you not know me? Do you not remember me?'

Neither Ben nor Nicky could answer. They both did recognise him, but, given the option, neither could have said where from.

'Remove the child from my sight... I have no dealings with her.'

Nicky, acting as though she was on autopilot, got up and took Carla out of the room and up the stairs to her bedroom. She put her into her own bed and tucked her in. Once the infant was safely encompassed, she obediently came back down to the front room.

Why can't I move? Ben thought. *Why is she doing what this thing's asking? Why didn't she run?*

'You both stand on the verge of gaining everything you ever wanted...'

Every time the thing spoke, more and more black blood spilled down his pallid white chin, and seeped from the fish-belly wound in his neck. Even though he had very few teeth and a ruined mouth, his speech was perfectly legible.

'I, on the other hand, have nothing! Only you...'

'What do you want? Please, don't hurt us!' Nicky pleaded, Ben watched her as tears streamed down her face. 'We'll do anything you want, please don't hurt us, or our baby.'

'The child is safe. You two on the other hand… are not!'

The ghost stood up from the chair he was sat in, as he did, Ben and Nicky both witnessed something that triggered a memory, a memory long forgotten, almost repressed, and with good reason.

As he stood, a flap of his hooded top fell away, revealing his naked torso beneath. The skin was white and mottled with old scars.

The scars all began to open, each one of them pouring more of the vile, dark blood down the boy's stomach. The folds of skin flapped away revealing the rotten flesh underneath. The motion of his movements caused chunks of the flesh to fall from the wounds in his chest to land in a stinking pile of offal on the floor. The mound of steaming innards formed on the carpet as the boy advanced, slowly upon the besieged couple.

Nicky was first. She couldn't move, her arms and legs were fixed to the floor and her sides. Her whole body began to shudder as convulsions, brought on by fear, fear of this thing from… she just couldn't think of where she knew him from, but whoever, or whatever it was, was moving in on her… to kill her.

The clock on the mantel piece read three-fifteen am. Ben's heart sank as he thought about Carla's revelation that the boy only turned up when her clock had a three at the start.

He watched, helpless as the gruesome figure advanced upon his wife. The only organs that he had a modicum of control over where his eyes, he exercised that control and closed them. He didn't want to see what was about to happen.

Beads of cold sweat stood out on Nicky's forehead, and steam rose from them as the room was so cold. She could hear herself screaming for mercy, repeatedly. Terrified by what was about to happen. In reality, not one sound made it out of her mouth. The screams were all in her head.

Ben tried to move, tried to shout, tried to stop the filthy spirit from doing what he was doing to his wife. Total paralysis was dooming him to witness the oncoming demise of the woman he loved, the woman he had loved since they met in university all those years ago.

I do know you... I do know you, he thought almost incoherently.

I DO know you.

As this thought flared into existence, his face instantly lost all colour. His knees went weak, and this time he didn't just lose control of his bodily functions momentarily, he lost total control.

As the warm stream of urine poured down his leg, he couldn't tear his eyes away from what was happening in his living room. Even though it was disgusting and distressing in equal measures, he was morbidly fascinated with what he was witnessing.

His mind cast back to their days in university, suddenly what was happening here made, a modicum of sense.

'Oh, my God, I'm sorry... I'm so sorry,' he spat as the salty concoction of mucus and tears streamed down his face, towards his remorse filled mouth. It was The Twelve's fault, he knew that now, but he couldn't quite understand what The Twelve was. He couldn't quite remember the reference.

Then names began to filter into his head one by one. 'Fuck you Robert. FUCK YOU!!! I hope you're cursed into HELL!' He didn't know if he was whispering or shouting this, but the words were cathartic nevertheless. 'Why did we follow you? This is your fault! Wherever you are right now I hope you're in fucking agony.'

Nicky was still trying to scream. The thing was almost upon her now. It turned towards Ben and offered him a disgusting smile, making a show of the fingers of his hand as he did. The dead skin of his digits stripped away as they transformed into bony talons, and his mouth and ripped neck stretched, impossibly wide in a rictus. 'You know me now, don't you?' He hissed. It was a maniacal whispered voice, a voice like something way out of the realms of normality.

The talons began to tenderly caress Nicky, touching her almost lovingly, although they left long, deep red welts in their wake on the white, drained skin of her face.

'You know me now and you fear me, don't you?'

He was whispering, intimately into Nicky's ear, like a lover whispering sweet nothings to his sweetheart, but all the while his glowing, silvery eyes were intent on Ben.

Terror engulfed her. Ben could see the struggle within her as she could do nothing to stop what was happening. He could tell that she was trying to speak, to shout, but the fear and the revulsion of the talons were, literally, taking her breath away.

The fiend smiled again, and more blood poured from his mouth and wounds, dripping down his skin and mingling with the sweat of her body. She jolted each time the foul-smelling filth landed on her.

'Well you should,' he continued.

Ben could do nothing but watch as the wraith's skeletal hand traced her features, touching her like a delicate lover. The smell of rotting meat was overwhelming, emanating from the boy and from the black, rotten trail he had left behind him.

The boy then flexed the talons and the bones in his fingers creaked as he waved them in Nicky's face. A small whimper escaped her as her eyes traced the lethal looking fingers.

All Ben could do was watch in dismay as the sharp tip of one of the dagger like talons, slowly pressed into Nicky's neck. With a small pop her skin and flesh were pierced and a single drop of fresh blood seeped out of the wound before trickling down her neck.

She stopped trying to scream and her eyes rolled over towards the back of her head. Another spasm gripped her as she succumbed to the beast's touch. Ben witnessed, in sorrow and disgust, as he wife's legs buckled from underneath her.

With unprecedented grace, the boy wrapped his arm around her back, taking her weight. He laid her gently onto the floor. As he did, he looked back up towards Ben and smiled, a smile filled with smarm. *Look at what I'm doing to your wife*, the look spoke to him, as he began to remove the talons from her neck.

'Why are you doing this?' Ben hissed, using all his strength to form the words. 'You're supposed to be…'

'Dead?' The boy finished for him as he tore through Nicky's clothes, ripping her blouse right off her body. The pressure of the pumping blood from her neck caused it to spray over the walls and the carpet. Her eyes were leaking blood filled tears as all fight flowed out of her via the hole in her neck.

Ben longed to be able to wipe the tears from of his own eyes; he needed to see what was happening. He felt like he had to witness this, but he still couldn't move a muscle.

'Patrick, Gill, Carl… fuck you, fuck the lot of you, especially you Robert, you piece of shit.'

He hadn't spared these people a second thought since they had left university, years ago, but now, suddenly the thought of them was of great importance to him.

The ghost looked up from Nicky, right at him, his silvery eyes held Ben's in their gaze for more than a few seconds. The same, smug grin pulled his skin taught over his dirty, bloody face. 'Why not add Debbie to that list Ben?' It whispered before looking back towards Nicky. 'And…'

Ben was suddenly able to watch what was happening. With dawning terror, he gawked as the boy put his red stained, bony, talons together, the sharp points fitting together to form a single, deadly stiletto. With his dead, silver eyes still holding Ben's, the ghost began to lower its hand towards Nicky's naked stomach.

Please… NO… he screamed within the confines of his own mind. Nicky's face was awake and aware, and she too was watching the progress of the hand journey lower. Helpless to do anything to stop, or combat what was happening to her, her breathing became increasingly laboured, short, fast and shallow. The tip of the dagger hand pressed into her skin.

'Nicky!' The ghost concluded in a sharp whisper. His eyes never leaving Ben's, still smiling a parody of a smile.

A small amount of pressure was applied and with another popping noise, the sharp tip pierced the skin of her belly.

There was an audible rip, followed by various squelching sounds, which were quite possibly the worst sounds Ben had ever heard in his life. His eyes finally broke from the boy's and switched to what was happening to his wife. There was no blood, yet, but the horrible, deformed fingers were deep inside her body now, up to his second, bony knuckle.

Nicky coughed and Ben's eye flicked to her face, just in time to see her own dark, but fresh blood spurt from her mouth.

The Twelve

He closed his eyes again, he didn't want to see what was happening, not to her, not to the love of his life, but not seeing, he found out was a lot worse.

Nicky's scream eventually ripped from her vocal chords, it had been coming for a while, and when it did, it came with gusto. It was ear shattering, blood curdling and wet. More blood projected from her mouth as she shouted at the top of her lungs, joining the arterial spray that was currently adorning the walls and carpet.

The scream was too much, and Ben couldn't help himself but open his eyes and watch.

Strangely, Ben's first thought was *Hush Nicky... You'll wake Carla.* As the ghost's hand pushed deeper and deeper into her stomach. The blood had begun to flow now, and it was seeping from the rough hole that was only semi-plugged by the boy's talon fingers. He thought he would faint, he wanted to faint, but he somehow knew that he wouldn't be allowed to. *He won't give me any relief, not after what we done to him, not if this is all about revenge, and this IS all about revenge*, he thought.

The ghoul had wanted him to witness the horrific disembowelling of his wife. He had kept him awake specifically to absorb every moment of the grisly madness that was happening not five feet from where he stood, paralysed by some unearthly force.

Blood was pumping faster and thicker from Nicky's stomach now, completely ruining the new carpets that they had had laid less than a month ago. The boy's hand was now completely inside of her.

Ben's stomach did somersaults as he watched the filthy, contaminated blood drip from the boy's mouth and neck, he watched it dribble into his wife's deep wound and mingle with her own. This was the moment that it finally dawned on him that neither of them were going to wake up tomorrow. He was never going to take that exam to become dean of the faculty, and Nicky was never going to be the TV star she most desperately wanted to be. Worse than all of that, Carla was going to wake up tomorrow an orphan. He hoped that his boys would be able to step up and take responsibility for her. He knew that one could, but he wasn't so sure about the other.

Nicky's body was shaking violently again as she succumbed to shock. Her skin was now an ashen grey, her pink eyes were open but sightless, and her blood-stained tongue was lolling from one side of her mouth to the other, leaving streaks of red in its wake.

Ben knew that she was beyond help now.

The boy forced his other hand inside her wound, tearing her flesh deeper and wider as he did. There was no precision in his work, he just forced himself into her, tearing her as if she was a package that needed to be opened.

He lowered his face and pulled aside the folds of skin of Nicky's gaping wound. He was looking inside her as Ben stood on, helplessly watching his wife and the mother of his children being gruesomely murdered in their front room. When her violent shaking began to subside, Ben knew that his wife of nearly twenty years was truly dead. He lowered his eyes and mourned.

The boy was still rummaging inside her stomach. He looked like a child trying desperately to get the last, elusive present from the bottom of the Christmas stocking. He began roughly removing the contents of her stomach through the wound, Ben could hear the sickening 'cracks' as her ribcage was pulled apart. The dirty, blood stained face looked up from its grisly duty, and stared right at Ben.

Even though he knew that she was now dead, the thought of this thing's dirty blood mingling in with his wife's clean, fresh blood sickened him to his stomach.

A terrible smile ripped the boy's face further, it seemed that he'd found what he was looking for. 'There

The Twelve

you are,' he whispered reaching deep inside Nicky's, now motionless body, once again. His arms rummaged for a second or two before it stopped, retrieving something from deep inside her. To Ben's eyes it looked like a big bloody lump. He held it up into the light, turning it around and around as he gazed at it as if it was a solid gold nugget.

'Ben Lomax, you have something that is mine too, and I will have it back.'

He noticed, just as boy grabbed him, right before the rotten meat smell coursed into him so thick that he thought he could actually taste it, before he felt the ice cold, but perversely strong hands penetrate his stomach, and of course the inconceivable pain that this caused, taking him to the very edge of consciousness, almost, but not quite tipping him over into the blessed black oblivion of death; but before all that, he noticed that the ghost had one more tooth in his mouth than it had had just a few moments earlier.

'I'm so glad you remember me now. It would have been rude of you to forget me, after my... sacrifice.'

After retrieving what he wanted from his stomach, the ghost dropped Ben onto the floor next to his wife, like a misused and outgrown toy. He smiled another hellishly satisfied smile, then simply shimmered out of existence leaving husband and wife, Ben and Nicky Lomax dead and dying on the floor of their own front room.

Redford University, South London
20 years earlier

43.

MICHAEL BROOKES WAS a self-made millionaire; he'd made his first million setting up a company that specialised in repackaging name branded products into cut price superstore's own packaging. He started this when he was thirty; by thirty-five he had 15 factories across Europe. He then put money into real estate, and this tripled his investments. His next venture saw him take advantage of the potential in a small start-up company on the Alternative Investment Market and loaded a couple of million into that. This investment paid off too, and he made returns in the region of three hundred percent It wasn't bad going for a boy from the poor end of Plymouth docks.

Because of all his hard work, his only child and son, Carl, didn't have to worry about finances.

And he didn't, in a rather spectacular way.

His father had bought and maintained a massive duplex apartment in Mayfair, and had gifted it to his son. It was thirty miles away from his university, but when that thirty miles was spent in a Porsche 911 convertible, then they were absolutely, ultimately bearable.

So, in that same vein, Carl had thought nothing of purchasing a massive storage warehouse in the East End docks under his father's name. *Why not?* He thought, *Dad won't even notice.*

For his own purposes, he was able to locate and procure a huge antique, oak circle table, and have it delivered and installed within the warehouse. He had found a unique carpenter who specialised in occultist ornamental carvings, he hired him to work on the table to a specific set of instructions straight from Robert. Both had overseen everything, from the fitting of the huge red velvet curtains, incense, all the ornate objects required for the completion of this ritual, to finally having a state of the art PA system and the fitting of a rather intricate lighting rig. Finally, Brenda had done a fantastic job of designing and making the costumes that were required to be worn by everyone present.

Basically, everything was in place.

Tomorrow night, Friday, was to be the first, official meeting of The Twelve. This was the only meeting required prior to the actual ritual they were about to undertake. Tomorrow, everyone would make their pledges and reveal their individual wishes.

There was only one part of his spending spree that they hadn't yet received, and it was the one that both he and Robert were both worried about. It was the small individual sacks they had bought, at great expense. These were integral to the whole of the ritual.

Robert had been rather specific in the design, the materials and the specific sizes of these sacks. They had scoured everywhere to find them. Small sacks about 2cm x 2cm made from a specific reed only found in a small area of the Tibetan mountains. He'd read about them in a few select scripts, but had found them immensely difficult to locate and to procure.

After a lengthy search, he'd finally been able to track them down to a mystic occultist who lived in San Diego, USA. This guy made them himself from regular visits to the Tibetan mountains for his own solitude rituals.

One dozen of these small sacks had cost Carl, or rather his father, just shy of £50,000. If they were to come in time, then they would be worth every penny of that small fortune.

44.

ROBERT AND CARL were busy making all the final preparations for their first meeting, as Gill and John were getting ready for date night.

At seven thirty, prompt John pulled up to her house in a black taxi. He got the driver to beep as they'd arranged. She didn't respond immediately, so he asked him to beep again. There was still no reply.

'I've got other fares to pick up you know mate, I can't be hanging around here all night,' the taxi driver snarled at him, obviously unhappy at hanging around on a Friday night.

'She'll be out in a minute, beep again.'

He did and this time there was a flicker at the window.

'See, I told you she'd be ready.' John physically relaxed and sat back in the seat.

A minute, or two later, Gill opened the front door and stepped out of her house.

'Jesus!' The taxi driver exclaimed. 'There's no-way on God's green earth a runt like you gets a bird like that.' He said it with real exasperation in his voice, probably not even realising that he had just talked himself out of a tip.

John looked out of the window at the vision closing the front door to her apartment block.

'You're getting paid to drive, not to look at my girlfriend.'

'Mate, if my girl looked like that, I'd never leave her on her own.'

John looked at him with a small confused look on his face. He thought it was a funny thing to say and something about it hit him, not like a déjà vu feeling, but something rather akin to it. He put the unsettling thought out of his head immediately as he saw why the taxi driver had commented.

Gill walked out of the front door. She was wearing a skin-tight black dress that was cut to half way down her shapely thighs; her high heels complimented the dress perfectly. The neck line plunged so low that even John didn't know where to look; well, he did and he was guessing that the taxi driver knew where to look too. Her long auburn hair was loose, it had been waved and there was a, natural looking curl running through it as it blew in the breeze. As she made her way to the taxi, smiling, John was appreciating her, he had always loved the colour of her hair, it was almost his favourite of her, apart from her lopsided smile obviously.

As she climbed in the back of the taxi, John almost scoffed to the driver as she leaned in and gave him a kiss on his lips.

The driver harrumphed, shaking his head, before checking his mirrors, indicating and then driving on.

Every bar they entered, they got the same reaction. Everyone stared at Gill fascinated, and everyone looked at John, wondering why a stunning girl was spending a pleasant evening with a skinny geek.

Gill was completely oblivious of the attention, John thought that she had probably gotten used to it after all the years being on the receiving end, but to his amazement and satisfaction, it seemed that she did only have eyes for him.

'Are you looking forward to tomorrow?' She asked while they were sat in a quiet, but rather expensive, bar.

The Twelve

John shrugged the question while sipping at the stupidly shaped glass, his stupidly named, and priced, cocktail had come in. 'Yeah, a bit. Do you know what your wish is going to be?'

Gill looked him straight into his eyes, and smiled a bright, beautiful smile. Her green eyes lit up, thus lighting her entire face with enthusiasm towards the question.

'I know exactly what I want. I think it'll surprise a few people though. What about you?'

'I've got a feeling that mines going to be a bit boring, probably won't be much different from everyone else's I'd say.'

Gill shrugged and took a sip of her, equally ridiculous named and priced cocktail.

'Well, both Carl and Robert have said that we need to be at the location for no later than eight pm. I really can't wait for it. After this the only thing left to look forward to is graduation.'

'Hey,' John said suddenly, looking over the club towards the bar. 'Isn't that Jenny over there?'

Gill looked in the direction he was indicating and saw the athletic and gorgeous figure that was, unmistakenly, Jenny Weaver. The sports sciences girl, the one who'd been so rude to Kevin, and then given him her number, right after he'd been beaten up.

He hadn't really cared for her after that night. *Come to think of it*, he thought, *I don't really like any of them except Gill. Maybe Ben and Nicky are OK, a little weird, but OK. Other than them two, I couldn't, say that I liked any of them.*

'Let's call her over,' Gill said, turning back to him, there was more than a hint of excitement on her face. 'Just to see what her take on tomorrow is.'

'Oh no, let's not,' John replied frowning a little. 'Tonight's supposed to be all about you and me. Anyways she's with someone, look.'

They both looked out over the crowd to where Jenny was sitting on a high stool at the bar. She was attracting a fair bit of attention from the men dotted around the club, and a good chunk from some of the ladies too. It was a fair assessment to say that Gill and Jenny were the most attractive girls in the bar, which was filled with attractive girls. This fact did wonders for John's, always low self-image.

He was already losing interest in the girl that he thought of as rude and shallow, and was about to request that they move onto the next bar when he nearly dropped the expensive cocktail glass that he had to his mouth, as the person she was with revealed himself.

'Kev!' He almost spat.

'Oh, My God, look, it's your mate, Kevin,' Gill laughed out loud.

'I thought we weren't supposed to fraternise with anyone outside The Twelve? At least until the meeting is over?'

'Well, she's certainly fraternising with him,' Gill laughed.

Even from this far across the bar, John could see that Kevin was still sporting a few bruises from his beating, but other than that, he'd scrubbed up well. A haircut and what looked like some new, cool and semi-expensive clothes made him look like quite a catch. It seemed that he and Jenny were having a good time.

'Hey, should we follow them?' Gill had a devilish look on her face.

'What? No. I told you tonight's about us, not someone else who's having a good time.'

She pulled a little pretend sob face and looked at him with baby eyes. 'Oh, OK then. Well I'm a little bit drunk, a big bit horny, and a little bit impatient to get you somewhere where we won't be disturbed. What do you think about that?'

'I'm very much down with that.' John replied with a devilish grin of his own.

45.

THE SMALL, SPECIAL sacks arrived the morning of the first meeting. Carl and Robert were in equal measures relieved, and ecstatic with the delivery. Twelve tiny reed sacks, made with great expense, especially for them and their meeting.

The reason why these sacks were so important was due to the nature of the raw materials used in their manufacture. They were made exclusively from the only naturally occurring substance a human being can swallow and not digest, not pass through the digestive tract, and not cause any known problems with the natural course of bodily functions.

Tony Corliss had sourced and supplied the specific drugs that they needed to suit their purpose. Debbie Baines was going to stir the erotic levels of the evening to a peak and Carl had purchased expensive champagne by the crate full.

Everything was set, except for the one last, very important ingredient. One that was still yet to be secured. Robert and Carl had been very tight lipped on what this was, and no-one was to find out what it was until the actual ritual.

46.

THE DAY DAWNED of the first meeting. All twelve had been busy ringing each other and chatting with excited but hushed tones. They'd all written their pledges. They'd all been, or were going to the gym, to make sure that they looked and felt buff.

They all arrived at the location of Carl's warehouse on the Docks, at precisely the same time, seven thirty. Ten excited people arriving in various taxis and gathering at the doors to the massive and disused building. None of them really knew what to do or where to go, so they all just kind of milled around the grounds of the large building. A loud noise from behind the smaller of the two, metal doors caught their attentions, and their gabble quietened down.

The smaller door opened rather theatrically and Carl appeared behind it. He was completely naked beneath a red velvet cloak. The cloak had golden swirls and ancient symbols embroidered on it and it looked more majestic than comedic. On his head was a golden crown with horns that looked like goat horns.

As everyone regarded him, he addressed the attendees together as if they were strangers.

'Thank you all for coming, we are awaiting your pleasure within the main hall. If you would just follow me.'

He spoke formally, with a Queen's English accent, almost as if he was playing the part of a butler in a play or film. This elicited some giggles from the more nervous among them. Gill included.

He ushered them inside the warehouse, through a dark, narrow corridor that led into a large anti-room. The room resembled a gym changing room, with a long mirror that ran the length of one wall and a series of hangers along the opposite wall. On the hangers hung ten cloaks and ten crowns, all similar to the one worn by Carl. Each cloak and crown was labelled with a name.

He gestured to the wall with the cloaks. 'If you would all please undress and attire yourselves in the dress of the evening, we would be most pleased. Also, you will find a flute of the finest Champagne alongside your robes and crowns, there is more chilling in refrigerators at the back of the room.' He indicated towards the end of the room where there were five fridges with glass doors, each fridge was filled with bottles of the expensive Champagne. 'Please indulge yourselves, drink prior to entering into the main hall. You may not bring anything in with you.'

With a theatrical swoop of his cloak and a flash that he was indeed naked beneath it, he turned and exited the room.

Everyone stood around not really knowing what to do. There were more than a few embarrassed looks and quite a bit of shuffling of feet. No-one wanted to be the first to do anything.

'Ah well,' it was Debbie, of course, who was the first to react. 'It's not like you guys have never seen me naked before, eh?' She grabbed the flute of Champagne from next to her robe and downed it all in one swig, she produced a loud burp as the bubbles came back up, before proceeding to strip off all her clothes. Once naked she draped her cloak around her, and picked up the crown that was on the bench next to it. She took a second or two to look at it, it was almost identical to Carl's but instead of goat horns, her crown was adorned with rabbit ears.

The Twelve

'Well, if the shoe fits.' She nudged Nicky and pointed to the rabbit on the top of the crown, laughing as she did.

This broke the ice and both John and Gill cracked up laughing almost instantly. Soon everyone in the room was shedding their clothes, donning the robes and chinking flutes of expensive bubbly. There was an air of carnival in the room.

John's crown was a badger, Gill was sporting a small bird, maybe a robin. Everyone else had differing animals, ranging from a mouse for Nicky all the way to Patrick as a squirrel.

Everyone was half naked, each at least trying to cover their dignity, all except Debbie, who was openly flaunting her nakedness to everyone who'd indulge her. This basically meant everyone in the room, especially the males.

John couldn't help himself but sneak looks at Jenny, Nicky, Brenda and even Lynda With-a-Y. He had never envisioned himself to be in a room with so many beautiful, naked women. *At least without paying for the pleasure*, he thought with a smile.

A large golden sign with the word ENTRANCE carved into it had been placed over a door on the opposite end of the room from where they'd come in. This was the door that Carl had disappeared into.

A voice came over a loudspeaker system in the room, surprising them with its volume and the serious tone that emitted from it. They all quietened, as one, to listen.

'WELCOME MEMBERS OF THE TWELVE. I KNOW THAT YOU HAVE BEEN WAITING FOR THIS NIGHT FOR A LONG TIME. THE WAIT IS FINALLY OVER. PLEASE FINISH YOUR DRINKS AND ENTER INTO THE GREAT HALL.'

The excitement levels within the room had almost reached a fervour. They all drained their drinks as quickly as they could and filed through into the main hall.

The hall had been built into a round room with a huge circular dark oak table adorning the centre. It had been decorated with several, intricately carved figures into the wood. The figures were in various stages of copulation; some natural, some very unnatural.

Each person had a marker with their name written on the floor for their designated position at the table, they had been laid out in boy/girl order.

John was more than relieved to find his position was stood in-between Gill and Jenny, the two best-looking women in the group.

Everyone was chattering and nervous. Tony was flashing his privates at anyone who'd look, in a totally childish manner, and the mood had become more relaxed and jovial, which was possibly to do with the copious amounts of sparkling wine they'd all drank in the changing rooms.

Robert's voice then boomed out again from the loudspeakers that were, obviously, concealed somewhere in the ceiling.

Although it was Robert's voice, it sounded nothing like the voice of the person who had asked them all to enter the main room.

'Can I have everyone's attention please? If you could all fall into your designated positions, then we can begin.'

Robert was less authoritative on the mic than the previous speaker. Carl was the only other person not in the room, and the voice hadn't sounded anything like him either.

It seemed that John was the only person to notice this subtle change, as no-one else seemed in the least bit

The Twelve

interested. They all, obediently, fell into a hushed silence and stood on their markers at the table.

Robert's voice boomed out once again. Still not the same voice as earlier. That voice had a strange, serious and commanding edge to it, but Robert's sounded like he was reading from a script.

'Very soon we shall be in the presence of The Great Lord Glimm. He will appear to us in human form. You may gaze upon his magnificence but you must not look him in the eye. His spirit will select one of your earthly bodies to possess. This will be to test your resolve and, of course, to taste your offering. Behold the Great Lord Glimm!'

The lights lowered and the candles that were lit all around the room began to flicker at the same time, as if they were on a controlled dimmer switch. Sheer white lights, that must have been hidden under the floor, flashed into life. Their intense brightness travelling in straight beams towards the ceiling, giving the room a strange black and white feel. The only real colour was the dulled red of the robes each member was wearing.

Not for the first-time John wondered what they were all doing here, why he was playing around with these fools. He instinctively grabbed Gill's hand and squeezed it. As if in answer, she squeezed back.

In a hiss of smoke, Carl emerged from a hidden door that no-one had noticed was there. He was wearing his goat horn crown and his robe with the golden symbols in the trimming. In dramatic fashion, he climbed onto the table, his nakedness obvious and, maybe more than a little uncomfortable for the male members of the group.

He stood with his hands on his hips and surveyed the room around him. He then began to walk around the circumference of the table, his twitching genitalia mere inches from everyone's faces. As he strutted, thrusting himself towards everyone, it was quite evident that he was rather enjoying himself.

'HAS THE GREAT LORD GLIMM CHOSEN HIS THRALLS?' The hidden voice boomed again.

Apart from feeling a little uncomfortable, John also become even more confused. As Carl was now in the same room as them, the voice coming through the PA system must be Robert's, but it didn't sound like him, not even a little bit.

'Yeeeeeesssssssssss….' Came a loud whispered reply. The word didn't come from Carl's mouth, but, seemingly from somewhere else, some undefinable location within the room.

'THEN ENTER THE GREAT LORD GLIMM!!!'

With that, all the lights blinked off and the room was suddenly pitched into sheer darkness.

A whispered incantation began to thrum through the speakers, very low and very repetitious. A wind seemed to whip through the room, and low, purple light began to pulse from the symbols carved into the dark wooden table.

John thought it was a great effect, but more than a little dramatic for his liking.

With another flash from the intense white beams in the floor, Robert made his grand entrance into room. He seemed to swagger in, like a world champion boxer entering the ring in a prize fight.

His crown was a stag. The antlers stood huge and proud protruding from his head. His robe was golden with red symbols, the exact opposite of Carl's.

He strutted around the table top twice, looking everyone up and down, summing them up before climbing on top to stand alongside Carl.

He whispered something into Carl's ear.

Carl then pointed towards Debbie.

The Twelve

Robert was now sporting a massive erection and in the purple glow of the illuminated symbols, he looked at Debbie with a mixture of lust and greed. Sweat had gathered on his brow in beads, and in the purple light, offered a gruesome interpretation of his, normally handsome, face.

He gestured for her to climb up onto the table. Without a moment's hesitation, she obeyed.

Well, no surprises there then, John thought to himself with a wry grin.

He turned towards Gill to gauge her reactions to the proceedings, but she had her eyes closed. He looked the other way and Jenny was the same.

The incantations were getting louder through the PA system; and smoke began to billow in from the purple light emanating from the carved symbols.

'THE GREAT LORD GLIMM HAS CHOSEN HIS THRALLS…'

The voice boomed out over the loudspeakers once again; John looked all around him, counting the bodies present. He accounted for all twelve.

If all of us are here… then who's that over the PA system?

He was just about to whisper his question to Gill, when Robert ripped Debbie's robe from her body in one violent jerk. The sudden sight of Debbie's complete nakedness made him lose what modicum of concentration he had left.

Carl held her thin arms with his huge hands. His thick fingers almost wrapping themselves completely around her as he forced her down, onto her back.

To be fair to Carl, John thought that she didn't offer any resistance to this roughness, whatsoever.

While she was on her back Carl prised her legs apart, and Robert dropped down on all fours. He took her legs in both of his hands, and lowered his head in-between them. Intrigued, and to his shame a little aroused, John watched as Robert performed oral sex on the girl, right there on the table. He regarded his colleagues around the table, and they were all watching the proceedings with rapture. The males in the group were all, obviously, enjoying the show as much as he was.

Robert then removed his head and moved his body upward. He guided his erect penis in-between her legs towards the dark, wetness of her intimacy. He paused for just a second, before entering her, with some force, in front of them all.

As he did she screamed. The scream was loud and shrill. A scream of pain and of delight in almost equal measure.

Robert's face changed instantaneously. The snarl on his lips altered the whole of the bottom half of his face as he continued to plunge into her. After a good few deep, penetrating thrusts, he turned to the group and shouted.

'ALL HAIL TO THE GLIMM'

Debbie screamed in pain, agony and ecstasy again as Robert seemed to reach orgasm inside her.

This sight was enough for John, he felt dirty even being here, never mind standing around idly while one of his, so called friends, raped another one of his friends. He was just about to give up and leave the table when Debbie scrambled away from a panting Robert, to re-join the group on the floor. She picked up her robe and wrapped it around herself, shaking as if she was cold.

Robert stood then, his erection was still powerful, and his malevolent face regarded the group one by one.

The voice boomed over the PA system, cutting through the rhythm of the incantations, once again.

'WHO WILL BE THE NEXT THRALL FOR THE GREAT LORD GLIMM?'

John had a horrible moment, as did Ben by the look on his face over the table. They both thought that they might have to give up their girlfriends to the Glimm. This was something that, right now, John didn't think he would be able to do.

Carl was still stood on the table, hands on hips, his massive penis was fully erect. He was looking around, when Debbie, still wearing her cloak and still shaking a little, climbed back onto the table.

'DEBORAH BAINES, YOU CARRY THE SEED OF GLIMM. IT IS UP TO YOU TO CHOOSE THE SECOND THRALL?'

Debbie's face was vacant, like she was in a daze, her eyes in the purple glow were lost, uncoordinated. With growing unease, John scanned the room around him. Except for him and possibly Ben, everyone else seemed to be in the same daze she was. They were all swaying with the rhythm of the incantations, lost within their own music. Gill included. She was swinging her body from side to side, the cloak no longer performing its duty and covering her nakedness.

A panic began to rise in his chest, he was way out of his depth here, everything felt alien and... wrong.

'Carl will be Lord Glimm's second thrall.' Debbie shouted. Her voice wavered half way through the shout, and she sounded confused, almost as if it was a question, not a statement. She turned and grabbed Carl around the back of his head and swung her legs underneath him, like a martial artist performing a professional display. This caused the big man to fall on all fours. His face was both shocked and frightened as Debbie held him in place with her legs.

Robert, still sporting a mighty erection, idled up to Carl's exposed rear.

Debbie's was now swaying along with the incantations; her face was in a carnal ecstasy. As she looked up towards Robert's thick, throbbing member she licked her lips.

Robert grabbed her hair and pulled her head over towards him. Enjoying the rough treatment, she went willingly and took the whole of his erection in her mouth. He pulled her away from him again and John, in his disgust at what was happening, had just enough time to see a thin rope of saliva from the end of Robert's penis to her mouth snap. Disgusted as he was, he couldn't help but marvel at the glistening end of Robert's erection as Debbie wrapped her hands around the thick shaft. He assumed that she was going to put it back into her mouth, but she surprised him as she guided it towards Carl's exposed behind. With a lustful roar, Robert thrust himself towards Carl's offered sacrifice.

He entered him.

As he did Carl's scream was louder and more ferocious than Debbie's. It was more sickening than anything John had ever heard in his entire life.

Disgusted, John looked away, casting his glance towards Gill. Her eyes were wide open and she was still swaying with the rhythm of the incantations playing over the PA system. Although looking unfocused, she couldn't take her eyes away from Robert and what was happening on the table.

John looked frantically around once again, no-one in the room could tear their gaze away from the bizarre and sick spectacle that was happening above them. Even Ben was now fully enthralled with everything unfolding in front of him.

Robert was now pulling the same concentrated face as he was sporting earlier. Carl looked to be in great pain and discomfort. John fancied that he could see tears glistening in the big man's eyes through the purple glow of the lights. If he could, he couldn't blame him.

After another few thrusts Robert, once again, came to orgasm, this time inside of Carl. He threw one arm in the air, in a gross parody of a tennis player winning

The Twelve

an important and hard played for point. Looking down towards everyone on the floor he shouted, 'Hail to the Glimm.'

As he pulled away, Carl fell flat on his face, squashing Debbie who was still wrapped around him. The purple light from the table intensified as the rhythmic incantations from the speakers grew louder and faster.

John could feel himself beginning to sway with the rhythm now. He was feeling helpless as the, seemingly nonsense words coming through the speakers, began to speak to him. They had started as gibberish, but slowly they began to make sense to him, to talk to him... he began to repeat them.

'Hickula, tragantie a billinctus, shakker, toogorey'

'Hickula, tragantie a billinctus, shakker, toogorey'

'Hickula, tragantie a billinctus, shakker, toogorey'

Over and over again...
He smiled and closed his eyes, unaware of any unsavoury acts that had been, or were being performed around him, or even to him.

The words formed in his head, he was happy to hear them, he embraced them and put them in a special place in his heart.

'Twelve, destiny calls, fulfil, encapsulate, embrace!'

'Twelve, destiny calls, fulfil, encapsulate, embrace!'

'Twelve, destiny calls, fulfil, encapsulate, embrace!'

A white sheen fell over his eyes hampering his vision. He could sense Carl talking to Jenny, and he knew that she was nodding in agreement to something. He was also aware that Robert was talking to Brenda and Patrick, both were nodding too.

A state of fluffy euphoria fell over him and he was happy that everyone was compliant and convivial. He knew for certain that right now he'd be compliant too, he wanted to fulfil, to encapsulate, and, most of all, he wanted to embrace.

Before everything went white, he felt something wrap around his erect penis, the feeling that the sensation gave him was joyous, he looked down but couldn't tell who, or what was giving him this pleasure.

And he didn't care…

~~~

John awoke, or rather he emerged, a short while later. He was lying on the floor with his red robe spilled all around him, Gill was lying next to him, her robe had fallen away exposing her breasts. He sat up a little too fast and marvelled as the whole room began to spin around him. He put his hand to his head to try to stop it, to control his brain. It worked, but only to a degree. He leaned over and fixed Gill's robe, mostly to hide her modesty even though he thought it was all a little too late for that.

Everyone else seemed to be rousing at the same time, they all looked dazed, and more than a little confused. Even though he had woken up semi-naked in a room filled with semi-naked people, he was having trouble convincing himself that he had seen what he thought he had seen. Leaning up on his hands, he gazed around the room at the groggy faces of everyone else, they all seemed to be either OK with it, or had maybe even missed it.

Robert looked worse than all of them, but he endeavoured to get up, fix the crown back onto his head and climb back onto the table. John noticed that he seemed more like the Robert of old rather than the one he'd just witness rape two of his friends.

The Twelve

'OK everyone,' he announced, his voice sounding a little weak and croaky. 'It's time to make your pledges to The Great Lord Glimm.' John could hear levity in his voice, a playfulness that hadn't been there earlier. 'It's time to put your wishes into the pot. Let's all become successful people eh? Everyone get back in their place and Debbie will walk around with the pledge pot.'

The pot was passed around each member, they then had to place their crown into it and say out loud what their wish was.

Robert went first, as he placed his crown into the pot Debbie offered to him, he wished to become the most distinguished judge in the British judicial system.

Carl was second, he wished to become a top-flight football manager for a big team.

Next was Ben, his wish was to become the Dean of a university.

Nicky wished that she would be a top actress with her own show.

Jenny wanted to become a fitness guru with her own range of videos.

Tony wanted to be a toxicologist.

Brenda was all set to be a society bride wedding organiser, the best in her field.

Patrick wanted to be a nuclear civil engineer specialist.

Debbie wanted to run her own nightclub, or maybe even a string of nightclubs.

Lynda wanted to make it as a top TV chef with a string of restaurants.

John said he wanted to be, at least, partner in a multinational IT company.

Gill said she wanted to be…

John was momentarily distracted from the proceedings as Debbie dropped one of the crowns, his crown, from the pot. He turned to look at what had caused the clatter, and he went to bend down and pick it up for her, but before he could Jenny had already gotten it for him. As she did her robe fell open revealing her fantastic naked body underneath, and he couldn't resist looking. She caught him and gave him a cheeky little smile. John blushed and looked away.

As his attentions focused back upon Gill, she had already put her crown in the box and was now sporting a great big smile on her face.

'Now we've declared our wishes to The Great Lord Glimm, they must NEVER be repeated by anyone or to anyone until the time of their passing. Their time of passing will be a minimum of twenty years from now. Until that time, we will all work hard and live fruitful and fulfilled lives.'

John looked over at Carl and Debbie, they both looked happy, but also looked to be physically uncomfortable. Carl was having trouble standing up straight. *I'm not surprised*, John thought with disgust. Filthy animals, the lot of them.

47.

THE NEXT EVENING, Gill and John were lying in her bed. The events of the night before were still playing on his mind. Gill had also been somewhat quiet and withdrawn.

'Did you not find some of that...' John made speech marks with his fingers, 'meeting, last night disturbing?'

'I'm disturbed by the fact that now I know you look hot in a red robe.' Gill was chiding him, obviously trying to make light of the whole situation. 'Plus, I couldn't get over the size of Robert's...'

'Gill!' He interrupted her, not laughing. 'I'm trying to have a serious conversation with you here.'

She looked pensive for a second or two before finally answering him. 'Well, yeah, there were parts I wasn't quite ready for, like all this Great Lord Glimm business. The funny thing is, I don't really remember much after Debbie getting onto that table, until I woke up next to you on the floor, and we did our pledges.'

'Are they really the only bits you remember?'

'Yeah, why? Did I miss something else?'

It was John's turn to become pensive for a few seconds before answering. 'Eh... no, not really.' He lied to her. *Only rape*, he finished off in his head.

'Well, I'm not staying lying here in bed all day. Are you up for a drink?' She asked while hopping out of the covers. John was always surprised by her nakedness, at how very beautiful and graceful she was.

'After that last night, I'd say too right,' he replied getting himself up and out of the bed. They both dressed almost in silence, there didn't seem like there was much to say, before leaving her house to walk down to the local pub.

The bar area was busy for a Thursday night and there was only standing room left, but they didn't mind too much as the plan was to only have a couple before either going home or moving on somewhere else.

'What do you want?' John shouted over the general hubbub.

'A brandy and Babycham please.'

John grimaced a little at the thought of how much one of them cost. She flashed him one of her lopsided grins and mouthed, 'I'll make it worth your while later.' Then she winked at him and all the strangeness of earlier seemed to melt away. He shook his head as he faced the bar, knowing that he was a lost cause. *Jesus, I'm too easy...*

He did his best to push through the throng in the pub as he made his way over to the bar. He managed to squeeze in through a small gap between two large men leaning against the bar, chatting. Both pulled a face at him as he did his best to get the eye of the single barman on duty.

As he tried in vain to get served, he spied Kevin sitting in a booth in the opposite barroom. He was facing him, so John couldn't quite make out who his companion was sat opposite him. Whoever it was, they seemed to be having a few drinks and a good time.

He eventually got served and began the arduous journey back through the crowd towards Gill. He took another look over towards where Kevin was sat. He could just about make him out through the crowd, from this angle it was not difficult to make out who it was he was sat with. It was Jenny. *Happy days*, he thought, *go for it*

Kev. As he looked back towards Gill he had a big beaming smile on his face.

'What're you so happy about? I'm not that easy for a brandy and Babycham you know,' she joked.

He raised his eyebrows and took a sip at his pint. 'Yeah don't I know it? No, I just saw Kevin over there in the corner. Guess who he's with... again!'

Gill shrugged as she sipped at her drink.

'He's with Jenny! This must be like their second or third date or something.'

Gill suddenly looked interested. 'No way! Where are they?' She asked, straining to look over the large crowd in the pub.

'In the corner of the bar, over there. Do you know what? I'm made up for him you know. After the way she treated him in the club that night. But, it looks like he stuck by his guns and carried on. He's ended up with what he wanted.'

Gill looked at him, pulling a face as if he had just said the most ridiculous thing she had ever heard in her life. 'You make her sound like she's a prize.'

'To him, she probably is. In the three years of this course, I think I've only ever seen him talk to about five other people, other than me and lecturers. He's just painfully shy or something, but you wouldn't think so to look at him over there with Jenny now.'

For some reason the opening of the pub door caught his attention and his heart sank as he saw Carl, Robert and Patrick all walk in together. With rising panic, he gave a quick glance over to where Kevin was sitting and then back to the three of them. They were searching around the crowd for someone, John had a very good idea who it was. He wouldn't have time to stop them, or even to warn Kevin.

'Shit! It's Carl and the others. I think they're looking for Kev.'

Gill put her drink down on the shelf next to her and tried to get a better view over the crowd.

To John's surprise, he watched as Kevin stood up and beckoned all three of them over to their booth. He shook them all by the hand with big smiles and, to John's complete surprise, big hugs too. Carl broke away to the bar to order the drinks. John noticed with a hint of anger that he had been served almost straight away, but then he also noticed that he was still walking a little funny, like he had been doing some strenuous exercise. Eventually they all sat down together and proceeded to have a good time.

'What's all that about?' John asked Gill.

Gill had lost all interest in the proceedings and was now sipping at her drink. 'I don't know,' she shrugged, 'maybe they've got course work to talk about.'

'No, none of them share classes with Kevin. It's got to be something else. Maybe it's something to do with the beating he took the other week.'

Gill looked over and pouted a little, not really showing any interest at all.

'Do you think someone's dropped out of The Twelve, and they're recruiting a new member?'

'No, no-one can leave once we've had the first meeting, you know that.'

'John!' He looked around, surprised at the fact that someone was calling his name. 'Are you John?' The barman had come from behind the bar carrying two drinks.

'Erm… yeah, I am. Why?'

'The big guy over there asked me to bring these over to you two.'

'Oh, right. Yeah, thanks.' John said accepting the two, large vodka and cokes.

'Should we go over and thank them, see what's happening?' He asked Gill, placing the two large drinks on the shelf.

'Let's not. They know we're here, and that's enough. Let's drink these and go home. I want something to eat before I fuck you into oblivion. You can buy me some chips on the way back.'

John smiled as they knocked back their drinks as fast as they could. As they got up to leave John offered a quick glance back into Kevin's direction. Robert was looking directly at him, and he offered up his drink to him in a salute.

He nodded, offered him a small salute of his own, and then left to follow Gill home.

Present Day

48.

SHIT, THREE FIFTEEN again? John thought as he woke, alone in the darkness of his bedroom, *this is getting too much.*

Knowing that sleep was currently languishing in a merry little world miles away from where he currently lay, he flipped the covers off his side of the bed and clambered out. He went downstairs to prepare himself the obligatory cup of hot milk, and maybe watch some awful late night TV before, hopefully, falling back into some sweet oblivion.

'I had another one of those stupid dreams,' he spoke out loud to Gill.

He knew that she wasn't going to answer, and an absurd thought popped into his head. What the hell would he do if one night she DID answer? This made him smile, but it was only a brief reprieve from his misery. He still wanted to talk to her, especially after all the recent events.

In his dream, they were all back in university, but The Twelve were all zombies, or cannibals, or something like that. They were running around the campus, all thirteen of them... sorry, no, not thirteen, all twelve of them.

'There was only ever the twelve of us, wasn't there?' He asked Gill again, again, not really expecting an answer, but it gave him something to ponder on. In the dream, there had been thirteen of them... his confidence of this point was beginning to waver, the way dreams often did, with every slip of the second hand of the clock.

Anyway, they'd been running around the campus attacking the other students, just grabbing them randomly and biting into them. Then Ian from work turned up, John was just about to sink his fanged teeth into him, when he put his hands up in surrender and asked if he could join their group. He wanted to be in the meetings, he wanted to be... John searched for the word he'd used in his dream.

Was it encapsulated? He'd grown to hate his dreams.

He was snapped out of this reverie as the microwave beeped indicating his hot milk was ready. As he made his way back upstairs, he stopped halfway and turned around.

He'd had a feeling like he was being watched, it had gone on for a few days now, but it had been more intense since his visit to the police station and finding that picture.

Satisfied there was nothing or nobody down there, he continued to make his way back to the bedroom. Once there he flicked on the TV.

That was the last thing he remembered before slipping back into that horrible dream about university. His milk went cold at the side of his bed.

49.

THE NEXT MORNING, he awoke with a start at ten-thirty. As he lay in bed rubbing his tired eyes he realised that he wasn't in any way ready to go back to work today, not after everything that had happened over the past few days. He decided to ring the HR department and give them notice of one more week.

When it was done, he sat by the phone hanging his head in his hands. The thought of going slowly and quietly insane in this house depressed him even more than having a mental breakdown in-front of his work colleagues. *I really can't go on like this for much longer,* he thought.

He realised then that the TV was still on. The low sound was drifting in from the front room. It was the morning local news.

'… Looking for their son, William, who is of no fixed abode. Neighbours say that historically, he was likely to turn up at odd intervals demanding money, or somewhere to stay. When he stayed, there would always be a spate of burglaries in the local vicinity. Although no one could ever prove that it was him perpetrating these petty crimes, local feeling purveyed that he was to blame.'

John was just about to press the button on the remote control to turn the TV off, when something caught his attention. A shot of a large, nice house ensued, and a very pretty, female reporter standing outside a wrought iron gate flickered onto the screen.

'William Lomax is thought to be about six-foot-tall with of a large firm build, dark brown hair and blue eyes. If seen, please do not apprehend. Please report his whereabouts to the local police, he is still a suspect in this grisly crime and is thought to be…'

'Lomax?'

John's heart sank down into his stomach.

'What about Lomax? What's he done?'

He realised he was shouting at the TV screen, and, feeling a bit foolish he grabbed the remote control and began flicking through all the other channels, hoping to catch some more local news.

He found another local news channel and stopped there. A reporter was stood outside the same nice house on the same nice street. The house had blue and white tape all around it, and people in scientific forensic suits were passing back and forth in the background.

'There has been no motive brought forward as yet as to why Benjamin and Nicola Lomax were killed. No evidence of a break in, or indeed anything of note missing from the house. All we know is that Benjamin Lomax, a respected university lecturer, and his wife Nicola, a radio and TV personality were both found dead today, in the living room of their house in West London. Their five-year-old daughter was sleeping in an upstairs bedroom; she is currently being comforted by family members. The police have issued a picture of William Lomax, the couple's estranged son, and a person of special interest in this case.'

'HOW DID THEY DIE?' He shouted.

Frantic now he began pressing random buttons on his remote control looking for more information.

A terrible thought then occurred to him.

'Oh shit, the photograph!'

He began to search the house, frantically for the photograph. He remembered that Ben and Nicky's images were beginning to blur the last time he looked at it. It was all becoming far too much for him to process now.

He couldn't find it anywhere.

He scoured the bedroom, the living room and the hall way looking for the damned thing before finally finding it above the cooker in the kitchen. He couldn't even remember going into the kitchen with this stupid thing.

The frame and the glass were once again covered in an icy sheen, the metal was painful to touch, such was the cold. With a shaking hand, he rubbed away at the frost and condensation on the glass and peered into the picture.

Ben and Nicky were gone, blurred out of existence, and it looked like Brenda was next.

He sat down at the kitchen table and put his head in his hands once again.

He expected tears, but they didn't come. Instead, a deep melancholy encompassed him, biting into him like a frost.

He got up and began to search for his mobile phone. 'Fuck! Why don't we just use bastard tethered phones like in the old days? You always knew where they were.' He ranted this at himself in total frustration, while searching the house once again, this time for his mobile phone. He found it in the kitchen again. *What the fuck?* He thought. *Why does everything seem to end up in the kitchen?*

He clicked the device into life and searched for the number of Detective Addison, the nice policeman who asked him all nice questions regarding Debbie... and Gill.

It was answered on the third ring. 'Hello, hello... Yes, I need to be put through to Detective Addison please, it's an emer... yes... yes, I can hold but it is an...' The line went dead as he was put on hold.

'Oh yes, thanks. Eh... no, no he isn't expecting my call, but it's regarding an ongoing investigation. It's the Debbie Baines case... Just a few days ago. John Rydell, I think he'll remember me, yes, I'll hold again. Thank you.'

After what seemed like an eternity in the silence interrupted only by intermittent beeps, the line kicked back into life.

'Mr Rydell, thank you so much for reaching out to me. What can I help you with today?'

'We need to talk, as soon as possible.'

50.

JOHN WAS SITTING in the same bland, beige police interview room he had been in only a few days previously. He was nervous and twitchy, he had the photograph in the inside pocket of his jacket and kept touching it, just to make sure it was still there.

'Please tell me that you've still got that photograph you took from me last week?' John sprang at the detective the second he walked into the room. He was feeling sick to his stomach, and it was evident from the desperation in his voice.

Addison eyed him suspiciously, he could see he was a nervous wreck. He rather fancied that he was about to get some sort of confession from this John Rydell, and he maybe in a great position to close two cases in one go.

'I should think so, it was put into the evidence room right after our interview. I put it in there myself actually.' The Detective looked at him, shifting his head a little as he did. A thousand questions began to develop in his head. The most obvious came first. 'May I enquire why you're asking?'

'Yes, but I'm not sure the answer is going to make any sense. I asked you because…' John paused to take in a breath. He couldn't believe himself what he was going to tell the logical man before him, and if he couldn't believe it, then how, and why should he expect Detective Addison to. 'When I got home, I found this next to the TV in my living room. I thought I'd heard somebody inside the house, but there wasn't anyone there, just this…'

He took it out of his inside pocket and threw it onto the table. He didn't want to look at the wretched thing, and was glad that it was now out of his possession.

Detective Addison leaned in and looked at it and then at John. His face was impassive, emotionless. He put his fingers onto the edges of the small photograph then spun it around to get a better look.

It was the same photograph; it was just a tad more blurred.

His face looked a little confused as he got up from the table, and without saying a word to John, he left the room.

This didn't help John's fragile state of mind one bit, being left in the cold bland room alone. He had somehow convinced himself that it had gotten colder in the interview room, and he tried to see if he could see his breath when he exhaled.

He couldn't.

Addison was out of the room for maybe five minutes and returned holding a large padded envelope. The words DEBBIE BAINES: EVIDENCE #78 (John Rydell) was written in red marker on the front of it. It was taped with yellow and black tape over the seal.

He tore it open, careful not to take his eyes off John. As he reached his fingers inside, his face changed.

He kept searching in the small envelope, with his probing fingers, but there was nothing in there. He picked it up and looked inside, there was still nothing. Finally, succumbing to frustration he tore the envelope open, causing all the purple fluffy stuffing to float around the room.

There was still no photograph.

'How could you have gotten that?' He asked angrily. 'I put that photograph into this envelope myself.'

With that Addison stormed off, out of the room and into the office beyond it. John could hear him shouting.

'OK, who the hell has been tampering with evidence?'

The accusation was greeted by silence in the open plan office.

'I asked who the hell has been tampering with evidence. I put this envelope into evidence last week, with a photograph in it, and now the photo has not only gone, but the person I took it off has it in his hands. If I find any association between the man I have in there and any of you bastards out here, your arses will swing...'

He stormed out of the open plan office and blustered back into the interview room.

He was swinging the torn empty envelope in front of John's face. His cheeks were flushed red and his, normally placid, eyes were beginning to burn pink.

'*How* did you really get hold of this photograph? Who gave it to you? I must warn you that tampering with evidence in a murder investigation can, and will, be dealt with severely. We're talking custodial sentences here. Give me that back...'

'Gladly...' John, calmly pushed the photograph back across the table. 'Can you see the faces of the two people there? Who last time were just about blurring? Well, look at them now. Can you see now that they're completely gone? Blurred out of existence?'

Addison picked the picture up and took a long look at it, then back at John. There was more than a hint of confusion on his features. 'Yeah, I can see that, what of it?'

'Well, would you be at all surprised to know that the two people whose faces have now been erased are Mr and Mrs Ben and Nicola Lomax?'

'What?'

The Twelve

Addison couldn't quite comprehend what he was hearing.

'I'm sure you heard me correctly Detective. Ben and Nicky Lomax. Both were good friends of mine back in university.'

Addison gave him a look as if to say *Please carry on...*

'Well, you know that all the ones on this photo, the ones with blurred out faces, you know that they're all dead too. All of them killed in the exact same way.'

Addison was sat opposite him. His arms were crossed on the table, and he was sporting the perfect poker face, cold and emotionless.

John didn't know how calculating this detective was, and in his own fragile state of mind, he didn't want to say anything that might incriminate him. He took a long, slow breath, before continuing. 'It's my guess that Ben and Nicky were killed in this same way too. They haven't mentioned anything about it on the news, but it's my bet that they were gutted, and then disembowelled. Am I right Detective?'

Addison's poker face crumbled and he flashed John a look across the table. 'I'm not at liberty to discuss an ongoing case Mr Rydell, you know that.'

John's anger flashed then, he had felt it rising, but when he thought about Gill's murder, with him so far away... it tipped him over the edge. He stood up and shouted. 'It's the same fucking case! Can't you see that? It is the same MO; the same killer is out there. Look,' he began to count on his fingers, 'Patrick Mahone, killed in an 'apparent' accident in his caravan that he used for a work base. He was found disembowelled... Robert Cobham, top judge, killed, and disembowelled in his chambers, Carl Brookes, disembowelled in his car, Gill Rydell...' he paused for a second, 'my wife, killed, and...' he had to pause in his rant again here, a single tear fell from his eye, and he was caught, momentarily breathless. He steeled himself and continued. '...killed at home. Debbie Baines, disembowelled in her club, Ben and Nicky Lomax, my bet they were both disembowelled in their home too. All of them quite literally gutted, all of them with the contents of their stomachs ripped from their bodies.' He calmed himself down a little now and spun the photograph back around to face him. He traced his finger over the blurred-out images, pausing slightly on Gill's silhouette. 'Can't you see this Detective? These are all the same case.'

Spit was dripping from his lip as he sat back down, opposite the surprised policeman. He hadn't meant to fly into that much of a rage, and had surprised even himself at the ferocity of his outburst. 'Look here,' he said, wiping his mouth and pointing towards the picture, specifically to the image of Brenda who was starting to blur, ever so slightly. 'Her name is Brenda Osman. She was also a friend of mine in university. I think she's going to die, and I'm guessing this by the fact that her face is starting to blur away.'

He sat back down, shaking his head, his eyes not leaving Addison's. His voice was now almost a whisper. 'Now, I don't know where she lives or even if she's changed her surname, but that's who she was, Brenda Osman, and I know she's going to die. It's going to be horrible and it's going to be soon!'

John closed his eyes and put his head in his hands, and rested them all on the table before him. 'I can give you the names of the others too.' He spoke towards the table-top, his voice sounding muffled. 'Tony Corless, Lynda Witherspoon, and Jenny Weaver. There were twelve of us then; now there's only five.'

Addison looked like he'd been slapped in the face, and in many ways, he felt like he had too. He coughed into his hand a little and straightened his jacket. 'Right,

I'm going to do some digging into all of this. What I need from you Mr Rydell is total co-operation and full disclosure, no holding back on anything, and I mean anything. If we're going to save this Brenda one, and you I'm guessing, then I need to know everything.'

'I don't know if I can give you everything Detective, most of it's still fuzzy, but I'll try.'

Part 3

Redford University South London
20 years earlier

51.

JOHN WAS SAT in one of the lecture halls, he was doing some last-minute cramming for the finals that would start the next week. Except for him, the hall was empty.

He'd had to cram, as since the meeting last week his mind had been on other things and for the first time in his life he'd fallen behind on his course. He couldn't get the image of the double rape out of his head, and his complacency, allowing it to happen and go unchallenged, was eating at him. He'd thought about bringing it up with Carl and Debbie, but neither of them seemed affected by what had happened, and there was an air of mystery to the whole thing too. He had witnessed two of his, so called, friends raped before the rest of the group and he seemed to be the only one who could remember what happened.

The slamming open of the main door to the theatre surprised him, and he jumped at the noise, snapping himself back into reality.

Feeling a little foolish, he looked up to see if he could see who had just entered, as he could hear footsteps, and they seemed to be getting nearer.

There was no-one in the hall, and the hairs on his arms, and the back of his neck began to stand up, as his skin began to goose-bump. It was a horrible sensation.

The footsteps sounded like they should be right on top of him by now, but he still couldn't see anyone.

'Hey John!' The voice, it was almost a whisper, came from behind him, and it caused him to jump again. He felt his heart hammering away in his chest.

'Jesus...' He looked around to see Kevin stood behind him with a grin on his face.

'What's the matter man? You look like you just saw a ghost!' His friend laughed.

'Oh nothing, I was miles away then and you scared the shit out of me, creeping up like that.' He was laughing too now. 'Hey, I've been meaning to ask, I've seen you out a few times with Jenny Weaver.' He smiled and nudged Kevin theatrically. 'So, what's going on there, lover-boy?'

Kevin blushed a deep red. 'Ah, well, you know, it's nothing major,' he openly lied to John's face.

'Well it sure looked like something major the other night in the pub.'

'Nope,' he said sitting down next to his friend. 'It's nothing more than just a laugh.'

'It looked like a lot more than just a laugh the other night,' John said smiling now. He was teasing him, but he didn't know if Kevin was aware or not.

His face suddenly changed, the humour went out of it, and his features turned serious. He shuffled about a little, looking like he wanted to ask a question but didn't know how to go about it. Eventually he just asked.

'John, what is it with all this Twelve stuff?'

He wasn't quite sure how to go about answering this question. He remembered asking the same question himself not so long ago.

'I... eh!'

Kevin laughed. 'It's OK man, I know who you guys are. I was just wondering how I went about getting in? Jen told me that there can only ever be twelve. How did you get in?'

The question stumped John, and he had to pause for a while, thinking about how he could answer. 'I just sort of fell in.' He didn't feel at all comfortable talking about this to him, especially after seeing him with Carl and Robert the other night.

'Do you think I could just fall in? Jenny was saying that she knows at least one person who wants out. What do you think?' Kevin asked, his face and body language tell-tailing that he was brimming with a nervous enthusiasm. 'Hey maybe I could get myself some real mates, in these last months of university.' He was laughing as he said this, but John could see the underlying sadness of this painfully shy person. He looked like he was seeing a glimmer of light at the end of a long dark tunnel.

'If it was up to me you'd be in, in a flash.'

'I know, but it's not up to you, is it?'

'Well, pretty much, no. It's not'

'Well I thought I'd ask my best mate. If anyone was going to get me in, I thought it could have been you.' He looked like a broken man, almost. 'Right, well I've got to get off now anyway, I'm meeting Jenny in the Cooler. You fancy joining us for a few?'

'Yeah, why not eh? I'll just finish up here and I'll meet you there in about half an hour.'

As Kevin walked off John watched him. He noticed something a little bit different about him, maybe there was a little bit of a swagger to his walk, and an air of, dare he say it, confidence. *Well he is off to meet one of the fittest girls in the whole university,* John thought with a smile. His mind wandered off to the other night when she bent over to pick up her crown. He closed his eyes, recalling the view, and he had to fight the twinge he

The Twelve

was feeling in his trousers. He smiled and shook his head, knowing that there was no more revision for him today.

He did meet up with them in the Cooler and stayed for about an hour or so. He was more than curious about how this unlikely couple dynamic worked, and was pleasantly surprised by how dynamic they were.

During his short time with them, the topic of The Twelve never cropped up once.

Present day

52.

AFTER UNIVERSITY BRENDA Osman moved up north to Stoke on Trent. She opened a small shop offering up her services as a seamstress, making her own bridal gowns. It was something that she'd always wanted to do. Not long after the opening of the shop, it started to become successful. The logical next step was to expand the business to encompass her own party planning company too. Killing two birds with one stone.

Such was the quality of her work, news spread about her and very soon her celebrity clientele list was prestigious and as long as your arm. Top models, TV and radio presenters, movie stars and footballer's wives. Her list was an endless who's who of current celebrity.

She was now wedding go-to girl.

The day that she'd been waiting for all her professional life was almost upon her. Tomorrow she would find out if she'd landed the biggest client of them all.

The Duchess of Kent was marrying her rugby playing boyfriend next year, and her tender for the dress, and party, had been accepted as a potential. The budget was unofficially, name you own price, but it was the prestige that went with it, that's was the real prize.

Osman's had been narrowed down to the last two, but Brenda was quietly confident of securing the deal, as recently it had become clear that the other company in the running had made a lot of their money doing cash deals with travellers, for a low-grade Gypsy Weddings programme that seemed to be popular on TV.

It had been known in certain circles that the Duchess didn't want to be affiliated with that sort.

Brenda's husband was currently in Afghanistan, heading a logistics company for the British Army and their allies. He was sat behind a huge desk getting paid a fortune for not doing an awful lot … She didn't mind it though, even though she loved him more than anything, it kept him out of her way for months on end. Allowing her to concentrate on the important things, like her career.

53.

TONY CORLISS LIVED for his work. And his work was his whole life. He was a leading toxicologist for one of the three largest pharmaceutical companies in the world. Even though his title mentioned the words, he no longer worked as a toxicologist per se; he had risen through the ranks to become an executive director of the toxicology department. In short, whatever he said got done, and he liked it like that.

His penthouse office in Canary Wharf had the second most stunning view in all of London. It was the fact that it was only the second best that bothered him the most.

He was in line to become executive director of operations within the company and therefore a major private shareholder and senior board member. All he was waiting for was the say-so from the current CEO, which should be anytime in the next few days.

He liked the term 'current' CEO, because in all truth, Tony had his beady eyes on that role too. He wanted it all and he was ruthless enough to get it.

He didn't have the time for a wife or children, but he did have a string of loose, semi-serious girlfriends, that he could call upon any time that suited him. He had a black book with a long list of call girls that would cater for his every mood and every, wicked whim. He also had a major, Class A drug habit.

Luckily, he had the wealth and the contacts to cover both.

54.

LYNDA WITHERSPOON HAD always loved working with food, she'd been working in kitchens ever since leaving university. Working her way up from pots and pans to full chef in the top restaurants of London. She'd excelled in every discipline and earned herself a placement as assistant sous chef in a prestigious London hotel.

From there she went from strength to strength, rapidly progressing to full sous and therefore gaining the respect of everyone she worked with, on every level.

By reputation alone she managed to find the financial backing needed to open a small café on Milk Street, right in the middle of London's financial district. When she opened it, the naysayers had scoffed, saying that a café would never work there. That level of clientele didn't want bacon and sausage on toast, they wanted finger sandwiches, and natural yogurts with granola.

Lynda proved them all wrong. She sourced the finest cured bacon, and her cousin, who was a butcher, supplied her with the most exquisite homemade sausages. Free range eggs, organic tomato ketchup, the finest black pudding imported all the way from Scotland.

The café was a roaring success.

She was a roaring success.

She opened another café in Canary Wharf, to the same public aplomb and, maybe even further levels of success. Everything she touched turned to edible gold.

Four cafés later she tried her hand at taking over a small, failing restaurant off Drury Lane. Within six months of opening, it was another triumph due mostly to her shining reputation, earning her a Michelin Star.

She'd never had time to marry. 'All that malarkey just eats into your social life,' she'd say when asked about it. Plus, the fact that she'd never quite found the right man to be fair. Although she had found the right woman a few times along the way. It had been a long time before she decided that she must have been gay all along.

Almost inevitably, TV came calling for her to produce and star in her very own cookery series. 'With A Spoon, Will Travel'

The premise; for her to travel around greasy spoon cafés all over the UK and help them change the image of the whole industry to boot. The money was fantastic, and fame and fortune was only around the corner.

55.

BRENDA LIKED TO work late nights, she loved the solitude and the fact that there were never any distractions, plus it had the added bonus of her being in the same time zone as her husband overseas. He knew he could ring and talk to her whenever he wanted.

She had been working late into the night on the project for the Duchess. The design had to be finished and it had to be perfect. Her whole future, and the future of her company hung on it. If she won this tender the royal office would want the full designs and intricate samples the very next day.

She had plenty of staff about, more than enough to do this kind of thing for her, but something as big as this; it required her personal attention. There was also the fact that she wanted most, if not all the glory of being able to say, 'I made that. Every bit of it,' whenever the dress appeared on TV.

'So, what happens now? You've been away for so long.' She was talking on the telephone to her husband, Brian, in Afghanistan.

He was four hours ahead of her, making her late night and him early morning, both were very tired.

'Two more months and then we should be sorted over here, then home for good. Back to my Brenda.'

His normal, jovial voice changed then. He had things on his mind that he wanted to ask her, serious things.

'Have you been having any more of those... episodes?' There was an inflection on the word 'episodes' in order to lighten the sentence and hide the deep concern he felt for her.

'Well, yes actually. Have you got time for me to tell you about it?' She wanted to tell him all about them, as they had been freaking her out, but there was nothing that he could do while still so far away, and she didn't want to worry him.

'Honey, I always have time to listen to you, especially when you're miles and miles away.'

Her smile was evident in her voice. 'I knew there was a reason I loved you,' she laughed a little nervously. 'Well, you know I've been having these strange dreams? If I go to sleep early, I keep waking up about… well, about this time! Every time I dream, whenever I wake up and look at the clock, it reads three-fifteen exactly. It's bizarre because, it's never fourteen or sixteen, it's always dead on fifteen.'

Brian laughed a little on the other side of the world. 'Honey, that's normal, you're just missing me and your body clock is becoming sympathetic for what time I'd be getting up.'

She would have liked to share his enthusiasm, she would have loved to have shrugged the whole experiences off as just missing her husband, but she couldn't. 'It's a bit more than that Brian. The dream I was having the other night, the stupid wedding dresses were eating me, swallowing me up within them. I was screaming and struggling but they just kept on coming and coming. This dress for the Duchess, shit, I really think this project is going to kill me. I know how stupid that sounds … but it's how I feel.'

Brian laughed again. 'Bren, you're working way too hard. You need a break.'

She tried her best to sound a little more upbeat, but she knew, deep down, that she was failing miserably.

'I know, and I will. If I get this tomorrow, I won't have to work ever again, and neither will you.'

'Are you having a laugh, you're on the verge of fame and fortune, you're brilliant at your work, and you love it. If you gave up on this dream you'd be insufferable to live with, and I'd probably just move back here with the ungrateful Afghanis just to get away from you. Anyway, I sense there's more to this story. What else happened?'

'Well, the stink I was telling you about has been back, this time it smelt so bad, it was like real poo. I mean a deep shitty smell. I'm buggered if I can find where it's coming from. It made me retch, it really did. I've searched high and low, but there's nothing. Plus, the air conditioning unit in this building has just got to go, it can be the first casualty of our new regime when you get back home.'

'Oh yeah, something for me to really look forward to,' he mocked. 'Listen, I really have to go now, I've got a seven am meeting and I need to get a bit of prep in. I'll call you later today, OK?'

'OK.'

'Don't work too hard or too long now, OK? I love you.'

'I love you too. I think I'm just about done here anyway, so... I'll speak to you later?'

'Yeah, you can bet on it, talk later... I love you!'

He whispered the last part before disconnecting the line and was gone. The distance between them was back and now she was all alone again. *I love you too honey, I can't wait to see you again. I know the drill, the line goes dead but he's still about, he's just on the other side of nowhere*, she thought, in deep melancholy.

Wiping a tear from her eye and smiling a brave smile to herself, she put her phone down, adjusted her desk lamp and to continue to work on the samples.

Tonight, she was going back to the golden days of sewing by hand.

Her office was out in the sticks, far away from the traffic and the noise of Stoke on Trent. She liked it that way. She loved visiting the big city every now and then, especially London, but found early on that she couldn't live or work there to the best of her abilities. So, she'd set up shop in the back of the factory that she'd rented, at great expense, for this tender. It had been a gamble, and it had almost blown her entire budget for the whole year, but the odds on this gamble coming off were just too good not to give it her all. The publicity alone that would come from 'nearly' being the designer for the dress would be almost as good as if she had won the contract in the first place.

So, here she was, all alone in her dimly lit factory in the wee small hours of the morning. The nearest living person would be about two miles away in any direction, the nearest, awake living person would have been further still.

'What a chilling thought,' she said out loud, scaring herself just a little bit. She glanced over at the clock, it read five past three am.

'Damn it's cold!'

She hadn't noticed the cold creep up on her while she'd been on the phone, or the smell.

She began to gag a little as the stench crept up her nose. Fuming that it was back, she put her work gently down on the table and stood up. Her hands went to the small of her back, as she stretched it out a little. 'Maybe it is time I was off to bed,' she said, looking around the room at the layers of fabric and samples lying around haphazardly. 'I think I've got enough done for tomorrow now anyway.'

The Twelve

A shadow passed by her window, she caught it darting away out of the corner of her eye. She turned to see what it was, but it was gone, almost as fast as it came.

That was when Brenda noticed just *how* cold it had gotten in her factory.

56.

TONY LAY IN the huge king-size bed in his plush apartment overlooking the Thames. From the window in his room he had an excellent view of the Shard and London Bridge. His massive TV was on; he'd been watching his beloved Southampton kick lumps out of Bordeaux in some boring pre-season friendly on the other side Europe, and all the while having a prolonged drug and sex session with his latest conquest. He must have fallen asleep at some point because some stupid talk show was now playing on the TV. He hated that crap!

This is what Wednesday nights are for, he thought dreamily to himself, wiggling his toes against the silk of his bedsheets. As he clambered out of the large bed he slapped the naked bum cheek of the girl who was sharing it with him tonight.

'Oy, you, whatever your fucking name is, get out of bed, get dressed, and get lost!' He snarled at her.

He sounded like he was joking, but when she didn't move a muscle Tony lost his short-fused temper. He reached out and grabbed her by her long blonde ponytail and physically dragged her out of the bed.

As her beautiful, perfect body bounced off the expensive, thick piled carpet her face was filled with surprise and anger.

'I SAID GET OUT!!!' He shouted as he stood, looming, over her.

He grabbed her hair again and began to pull her out of his room. The poor girl was dragged, naked and kicking, across the carpet, giving her multiple carpet burns on her skin. He let go of her on the cold black tiled floor of his en-suite bathroom.

'Shit Tony, you fucking asshole. What are you doing?' Her American accent riled him even more than he already was.

'Who are you anyway? Who are you but a stupid fucking WHORE?' He shouted the last word, his anger was boiling within him now. He always got like this when he had been using too much, it usually served him well in the board room, but could be a strain on his personal relationships. 'Stop sponging off of me, you slag, stop it or I'll fucking kill you.'

He was leaning in close to her, she could see the anger and the psychosis on his face, this coupled with the two fists he was clenching was enough to make her know better than to argue with him.

Katie was physically beautiful, with her long blonde hair and athletic figure, but there was something about her that was broken. Mostly it was her personality.

She'd been his on-off girlfriend for about two years now; she worked as a PA in his office. Everyone hated her because of her arrogance, and the horrible way she treated people. She was always late, and it always seemed to be either due to drink or drugs.

She'd figured Tony out within a few weeks of being in the office. His tardiness, the fact that he'd sometimes be in the office with the same clothes on for three days at a time, and his continual sniffing and jaw movements. He was just like her, broken but high-functioning.

She made herself available to him. She was aware that he was with several other women in the office, but she didn't care, she didn't love him and never would. She thought herself incapable of love. The other girls were only there because they flattered him and he knew he could have them whenever he wanted. She was with him purely for the money, the drugs and the power.

Right now, her life experience had taught her that when he was into a meth induced paranoia rage, it was not advantageous to argue back.

'OK, OK... I'm going. Oh, and I'm Katie by the way. Your fucking girlfriend!'

She headed out of the bathroom, back into the bedroom and grabbed her clothes. It was still the middle of the night, but she had syphoned off a large chunk of cash from him tonight, so this little detail didn't really matter, she could afford to get to wherever she needed to be.

'It's always too fucking cold in here anyway,' she snapped back at him.

She ran from the bedroom, still naked, and down the stairs into the living area of the duplex apartment shouting back over her shoulder as she did, 'And it stinks in here too, you fucking animal.'

Tony was indeed in the middle of a meth induced rage right now, he knew it was for no reason, other than this *'slag'* had just had the audacity to call him a filthy animal. He jumped off the bed and ran into the living room, his mad eyes were a deep red and thick, white froth was foaming from his mouth.

Katie had seen all this before, and she knew that if he caught her he would quite capable of killing her. She also knew that when he'd been on a meth binge his reactions were always slow. So slow that when she saw that he was really coming at her, she easily side stepped him, laughing out loud as he went flying into the coffee table, the very same table that they'd both snorted coke from, and then had weird sex on, a few hours earlier.

'I'LL FUCKING KILL YOU, YOU BITCH!!!' He shouted as he squirmed about on the floor, trying in vain to get up.

The Twelve

Katie shook her head and laughed down at him, he looked so pathetic on the floor, angry and helpless, like some fat cartoon character. 'No, you won't, you fucking loser! You and your limp, drug addled dick are going to stay down there. You prick,' she spat.

She hated him more than she hated herself, and that was saying something.

His arms and legs seemed to have a life of their own as they flailed about attempting to correct himself. In the time that he was squirming, and unsuccessfully trying to get himself up, she managed to get herself dressed and also had time to do her make-up, to a fashion. She knew she was safe while he was wallowing about down there.

In plain sight, she began to rifle through his trouser pockets looking to find his wallet.

'There's no point in spending my own hard earned cash is there?' She asked him. 'I mean, I just let you fumble about on top of me for two hours, so I figure you owe me this.' She showed him the thick wad of notes, which she guessed would be mostly fifties and twenties, before putting it into her purse with the rest of the cash she had stolen from him.

His mad, hate filled, eyes glared at her, and his face reddened as his anger boiled inside of him.

At the door, she turned around and looked at him, still on the floor. 'See you in the office in a few hours,' she said sweetly to him, blowing him a kiss. She knew that he wouldn't remember any of this after the rage had burnt out and he'd been asleep.

The exact moment that the door closed behind her Tony's rage depleted. It dissipated almost as rapidly as it had escalated. He assessed his situation, and he saw the funny side of it. He was lying naked on the floor with a massive grin on his face.

'See ya, Katie… Love you,' he mumbled to himself, spitting the thick white froth from his dry mouth as he did.

The temperature of his apartment hit him then. At first, he thought it was just him coming down off whatever he'd been pumping through his nose that evening, but he quickly realised that it was more than that, it was the whole room that was freezing cold.

His naked body had a sheen of sweat all over it, as it normally did during a rapid come down, and he began to shiver as the moisture on his skin began to freeze. He wrapped his arms around himself to stave it off. 'I love the cold, I love the cold,' he stammered as he tried, once again to get up.

This time he made it, he eventually got to his knees and looked around him. Drug paraphernalia was strewn everywhere, his glass table was now broken, and he had a feeling in his stomach that told him he would probably be spending the next few hours racked in pain, sitting on the toilet. Unless he got right back on the gear.

He sat on his leather couch, wincing from the cold of it against his sweaty skin. 'Man, I really do need to sort this shitty life out,' he said to himself as another series of tremors ripped through his body. His bones ached.

He grabbed his expensive bathrobe from where it was lying on the couch and dusted it down of all the debris from his heavy night with… *Shit, who the fuck have I been with tonight?*
Normally this would have caused him to break out in a big grin at his varied and successful love life, but right now it scared him half to death that he genuinely couldn't remember.

'I fucking hate the cold…' he mumbled.

A strange, paranoid feeling washed over him then, it was a feeling like he wasn't alone. Paranoia was normal after, whatever he'd been doing tonight, but this feeling was different somehow, more intense. He looked up towards his bedroom door on the second floor of his duplex, hoping to see who he'd spent most of the night with.

    The light from the bedroom revealed a silhouette. There was someone standing just inside the door, half hidden in the glare from the light inside.

    The clock on his wall read ten minutes past three.

    His paranoia induced rage returned, all at once.

    'Who the fuck are you? And what do you want?'

57.

LYNDA AND HER camera crew were set to start filming in a café in the middle of nowhere, somewhere in the Scottish Highlands. The café opened its doors to customers at five am, seven days a week. They baked all their own pies and cakes too, so the staff's working day began at three am.

Lynda had never been good with early mornings, so when she found out that this was the first assignment for her new TV show, she was excited, but also quite a bit apprehensive.

Ever since she was ten years old she'd always been what you might call, a robust girl. Broad shoulders, sturdy legs, small breasts, and she'd always had an issue with getting out of bed early in the morning. This morning however, at three am, which she still considered the middle of the night, she'd had her hair done by professionals, she'd had her make up done by professionals, and they had dressed her in size appropriate, flattering clothes for the camera.

She was looking and feeling good about herself for the first time in quite a while. Over the last few weeks she'd not been getting a lot of sleep, she'd been plagued by crazy dreams, seeing shadows and experiencing crazy, sickening smells that follow her around wherever she went.

The dreams, she put down to anxiety about the show, the shadows were obviously because she wasn't getting enough sleep. But the smells? Well she supposed

The Twelve

she'd been smelling rotten meat most of her life, in one form or another.

It had started getting bad just lately, mostly on the run up to the filming of this show. *Just my luck.* She thought to herself one night, a few days earlier. *All this time I've been waiting for my big break, and here I am getting a frigging brain tumour.*

'Ms Witherspoon, you'll be required on set at three-thirty… it's now five-past, is that good for you?' One of her aides informed her as she popped her head through the trailer door.

She smiled a nervous smile. 'Yeah, I'll be there Joan, but can you do me a favour in the meantime? Can you get someone to have a look at the heating in this van? It's freezing!'

Joan looked at her a little concerned. 'Lynda, the heating's on full… and the gas cylinder is new, therefore full, are you sure you're feeling OK?'

Joan stepped into the trailer to take a closer look at her. She leaned in and placed her hand on her forehead, like her mother used to do. 'Well, you're not warm, but Jesus, you're right; it *is* cold in here. I'll go and see what I can do.' She looked back out of the door before leaning in and giving her a kiss, she pushed her hair gently behind her ear, and winked at her. Lynda held her hand and smiled at her.

Joan then left the trailer lifting her collar up on her coat as she did. This left Lynda sitting in the cold, alone… or at least she thought she was alone.

'You can do this, you can do this, you can do this, you can do this…' Over the last few years, since listening to a self-help tape somewhere or other, this had become her mantra to get her through stressful situations, and now, sitting in front of this big mirror, she felt stress starting to envelope her.

She closed her eyes as if in meditation and began to suck in deep breaths. As she did, a waft of rotten meat, excrement, and something that smelled like vomit washed over her. Her eyes opened in an instant, as her stomach rolled with the assault on her senses.

The mirror she was looking in began to fog over, it went further than fogging, it started to freeze in the corners. She watched in amazement as ice tendrils began to form, crawling their way towards the centre of the mirror like alien fingers, clawing their way towards her reflection in the dead centre. To her, it was as if she was watching a time-lapsed film, they were moving that fast.

The icy fingers stopped their advance when they reached her reflection. They formed a kind of shroud around her image. The scene was a lot more than unnerving.

Her confused face stared back at her from inside the mirror, but the confusion soon changed to terror.

In the mist behind her she could see a blurred reflection of something, or someone. She couldn't take her eyes of it. She moved, slightly to the left but the shadow moved with her. This was no trick of the light. Knowing that there was no-one else in the trailer and the curtains were drawn due to the hour, her brain couldn't comprehend what the shadow was.

As if glued to her chair, her wide eyes attempted to make some sense out of what it could be, when it moved. Arms seemed to form from the dark, hooded shape, arms that were reaching out towards her.

Scared, petrified even, she whipped her head around to see who, or what was there. As she did, the something or someone grabbed her head and neck, stopping the rest of her body from spinning around to catch up.

The feel of the cold, clammy hands on her skin made her feel dirty and empty inside. Without even looking at them she knew that they were filthy, rotten even, in every sense of the word. They were unbelievably strong, moist, and freezing cold. She realised that it was the hands, or the fingers that must have been the source of the vile smell she had been experiencing.

She couldn't move her face a centimetre in either direction, so she had no way to see who her assailant could be.

'Thiiiiiiiiiiiirteeeeeeeeeen!!!' Came the whisper, the whisper that seemed to resonate from all around her trailer.

Truly petrified, out of her wits, it was all she could do to whimper a pathetic reply. 'Who's there? What do you want?'

She wanted to shout this reply but couldn't, the disgusting cold hands were now covering her mouth, muffling her words. She could taste the smell, if that was even possible. The fingers had entered her mouth, and left a feeling that was turning her stomach. Shit, sweat, decay, vomit... Death!

'I want much,' came the spirit's scratchy, whispered reply. 'You have something that's mine, and I want it back.'

The hands left her face, and her head snapped almost comically back, so she was now looking at herself in the frozen mirror. She attempted to breathe deep relieving, breaths, but all she took in was thick, cloying filth.

Her reflection showed her that where the hands had touched the skin, they had left big red welts on her cheeks. *They'll be bruises by the morning,* she thought.

The strong hands took hold of her once more. This time they pulled her head back by her hair. She tried to scream again but her neck was so taut that it was squeezing her oesophagus tight, no sound could escape.

She didn't want to see who or what her assailant was, she didn't need that amount of horror in her life, but her eyes betrayed her and she looked up. There was an upside down, confusion of a face staring down at her. It was the ruined face of a young boy, a face she thought she might have remembered, recognized from a different time.

The destroyed features continued to stare down at her as thick, black, coagulated blood poured from the gaping wound of his mouth and from a deep gash within his neck.

As she opened her mouth to shout, the thick blood dripped in, causing her to gag as the disgusting copper taste of old, dirty blood filled her mouth.

The boy removed the hood that he had over his face, revealing himself fully to her. Recognition registered on her stricken face.

'YOU?' she croaked.

58.

'YOU HAVE SOMETHING of mine, and I want it back.' The whisper, although quiet and scratchy, seemed to bounce off every wall of the apartment.

'How the fuck did you get in here? You've got thirty seconds to leave or I'm calling the police.' Tony was shouting at the hooded silhouette upstairs in his duplex apartment, if he'd been particularly sober or had any of his faculties about him, then he would have run for his life, but still in that hazy twilight of being high and on a rapid comedown, he wasn't altogether present in his head.

'I will leave when I have what is mine.' The shadow whispered in response.

'I don't have anything of yours. What the fuck could you own that I could possibly want? You freak!' Tony's bravado was beginning to ebb now the more he looked at the thing, and the more of it, he could see.

With dawning horror, Tony was beginning to shake, he was holding his stomach as the cramps that were building up inside of him felt like they were attempting to tear him apart.

'What the fuck do you want with me?'

This was the worst come down from the meth he'd ever had in his life.

'I want... what is mine!'

'What the fuck does that mean?' He screamed. 'Are you going to stand in the shadows or are you going to come out here and speak to me? Come out here and face me you piece of shit!'

Tony's face contorted as the pain of the meth come down began to take its toll. 'Oh fuck!' He whispered dropping his face to the floor as another wave of cramp induced pain tore through him.

Crazy, weird images, or visions, or even memories flashed though his mind. His brain was so addled that he couldn't decipher between them. Colours, mostly reds and purples. There were some strange noises too, like gushing wind and chanting. There was blood, so much blood.

And screaming.

He had to cover his ears to drown out the rhythmic chanting that was now filling his head. It felt like his brain was throbbing and that any moment it would explode. He could see waves and waves of thick black blood.

It all seemed to be coming from the horrific, hooded, hallucination he was seeing before him.

'I want what's miiiiiiiiiiiiiiiiiiiiine!!!' The thing hissed at him, the sound swirling like a wind, rushing around his apartment, and his head.

Tony's eyes filled with tears, tears for his lost life, and tears for his lost innocence, tears of terror, and tears of pain.

'Leave me alone… leave me alone. I don't know you anymore,' he sobbed. The tears fell down his cheeks, leaving tracks down his sweat slicked face.

He wanted to scream, but he knew that if he started now, he might never stop; he'd scream and scream for the rest of his life.

However long that was going to be.

Another tear fell down his cheek, it was closely followed by another, and then another two or three.

A red one appeared in his eye well. The corner of his eye had begun to sting, and his vision turned mostly pink.

Soon both of his eyes were haemorrhaging red tears.

The only thing that he could see through the red hue of the room was the dark figure, the dark, hooded figure that he thought he recognised, it had advanced upon him, from upstairs in the beat of his heart.

He was freezing cold and all he could smell was shit. He opened his mouth, once again trying to scream, but it was difficult to scream when he couldn't get any air into his lungs.

Panic set in and he wiped the red tears from his eyes in a frenzy. He looked down at his naked body. In his fear and downward spiralling drugged fuelled state, it took him a few seconds to realise that he was dying.

He still thought the red was just coming from his eyes, but he soon realised that most of it surrounding him was coming from other parts of his body.

His stomach was a massive, ugly hole that was spewing forth blood, gore and remnants of undigested meals. His face filled with horrific surprise when he realised that it was *HIS* blood and gore that was currently decorating his carpet.

The last few beats of his weakened heart pumped jets of thick, fresh blood from the broken tubes of his arteries. With an almost serene clarity he watched it spray, decorating his white walls in what looked like a Jackson-Pollock work of art.

The figure stood over him, his hands covered in dark, dripping blood. Its deformed mouth smiled a gruesome grin down at him. Decaying teeth peeping through the folds of puffed up, bruised and purple skin that formed its mouth. Black, jelly like blood dribbled down the front of his filthy hooded top from the blackness of his face and the vicious looking slash in his neck.

Tony's eyes were wide open as his last breath forced its way out of his decimated body.

'Thiiiiiiiiiiirteeeeeeeeeen!!!' The figure whispered.

Tony Corless' last words in this life were…

'Thirteen, huh?'

59.

BRENDA WAS IN a complete mental breakdown over the shadow at the window. She was hoping that it was a figment of her imagination, but something told her that she wouldn't be having any such luck tonight.

A shadow watching her from a window had been one of her many phobias from an early age.

'Hello… Hello, who's there? Can I help you with anything?' Even at her most terrified, Brenda couldn't help being polite.

'Thiiiiiiiiiiiirteeeeeeeeeen!!!' Came a whispered reply. It seemed like it was coming from the walls inside the office itself. She whipped her head around, hoping to *not* see whoever had given her that creepy reply.

'Y…you want thu… thirteen?'

It wasn't just the fear that was making her stutter, although that was the main crux of it, but suddenly the temperature inside the office had dropped by at least ten degrees.

'Thirteen what? Please, if you wu…want money, there's a jar in the kitchen. Th… there's about three hundred pounds in it. T…t…take it, it's yours.'

'I don't want money… I want what's mine…' The strange whisper from all around her crawled into her ears again.

Along with the whisper, the shadow in the window reappeared. She had to blink, just to make sure that it wasn't all in her head, like in one of those stupid films that… Ben Lomax, used to make her watch back in university.

Where the hell did that name come from? She blinked again and shook her head, trying to rid herself of this shadow, and all thoughts of stupid scary films from long ago. *It's time to go home I think.*

She stood up from the table, intentionally ignoring the window, and picked up her coat from the back of a chair.

There was more movement from her peripheral vision. She froze and closed her eyes. She could hear her heart beating inside her chest, and it was too loud. She could swear that it could be heard from at least a mile away. Slowly she turned back towards the window, dreading what would be there.

The shadow had gone! If it had ever been there in the first place.

'Please don't let it come back… Please don't let it come back… Please don't let it come back.' She had found herself a new mantra.

After a short while she plucked up the courage to open her eyes and peeked towards the window. Her heart was now throbbing, at least double time.

Relief flowed over her. There was still nothing there.

Feeling better and more relaxed, she proceeded to put her coat on to combat the unseasonal frost in the air. 'Come on mouse, you know all you saw there was just a curtain or something equally as stupid,' she scolded herself, and shot a casual glance over to the window that had been causing her great anxiety for the last few minutes.

Her sharp intake of breath was twofold.

The first was due to the ice burn she had just received on her hand. The extreme drop of temperature had made the handle on the door dangerous to touch, her skin momentarily sticking to the freezing metal.

This was the minor of the two shocks that caused her to take in the breath.

Standing, apparently on its own, was one of the sample wedding gowns that had been folded over a rail in preparation for the morning.

The terror that gripped her now was an old one.

The person watching her from a window was only *one* of her childhood phobias, the other, strangely enough, was wedding dresses.

She knew it was silly, and she knew it was a strange career path to take, designing and creating wedding dresses, if she was so scared of them, but she'd always thought of it as therapy. And there was also the fact that she'd always been good at it of course.

Terror gripped her, as she looked down towards the bottom of the dress and noticed that it was floating at least a foot off the ground. Worse still it seemed to be floating, slowly towards her.

'Thiiiiiiiiiiiirteeeeeeeeeeen!!!' Came the whisper once more. This time it didn't come from all around her, it came directly from the wedding dress. She screamed and lunged at the freezing cold door handle. Her hands burnt on the metal once again and she was suddenly trapped. Trapped in her own office with a ghostly wedding dress chasing her.

Through tear filled eyes she watched as the dress continued to float towards her. In her dreams, even from childhood, this had happened many times, each time it ended the same way. The dress engulfed her and tore at her flesh.

She screamed, but even as she did she had the clarity of thought to think about what good it would do her. There was no-one around for miles. A small coherent part of her brain, and it was only small by this time, asked herself a rhetorical question. *Even if there was anyone about, who could save her from a man-eating wedding dress?*

It was a very good and pertinent question.

Her face was frozen into a rictus of terror. The small, coherent part of her had taken this time to decide to work a little overtime. *If this was a film I'd have turned it off by now for being rubbish, and unbelievable. Even Ben would have thought this implausible.*

She wished, more than anything, that it was a film. The dress stopped maybe five feet from where she lay. The smell that permeated from it was putrid, but it was, by no means the worst part of this absurd scene.

The dress was beginning to fill out; the bodice swelled as something inside it began to expand, to form. The whole brocade began to heave as if someone invisible were trying to breathe inside it.

From her low view point, Brenda watched, in denial as dirty boots appeared from underneath the skirt. Slowly she looked up to witness a dark head appear from the plunging neckline. That neckline was designed to show a fair bit of the delightful cleavage that the Duchess of Kent had in abundance. It was a little bit of a risk, but one that she was willing to take, knowing the Duchess' sense of flirty style. Now it was displaying something more horrendous than was ever intended.

She could only see the top half of the boy's face from her viewpoint. She was only, almost sure that it was a boy.

The skin on the face looked either dirty or a pale blue, or maybe it was both, she couldn't tell in the dim lighting and through the vividness of her fear. There was a slit across his throat, which was so deep Brenda could make out a small white bone inside it. Thick black goo was seeping out of the wound, dribbling down the front of the dress, destroying the cream silk brocade.

The Twelve

The rest of the boy/thing's head was covered in a dirty, grey hood. The only other part visible was his/its unearthly glowing silver eyes. When the head had emerged completely from the dress the hood was removed, and the vision underneath was far worse than the neck.

It *was* a boy. Ugly and dirty, and young. Everything from his nose down was destroyed and distorted. What was left of his jaw hung loosely from the dark, filthy abyss he had as an excuse for a mouth.

The rest of his face was just as bad, it was an evil, nasty, angry face. There was something else about it, something familiar, but she couldn't put her finger on what it was.

The whole apparition looked absurd, almost comical in the wedding dress; but the malevolence in his glowing silvery eyes soon washed away any thoughts of humour about this situation.

The boy or man, or whatever it was opened the flap that was his mouth, as he did an avalanche of the horrible dark gloop fell out in large clots, rather like raspberry jam. The dirty, crooked and broken teeth inside were few and far between, they were dirty and out of line, like they'd been roughly shoved into soft plastic.

As the thing attempted a smile, the skin from around the bottom of his face peeled away slowly, revealing large patches of raw flesh, and in some places, exposed jaw bone. His pale silvery eyes glowed further in the darkness.

'You have something of mine... and I want it back.'

Blood mingled with the spittle from the boy's mouth as he rasped. The voice hurt Brenda's ears, and she covered them up with her shaking hands. Hoping that this simple act could block out, maybe just a little bit of the horror that was happening all around her.

She was wrong! Very wrong.

The boy leaned in towards her, bringing all his stink with him. She couldn't help but look deep into his dark silver eyes, her face filled with deadly recollection.

Realisation dawned regarding what it was about this spectre. She did recognise him.

As if in a thrall, she continued to look deeper within his silvery pupils, there was something in there, she didn't know if it was a trick of the light or a vision or something else entirely, but she did know that it was disturbing. Something in the reflection of his eyes embarrassed, shocked and horrified her to the bone.

She saw herself.

She was naked.

There was a large man with her.

He was also naked.

They were doing an act, one that was bad, and one they were doing… willingly.

Something clicked in her head. She broke away from the glowing stare of the ghost before her and looked around her warehouse. With one sweeping gaze, she took in all the dresses that were hanging around on the rails, all the fabrics and samples on the tables, and all her plans and drawings.

She managed an almost sweet smile at the apparition, and to her shock he smiled back.

'All of this…' she gestured around the room. 'All of this is because of you, isn't it?'

His dirty grey hand moved slowly towards her chest, she was powerless to stop it. There was also a small part of her that didn't really want to.

His fingers stroked at her stomach, she could feel the cold of his touch even through her clothes. There was a small ripping noise and then her skin broke out in goose-bumps as the cold of the room bit into her.

He put his hand inside the small tear he had made and caressed her. The feel of his flesh touching hers was revolting, but she was too scared, and far too sad to care about that right now.

Suddenly his other hand grabbed at her blouse and with a powerful tug, he ripped it off her body, leaving her sitting on the floor in her jeans and large white bra.

The ghost stood over her, looking down. There was no mercy in his bloody face.

Brenda was frozen with terror, there was little she could do to stop this thing from doing whatever it wanted to do to her. As the ghostly boy continued to stroke her stomach, she felt something freezing cold pinch her, there was a moment of intense pain, but only a moment. Then there was only the cold.

The feel of the dirty, icy fingers entering her was strange and uncomfortable, not to mention painful, but the look on the boy's face was what scared her the most.

The serene look on his face had gone, along with all the tenderness of his fingers inside her. The worse pain that she could imagine ripped through her as he pushed his whole hand inside her stomach. Her breath was lost as the probing fingers delved deeper and deeper inside her, ripping her stomach wide open, like a plastic bag.

With a perverse sense of titillation, she felt the hand grab at her internal organs. *What a strange feeling...* she marvelled as wave after wave of pure unadulterated pain surged through her body.

Her face was as white as a sheet. *I'm guessing I'm going into shock,* she thought. *I really can't believe it's him. I thought he was dead, hah, maybe he is.*

Her thoughts were coherent, and she couldn't help but chuckle a little at her predicament. She guessed that in the balance of things, she deserved what was happening to her.   Another ripping sound followed by more searing pain coursed through her. Casually she looked down and marvelled to see her body torn open, and her innards strewn all over the floor.

The lower half of her stomach resembled a poor 80s video nasty special effect that Ben Lomax used to make her watch on the nights in with her and Nicky McEvoy, her roommate. The apparition's arms were elbow deep inside her stomach, now. The view was almost comical. *Who'd have thought that those rubbish looking effects were actually rather accurate?*

The boy was looking for something. Something that was apparently inside her.

He lifted his head to consider her face. He looked triumphant, almost happy, as he removed something from her torso, something small. With a contented look at what he'd found, he removed his other arm. It was dripping in… *Well, me I suppose.* She thought.

Whatever hold he'd had on her was gone now, and her abused, dying, torso curled up on the floor.

She regarded him, her eyes were already beginning to gloss over, and she needed to squint to see his face. She whispered something. The boy leaned in close to hear it. She whispered it again, and he nodded. He stepped back, admiring his work as she writhed in agony on the floor.

He raised one sharp, bony finger and slit her throat from ear to ear. She died instantly, bleeding out on the industrial carpet of her factory, surrounded by her life's work.

The words she had whispered to the apparition were… 'I'm sorry!'

~~~

Brenda Osman, incidentally, was due to receive a very important letter later that morning, it was a letter with a royal seal on it. It would inform her that after considerable debate, they were pleased to inform her that the office of the Duchess of Kent had decided to engage her designs for the royal wedding. This letter would have ensured great success in all her future endeavours.

    The only hitch to this was that Brenda Osman didn't have any future endeavours. Brenda Osman lay dead on the floor of her rented warehouse. The contents of her stomach decorating the ground around her. The royal wedding dress, now stained with thick, black blood and clumps of disgusting gore, was lying, destroyed, next to her.

60.

JOHN WAS RELIEVED to get everything he could regarding The Twelve off his chest, and Detective Addison lapped it all up. He told him about the exclusion of anyone else from their 'club', he told him about the sexual antics of Debbie, he told them about the meetings in the nude and about the occult ritual they had held prior to their main meeting.

Addison did not look impressed. John supposed that this sort of thing happened quite a bit in universities, where young people were opening their minds to new experiences and dabbling with all kinds of mind altering drugs and sexual awakenings. He couldn't see Addison as one who had ever opened his mind to anything new in his whole life.

Detective Addison was starting to see John as less of a suspect as the conversation continued. He had a nagging feeling that John was missing something out, maybe not quite holding back, but there was a little something omitted from this confession.

'Tell me about the meeting itself John, not the one prior, but the actual meeting. I want to know what happened, who was there, that kind of thing.'

John sat on the opposite side of the table looking at the detective. He'd heard the request and he'd fully understood what the man wanted to hear, but was almost dumbstruck in the fact that he genuinely couldn't remember.

'Do you know what Detective? I think I need to ponder on that question for a small while.' He shook his head and rubbed his eyes with his hands. 'I think I'm tired. My mind's a fog. All this reminiscing about Gill and the others has taken it out of me. Am I a suspect or can I go home and get some rest?'

Addison looked at him like a man looks at a stray dog on the street. Not one hundred percent sure whether to trust him or not. He sat back in his chair, pensive.

Eventually he shook his head and leaned forward. 'No, I don't think you are a suspect Mr Rydell, but I do think that you can fill in some of the blanks in these cases.'

'Cases?' John asked, a little taken aback. 'I thought this was just about Debbie Baines.'

'It was, but I've convinced the powers that be that this case and the one regarding G... sorry, your wife, are too close. Plus, what you've just told me about Mr and Mrs Lomax has made me think that there's more of a connection between them.'

John looked a little brighter, but not by much. Even though he wasn't officially a suspect, John was under the impression that somewhere down the line of these murders, and probably not too far down that line either, he would become a victim himself.

Addison took the photograph back from him, and made at least three people in the office witness while he inserted it back into the envelope after scanning it and saving it on his hard drive. He sealed the envelope, signed it, and then double bagged it before handing it back over to the evidence department.

Eventually satisfied, he dismissed John with the caveat of not going out of the country until this matter had been resolved, and the murderer of Debbie Baines and Gill Rydell, and possibly the others, had been apprehended.

John agreed and was more than happy to leave the station, without the photograph.

As he arrived home he felt the now familiar freezing cold bite into him through his clothes, almost as soon as he opened the door. He could also smell the familiar stench of rotten meat and excrement. It wasn't that this phenomenon didn't freak him out exactly; it was just that he was getting used to it, almost expecting it, and therefore had become somewhat apathetic towards it.

Keeping his coat on, and pulling it tighter around him, he walked into the living room, sat down on his chair and closed his eyes.

Before he did he snuck a quick peep at the clock. It read Twenty-five minutes past eight pm.

61.

AT THREE-FIFTEEN am, John awoke with a scream, he was drenched in sweat and his eyes were stinging as if he had been crying. He'd had a dream where he owned three dogs. He'd gone out somewhere, leaving them in alone, and on his return, he'd discovered that all three dogs had turned on each other, and ripped each other to shreds. All three disembowelled dogs adorned his kitchen floor.

Shaken, he had entered the freezing cold room and the three corpses instantly became animated, twitching and jumping, writhing in agony. Their bloody and torn faces all looked up at him with expectant, and accusing looks. Suddenly their faces began to turn; human features formed out of their ruined muzzles, complete with grimaces of pain and suffering.

Their canine bodies attempted to get up, each of them spilling their internal organs and entrails over the kitchen floor, via the slashes and tears in their abdomens.

Their bodies began to change then too, bloating and transforming into deformed half dog half human monstrosities. All three of them still whimpering in pain like dogs, but whispering conspiratorially.

'Thiiiiiiiiiiiirteeeeeeeeeen!!!'

At this point he woke up, screaming. The sweat on his face was freezing cold and he could see his breath. His pillow was crispy with frost and the TV screen had a thick layer of ice on it.

'Oh, for fuck's sake, that is cold!'

He struggled to get up out of his chair, but his back screamed in agony at him, scolding him for sleeping in a sitting position on a chair and not in a bed. Combining this with the total fatigue he was feeling, he failed to stand, and miserably flopped back onto the cushions. He sighed. A sad, resigned gush of air expelled not only from his mouth, but seemingly from every orifice that he could sigh from.

He closed his eyes in resignation when something fluttered down from the ceiling and landed on his lap.

He knew exactly what it was without even looking at it. By looking at it he knew that he would be damning at least one of his old friends to an unpleasant death.

He sat there, stock still for a few moments, trying to ignore the white piece of paper on his lap. It was a while before he finally succumbed to his own curiosity. He leaned over and turned the lamp on at the side of the chair. Even though it was dim, the sudden light hurt his eyes for a few seconds. He closed them, not knowing if he was doing it because of the sudden sting, or to procrastinate looking at what was on his lap.

Eventually he looked.

It was a photograph.

It was *the* photograph.

He closed his eyes and picked it up, it was the last thing in the whole world he wanted to look at, but he knew he was going to have to do it at some point. For the second time in a matter of a minute, curiosity got the better of him.

He looked.

It was not only Brenda's face that was completely blurred out this time, but Tony's *and* Lynda's too.

His heart sank.

It was too much for him to take in right now. He held the photograph up to his face in the dimly lit room and began to cry. He sobbed for everything that had been

The Twelve

lost. Gill, his beautiful wife, their nice successful, happy life together, his old friends, but most of all he sobbed for what he was in the process of losing right now.

His sanity.

Tears flowed freely and he worried that he wouldn't be able to stop them anytime soon. He held the photograph to his chest as the warm, salty tears streamed down his freezing cold cheeks.

Eventually, he eased up out of the chair, still holding the photograph to his chest, and still crying. He made his way to the stairs and began to slowly walk up, heading towards his bedroom. He didn't bother to get undressed before flopping onto the bed and curling himself up into a ball.

In his distraught state, he let loose a blood-curdling scream, crunching up the photograph in his fists. He sat up and began to rip the photograph into many, small pieces before throwing them into the air, letting them fall, silently to the floor.

Feeling a little better, he curled back up into a tight ball in his bed, hugging his knees to his chest. He closed his eyes again and cried himself to sleep.

As he lay in the bed, a short, dark hooded figure was stood in the shadows in the corner of his room. It stood in complete silence watching him lose his sanity. The ugly silhouette of the spectre's ruined face suggested it was smiling.

Part 4

Redford University South London
20 years earlier

62.

THE RITUAL WAS set for four days' time. Everyone was nervous about it, they were all either spending their time in the Cooler, talking about what this meeting entailed, or they were in the gym, trying their very best to look as good as they could while naked.

This was the meeting that involved all the sex.

John couldn't admit to being excited about it, he was more pensive than apprehensive, he still hadn't worked through his issues from the first meeting.

'Don't you think it's odd that no-one can remember what happened during the last meeting? I mean we all woke up on the floor for Christ's sake?' John asked Ben Lomax in a rare moment when there was just the two of them sat at a table in the Cooler.

Ben's eyes met his and John could see the excitement and the wonder within them. Due to his obsession with rubbish gore splattered, big-boobs films, this was almost a wonderland for him. 'I don't think about it. It was The Great Lord Glimm taking over our bodies and minds,' he shrugged. 'We don't need to know what happened.'

John felt a little disheartened by this response. He was hoping for a little more. Especially from him, who he saw, distressed at what was happening on that table. He was also troubled by his apathy to the whole thing.

'Listen, I don't really know how to mention this, but, I think I was a bit more lucid then everyone else that night.'

Ben looked at him over his plate of salad and his pint of lager. 'Go on man. Hit me,' he replied, nodding his head conspiratorially.

John looked at him, then all around him in the bar, finally happy that there wasn't anyone around listening to them, he leaned in closely and whispered. 'I'm sure I saw Robert rape Debbie on that table…'

Ben pulled back from the table, sporting a 'what are you talking about' face and vehemently shook his head in denial. He looked at John with a furrowed brow.

'That wasn't rape! She needed the seed of The Glimm.' He picked up his drink and took long swig from it. 'I'm a bit pissed though that I don't remember that bit, I'd have loved to see Debbie getting it banged into her.' Ben gave John a knowing smile and a wink.

'No mate, I'm sure he did, she was screaming.' *And I'm sure you watched that bit too Ben,* he thought.

He whispered again, shaking his head, knowing that this conversation wasn't going anywhere. 'That's not the worst of it, after he'd done Debbie then I watched him rape Carl too!' John gave great emphasis on the word 'CARL'.

'Whoa man, are you sure?' Ben backed away from him again, this time with his hands in the air in disbelief. 'That's crazy! Carl's not gay. Neither is Robert for that matter.'

'I never said he was gay. I never said either of them are gay. I think it's all part of this bizarre meeting we're having on Friday.'

Ben took another, long swig from his pint glass and laughed. 'Don't worry yourself too much John, I won't be banging it into you. Mate, you're far too ugly for me!'

John conceded to the humour of the situation and cracked a smile at Ben's joke, but he was far from happy about the proceedings.

Why do I remember all these things, and no-one else does? He thought taking a sip of his cold beer.

Just then the other members of The Twelve began to drift into the bar. They were all here for a small meeting that had been arranged by Robert. Some of them were still sweaty after just being to the gym or having been jogging. The atmosphere between them was convivial, and everyone was laughing, but there was also a nervous edge to it.

The last to turn up was Jenny.

John noticed her as she walked into the Cooler late, he was a bit surprised to see Kevin walk in right behind her. He didn't come over to the group, but went over to the other side of the bar, he ordered a drink and sat on his own.

John kept his eyes on him with interest as Jenny did the rounds with kisses and hugs.

After everyone was finally there and all the pleasantries had calmed down Robert stood up to address everyone. He banged his fist on the end of the long table and all the talking stopped as all the members of The Twelve turned to face him.

'Right, thanks everyone for coming tonight. I just wanted to go over a few things regarding Friday night.'

Everyone was silent as they watched him, he had their undivided attention. 'The meeting will begin at midnight exactly. You should all be at the hall for eleven thirty at the very latest. Any tardiness *will not* be tolerated and the meeting will have to be postponed, maybe indefinitely, and no-one wants that. Leave for the hall as early as possible to avoid any traffic related issues or any accidents. We'll all need to be changed and ready to partake by ten-to and in place in the main hall by five-to.

The Twelve

Midnight is a strict deadline, we cannot miss it and we won't miss it. Is everyone clear with that?'

There was a murmur of consent from everyone present.

'Good. Now, let's not get ourselves mixed up in any shyness or giddiness, the other night was for us to get over that shit. Remember we *will* all be having sexual intercourse, get over it. We've all seen each other naked, and the only difference now is that you'll all be expected to reach climax this time. Does anyone have any questions?'

John was tempted to ask if there was going to be any further homosexual intercourse involved, or even rape, but one look around at all the excited faces made him change his mind.

'So, let's drink and be merry, for tonight our future looks bright!' Robert shouted.

Everyone began to cheer as Carl picked him up and offered him up to the rest of The Twelve. They were shouting and throwing drinks over each other, until the barman came and threatened to throw them out if they didn't stop. They all knew this was an idle threat due to all the money they put behind the bar here, but they calmed down anyway.

It was a good time.

John took a sly look over at Kevin. He watched as his friend grabbed his jacket, slid off his chair and made his way out of the bar, taking one last, lingering look towards Jenny as he did.

Jenny, of course, was oblivious to this transaction.

Present day

63.

JOHN CAME AROUND on his bed, he was still lying in the foetal position, his back and joints were stiff. As he tried to unravel himself from his sheets he could hear and feel his bones creak and crack in his back, neck and legs.

Oh Jesus, I'm getting old, was the first thought that formed in his head that day. With a struggle, he managed to get himself into a normal sitting position on the edge of the bed, allowing his legs to dangle over the side. He rested like this for a few seconds, wiggling his toes in an attempt to get his blood circulating through them properly, before slowly standing up.

He stretched his arms in the air and then each of his legs in front of him, and let out a huge yawn. He ran his fingers through his unruly hair and scanned the room.

Then he saw it, and instantly knew that his day was ruined.

The photograph was lying on the floor, face up on the carpet. It was back in one piece.

His heart began to beat in his chest, his old friends, panic and anxiety, were back for the party. *I can't live like this. How the fuck could that thing have stuck back together?* He bent down to pick it up, trying his best not to look at it, but he couldn't help himself.

The small look confirmed everything that he'd noticed last night, everything that he tried to forget, the three faces were gone now, completely blurred out.

The Twelve

There were only two faces left, his and Jenny Weaver's.

Feeling calmer, maybe calmer than he should have felt, considering something that was supposed to be locked in an evidence locker, before being crushed and torn up by his own hands, was now lying on his bedroom floor. He tore his gaze away from it and looked at the clock. It was ten am; he knew Addison would be in work by now.

'Can you put me through to Detective Addison please? It's John Rydell, he'll take my call... Yes, it is an emergency.'

The woman receptionist put him on hold, but this time he wasn't there for very long.

'Hello Mr Rydell, I thought you might call today...' Addison answered with his usual charm. 'I've had our people track down your friends from that photo. You know some influential people Mr Rydell. The issue is that we've been trying to get hold of all of them since about eight o'clock this morning. Why do you think that is Mr Rydell?'

'Detective, I can't say for absolute certain, but I think they might not be answering their phones because they're dead!' There was a moment of silence on the other end of the phone, and it was John who broke it. 'Detective, do you still have the photo in your evidence locker?'

'I'd like to think so, unless you have it again.' He answered, there was a hint of sarcasm in his reply.

The sarcasm was lost on John. 'Well, that's why I'm asking you see, because I do have it again. I've got it right here in my hands. The three faces that were blurring yesterday are all gone now, completely lost. The only faces left are mine and Jenny's. I'm not one hundred percent sure Detective, it might be my old eyes, but I think that Jenny is already looking fuzzy.'

'Mr Rydell listen to me closely here, what I'm going to do is this. I'm going to send squad cars out to the locations of all four of your friends, one of whom is in Stoke, of all places. I'm going to ascertain if these people are safe and alive, and then we'll have to figure out what we are going to do with you. Please don't leave the house today Mr Rydell, I'll be in touch.'

Addison hung up the phone without a goodbye.

Slowly, John hung up too. 'What the hell am I supposed to do now?' He said aloud to, he hoped, no-one.

He went to his living room and sat down on his favourite chair. He put his head in his hands and thought. For the first time 'post Gill' he really tried to use his head. 'What do I know right now?' He spoke aloud to himself, counting on the fingers of his hands. 'Jenny is going to die sometime soon. I know that she'll be top of her field in some sort of sports or gymnastics area. So how the fuck do I track her down?'

He contemplated London, it was a huge place, with lots of Weavers scurrying about it. He grabbed his laptop and googled the phone book. He searched for 'J Weaver, London'. The report came back almost instantaneously.

There were seven hundred and thirteen J Weavers in West London alone.

He sat back, away from the screen and let out a deep sigh. He didn't even know if Weaver would still be her name. What he did know was that he couldn't just sit and wait for something to happen, he had to do something, but what?

Then a horrible thought occurred to him, something that maybe he should have thought about before, but he was probably too busy wallowing in self-pity to realise.

Once Jenny was gone, once she was dead, with her stomach ripped out and left to die lying in her own blood and filth, then he'd be the last one left alive on the photograph. It didn't take Sherlock Holmes' powers of deduction to figure that one out.

He was *next*.

Redford University, South London
20 years earlier

64.

'GILL, LISTEN TO me, I'm telling you, I saw it. I saw Robert rape Carl with my own eyes. Why would I lie about this?'

The argument had been brewing between them, to be fair it had probably been brewing since the first meeting. John had been sullen and brooding ever since.

'You're just paranoid about whatever's going to happen tomorrow night,' she shouted shaking her head in dismay. She put her hands on her hips, in John's limited experience, this meant that she meant business. Her face was screwed up in anger and suddenly she looked a million miles away from the stunningly beautiful girl he knew and… loved. 'You don't have to worry about it you know, it's not like I haven't had sex with Carl before. You knew that when we got togeth…'

'It's not about that,' he shouted his interruption. 'It's not about the sex, well, not *just* about the sex anyway. It's about the mystery that's surrounding everything. I get the reason why there are twelve of us, six girls, six boys, there are twelve months in the year, and there were twelve apostles, blah blah blah. I understand that it's a fucking mystical number or something. What I don't understand is why I saw what I know I saw.'

'Think about what you saw John. Just think.' She waved her finger in his face as if for impact, before storming off down the hallway into the small kitchen.

'I know what I saw Gill,' he whispered after her.

She stopped just before entering the kitchen, turned back and looked at him, the lopsided grin he loved so much was nowhere in evidence.

'Look, if Robert did rape Debbie, and then raped Carl, why would they still be hanging around together and the best of friends? If I know one thing that's for certain, it's that Carl's not gay, or the type to allow himself to be raped and not do anything about it. Jesus, it's usually him who pulls all the shots.'

She looked him straight in the eyes, her face unwavering in its anger. 'He's no victim!' She said shaking her head.

He looked away from her, he was disgusted that she didn't believe him, but he was even more disgusted that she wasn't willing to do anything about the information he was giving her.

'Look, we'd all been slipped a drug, you thought you saw something, it was a bad trip. Get over it.'

John's anger was building now, he never thought he'd be able to get this angry with Gill, but she was pushing him now to levels that he didn't even think he had. His voice was slow and filled with menace as he replied to the nonsense she was spouting. 'It wasn't a bad trip Gill, I saw what I saw, and now I'm having second thoughts about tomorrow night.'

Gill looked at him, her face was almost emotionless, all the anger that was there a few seconds ago had gone, replaced by a nonchalant passiveness. 'I think it might be best if you sleep in your own flat tonight, don't you? You know, get some rest, a bit of distance from tomorrow night, to clear your head. I'll see you in the morning, OK? Goodnight then!'

With that she turned away from him and slammed her bedroom door.

That was his cue to leave.

65.

BY THE TIME he'd reached his own flat he was fuming. It felt strange being back there alone, it must have been nearly a week since he'd been here last, as they seemed to spend most of their time together, naked, in Gill's place.

As he walked in he was confronted with a flashing red light on his telephone answering machine. He pressed the voicemail button and an electronic voice, that he hated, announced, 'you have… twelve… new messages.'

Ha, yeah twelve seems just about right… he thought with no amusement as he pressed the continue button. He hoped it was Gill calling to apologise, to tell him that all this The Twelve stuff had just been a big mistake. She would be telling him that she wanted to hurry up and finish university so they could just run off together into the sunset and live their long lives together, with all their babies, somewhere warm and inviting.

He didn't have any such luck.

'First message received on… Wednesday… at… eighteen-forty-two.' The horrible mechanical voice continued.

'John, its Kev. If you're there buddy, can you answer? No? OK man, I'll call you back later.'

'Second message received on… Wednesday… at… twenty-twenty-four.'

'John, it's Kev again, can you give me a bell when you get this? Just need to talk to you about something. Speak to you later man!'

The Twelve

'Third message received on... Thursday... at... zero-sixteen.'

'John, its Kev... can you ring me please mate?'

And so on, pretty much the same message until number ten.

'Tenth message received on... Thursday... at... ten-ten.'

'John, you're obviously away or at Gill's, I don't have her number so I can't contact you there. Anyway, I wanted to let you know that Jenny's asked me to come to your meeting tomorrow night. I can't tell you how much I'm looking forward to it man. I just wanted to ask you a few questions about what happens and stuff. I'm proper excited man. Ring me as soon as you get these messages.'

He listened to the last message again, confused and a little dumbfounded. Why would Jenny invite Kevin to a meeting of The Twelve? For one, he wouldn't have a partner; and it would put the whole twelve thing off balance.

Then he thought about whoever it was talking over the PA system. *If he's going to be the DJ for the night, why not just have him part of the whole thing from the start?* He thought.

He needed to talk to someone regarding this. He didn't think Gill would take his call right now, and the thought of calling Carl or Robert made him a bit sick. Ben and Nicky had said they were going away until tomorrow morning, and he just wasn't overly close to any of the others.

Kevin it is then... He decided, and dialled his number.

He answered on the third ring.

'Hello?'

'Kev, it's John, how's it going mate? Sorry you haven't been able to get hold of me, had my face in the books for a few days,' he lied.

'Did you get my message?'

Kevin sounded excited on the other end.

'Yeah I did all ten of them. What's all this about you coming to the meeting?'

'Well, Jenny and me are getting on really well, and she told me about all the occult thingy that you guys are up to. She asked me not to say anything, but I was just too excited not to.'

John put on an excited voice, in reality, he was anything but. 'That's great man. So, are you going to be Jenny's partner?' He asked.

'I don't know man. So, tell me, what happens? What do I need to do? You know you're the only one I can really speak to, well apart from Jenny, so I'm proper stoked that you'll be there too.'

'Well, I… eh, have you talked to Carl and Robert about it?'

His voice faltered a little. 'Yeah, they said that they always needed a reserve, just in case someone doesn't turn up. Carl was a little taken aback but Robert talked him around. Jeez, that guy has a way with words, doesn't he?'

John laughed, completely without humour. 'He sure does…'

'So anyway, Jenny told me that we all should turn up independently of each other, and not to tell anyone else where we're going… man this is all so secretive and 'Lovecraftian!' I fucking love it. So, it looks like I'll be seeing you tomorrow night then buddy?'

'Eh, yeah, I'll be there mate. I'll see you then eh?'

As he hung up, John sat down heavily on his chair and thought about that conversation.

Robert and Carl wanted reserves? In case anyone was a no-show? I thought no-show wasn't an option. This is getting stranger and stranger.

The Twelve

Even though he was feeling disturbed by what he 'thought' he saw at the first meeting, he still felt things had gotten too far for him to back out now, besides what would Gill think of him if he did?

He took himself off to bed, as he fancied an early night and an early morning gym session before he had to take his clothes off, once again, in the company of the others.

Present day

66.

'JENNY WEAVER, JENNY Weaver, Jenny Weaver…'

John was sat at home in his bedroom, he was obsessing over Jenny Weaver. He knew that he needed to get in touch with her as soon as possible, although he wasn't sure that warning her about what was likely to happen would be able to help her in any way. He didn't know if there was anything that he could do to help her, but he thought that he had to at least try.

Sitting at his laptop he was trying every possible search he could think of to find a Jenny Weaver that would match the one he went to university with twenty years ago. He thought about calling Detective Addison, but he didn't want him to think he was any crazier than he already did. He knew Addison had seen the photograph, the very same one that was in front of him right now, the very same one he'd ripped up only last night, but he still didn't think that the detective was on board with his theory that these people were dying *because* of the photograph.

He took another look at it, Jenny's face had started to blur quite noticeably.

He tried another search on an older site, it was a forerunner to the more recent FacePlace, called Pals-Found. He typed her information into the engine and pressed search. Once again, several hits listed on his screen.

The Twelve

He searched down as many as he could before his eyes began to hurt, he'd been at this for a good few hours, and fatigue was beginning to kick in.

Just before he was tempted to quit, a hit jumped out at him.

'Jenny Weaver... single, lives in Wantage, studied at Redford University, South London, works for West Ham football club, senior physiotherapist for the men's first team... gotcha!'

The social networking site wouldn't allow him to see any photographs until they'd 'friended' each other, other than her profile pic which was of a pair of running shoes. Cursing this stupid policy, he decided he'd have to bring Detective Addison into the fray after all. He really needed to get in touch with Jenny, and fast.

John rang the police station again. 'Detective Addison please... Yes, I'll hold, but could you let him know that it's John Rydell calling? Yes, it is regarding a case, thank you.'

He tried his best to be civil to the girl on the phone. Even though all he wanted to do was reach down the phone and grab her by the throat.

John was left on hold for two long and arduous minutes.

'Detective Addison speaking, Mr Rydell is that you?'

'Yes, it is. Look I think I might have found Jenny Weaver on one of those social networking sites... I don't know how to get hold of her yet, but you might. We need to act fast on this as her face, it's starting to fade from this stupid fucking photo.'

'I need to speak to you regarding that photo Mr Rydell, it's gone again from the evidence locker, I don't understand...'

'Detective, we can talk about the photograph all you want when you're here.'

There was a pause for a second before Addison continued. 'I can get to you in about twenty-five minutes, do you have an address for her?'

'No, just where she works.'

'Well, that'll do for a start.'

Addison hung up the phone, leaving John sat in the spare room upstairs with the computer still on. He was in the office chair looking at the photograph. All those blurred out faces, erased from their lives almost as fast as they'd been erased from his.

Why this photograph? He thought to himself. *What was it about that day that could kill off everyone in this pic?*

He thought about university again for a while, and thought about The Twelve. His memory spun backwards to the two stupid meetings they'd had, their dabbling in the occult.

He then thought about why they did it, what their motivation was for the meetings. He knew that it had originally been a bit of fun, so Gill had told him anyway, but eventually it had grown more serious, devious even. They'd been doing it for a reason. Something about bettering themselves, fulfilling their dreams maybe?

Or was it something else?

He racked his brains thinking of any other reasons for them other than the nakedness and 'getting ahead' in life.

Why had they gone ahead with those meetings?

Had something bad happened in that first meeting? Something that had disturbed him? Disturbed him enough so that he'd had reservations about the second one?

They did something at them… something else that was on the tip of his tongue. He felt like banging his head against the wall to release this memory.

Wishes!

The Twelve

That was it.
We made wishes!!!
He almost smiled at the thought, it made him feel a little foolish, *how childish was it to make wishes?*

He thought hard about what those wishes were. He sat back in his chair and gave it some deep contemplation.

He cringed a little as the memory came back to him. *Mine was to become partner in a multinational software company. Jesus, well that one nearly came true didn't it. If Gill hadn't have died then I'd be flying high right about now.*

He thought some more, Robert had wanted to be a judge, or something like that, in the Old Bailey.

He stopped himself there for a second. Maybe he was onto something with this train of thought.

There was something about that in his obituary. Something about him being just weeks away from inauguration or something like that. He did a quick search on his computer, and pulled up some of the newspaper reports on Roberts' death. The first thing he noticed, was that his death was still an ongoing investigation.

He continued reading down the article. There it was, in black and white. Robert was mere weeks away from becoming the youngest ever senior judge assigned to the Old Bailey.

He stopped for a moment to take that in, to digest this information.

Then he thought about Carl, he remembered that Carl was into his sports, football mostly, he was doing sports science classes.

He typed Carl's name into the search engine and it came up with several hits. Carl Brookes was the manager of Leyton Orient. Prior to his 'still unexplained' death he'd been linked to the vacant managerial position for Tottenham Hotspur. 'Football management!' He remembered.

He really thought he'd hit on something here.

Debbie Baines had wanted to own a night club. He didn't need to run a search to find out how that one ended.

All their wishes had come true.

He sat back in his chair and pondered for a moment. *Or very nearly came true.*

The loud knock on his front door made him jump, it also snapped him out of his reverie. He grabbed his coat and headed to the door. He opened it in an excited manner. 'Detective, you're probably not going to believe me on this but I think I've found a link...'

He looked up to see a solemn looking Addison looking right back at him. John's heart sank. From the look of him, he knew there wasn't going to be any good news. 'What's happened?' He asked, instantly regretting the question.

'Mr Rydell, there were three murders last night. When I saw the reports, I wanted to check, to see if there were any links to the names of the people in your group in university. I pulled in a few favours from the other forces.'

His head was low but John could see something in his eyes. Was it regret?

John didn't think so.

Steely determination?

Maybe more likely.

'I have some bad news Mr Rydell.' The Detective broke the silence.

Here we go, John thought.

'I'm not the type of person to beat around the bush Mr Rydell, so I'll just come out and tell you. Tony Corless was murdered last night in his apartment in London, Brenda Osman was murdered in her rented factory in

Stoke, and Lynda Witherspoon was murdered in her trailer while she was getting ready to present her TV show, in Scotland. I'm so sorry Mr Rydell.'

He was shaken, but he wasn't at all surprised. 'Well, this gives us more reason to find Jenny as soon as we can. Doesn't it?' He said. As he stepped out of the house, he swung his coat over his shoulder to put it on. 'Let's go then.'

Addison noticed the stink that was wafting from inside John's house. 'What is that smell?' He asked holding his hand to his nose. It was almost causing him to gag.

'I haven't got a clue Detective, but I think it'll follow me into your car.'

'You best hope it doesn't,' he replied. 'Or you just might have to get the bus.'

The smell didn't follow him.

67.

WHILE IN THE car heading to West Ham United's training ground, John relayed to Detective Addison all he could remember about the stupid ritual they'd performed as part of The Twelve. He told him about the wishes, and about his theory regarding the fact that they had very nearly, but not quite, come to fruition.

Addison wasn't overly impressed. He didn't have time for immature parlour games and sexual promiscuity that students got up to during their drunken formative years.

John looked him up and down. *It's my bet that you never had a full day of fun in your entire life,* he thought. The thought, right now, didn't cause him to feel sorry for the policeman, rather the opposite. He wished that he had led as quiet a life as this man seemed to have.

'Well, what did your wife wish for?' Addison asked, his face was stern but he wanted John to think that he was playing along with the story, for now at any rate.

'All I know is that I didn't wish for any of this.' He turned back towards the road before them, a wistful look filling out his face.

The rest of the journey was conducted in silence. As they arrived at the football training ground, Addison flashed his badge to get them past the security at the gate. A member of the PR team came down to meet them in the foyer of the administration building.

'Hi, I'm Mark Johnston, I work for the Public Relations team here at West Ham United. What exactly is it I can do for you officers?'

'My name is Detective Addison, and this is Rydell.' Addison spoke officiously towards the man and shook his hand with a tight grip. John noticed he hadn't let Johnston know that *he* wasn't a police officer.

'We're here to talk to Miss Jennifer Weaver, it's in relation to an ongoing case we are currently assigned to. Is she available for a brief chat?'

'Well, normally, she'd be in the physio room warming up muscles and stretching hamstrings by now, or out on the training fields.' Mark replied.

'I'm feeling a 'but' coming on here,' Addison interrupted. Mark give him an unrushed look.

'*But*, Detective, last week she secured herself a very nice and lucrative deal. She's a very attractive woman, as you may well know, and being a high-profile physiotherapist, she was offered a workout DVD deal. Six DVDs to be released over the next six Christmases. A six-figure deal... very nice.'

Six DVDs, six years, six figure sum! John thought almost laughing to himself. *If they hadn't recently changed the number of the beast, I'd have been seriously impressed right now.*

'So, she's no longer an employee here?'

'Nope.' He smiled at them. 'Her first shoot starts tomorrow morning, six-thirty am if I remember rightly.'

Addison offered his hand once again to the immaculately dressed man. 'Thank you for your assistance Mr Johnston, but there's just one more thing, can you please forward me her home address?'

'I can't, but if I can just see your ID please, I'll forward your query towards our HR department. You must understand, we get a lot of strange people hanging around here.'

Addison reached into his inside pocket and produced his police ID, he turned to John and said,

'Rydell, you get back to the car and call it in to HQ that her circumstances have changed.'

John, savvy to the misdirection, gave Addison a salute. 'OK sir,' he replied, and walked out of the foyer.

Ten minutes later both men were back in the car. Addison was in possession of a small A4 printout.

'She's no longer in Wantage, she now rents an apartment not far from Canary Wharf, in Shoreditch. The HR girls had said she was going away to the Seychelles until tomorrow morning. Apparently, her plane lands at half twelve, in the morning, into Gatwick. She should be home around three am. It's your shout Mr Rydell, what do you want to do next?'

John sat in silence for a while. His troubled mind was still trying its utmost to take in his current situation. It was still early in the day; he could try to grab a few hours' sleep before they went to her house.

'It would seriously put my mind at ease if we were there, at her house when she got home. That's if you don't mind Detective.'

'I'd be happy too Mr Rydell. Maybe we can get to the bottom of all this after all. How about I drop you off at your home now, and then swing by to get you about midnight?'

'That sounds good to me. I've just realised that I don't even know your first name.' John said trying to make some light of this situation.

'Yes, you're right, you don't. Let's keep it like that for now, eh?'

Another long, quiet drive later and the car pulled up outside John's house. 'Here you go Mr Rydell, grab a few hours' sleep and I'll be here to get you at midnight.'

John got out of the car and turned back to thank Addison but he had already pulled away from the kerbside, and was driving off in the direction of the main road.

He stood and looked at his house for a short while. It looked normal, nice, but nothing flash. He hated it with a passion.

When all this is over, I'll be putting you up on the market. Grisly murder or no grisly murder.

He put his key in the door and opened it. For some strange reason, he thought about Mick and Laura, he realised that he hadn't seen anything of them for a few days. He thought longingly, about ringing Mick and going to the pub for a few drinks. Yearning for normality in his life.

Tomorrow, he thought. *I'll ring him tomorrow. I don't want to smell like a brewery when Detective Addison pulls up tonight.*

He tried not to acknowledge the rest of the thought that brewed in his head. *If I'm still alive,* it continued.

He opened his door and the now familiar rotten meat stench hit him like a wall, he was quite expecting it. Although the day was a bright, August day, the house was dark and gloomy inside. Again, nothing new to him.

Something moved in the shadows, something that his peripheral vision couldn't make out, but he knew it looked big. Feeling his skin prickle, he stepped into the house. As he'd expected, he felt the temperature drop a good number of degrees. He had almost gotten used to these theatrics. What he hadn't gotten used to was the thought that some supernatural being might be lurking inside, ready to pounce on him and rip him apart, disembowel him on his hallway floor and leave him to die, screaming in agony surrounded by his own filth.

He wished he'd kept hold of the photograph now, just to see if his face had started to fade yet.

'Hello? Hello, is there anyone in here?'

The smell worsened the deeper inside he got. It was like vomit and shit, and… teenage adrenalin.

Right at that moment a flashback memory popped into his head.

He was naked, except for a robe. His hand was slick with dark blood, he was holding something small, sharp and bloody. He looked down at his body, his naked torso was also covered in blood... it was dripping from his hands and his mouth... and the smell, the coppery stink of fresh blood was thick in the air.

He was now back in his house, in the dark gloom of the sunny day. The flashback had popped out of his head just as quickly as it had popped in. His breath was pluming out in front of his face every time he exhaled. The mirror on the side of the hall was frosted over with small icy fingers.

'Who are you?' He whispered, his eyes roaming the room. 'Why are you doing what you're doing? Why do you want everyone dead?'

He didn't know where he was getting this burst of courage from, but here he was, confronting a...

A what? He asked himself. *A ghost?*

He didn't want to believe in ghosts, he never *used* to believe in ghosts, at least until he was haunted himself.

Fuck this... he thought, *if I'm going to die, at least I'll be back with Gill.* This thought made him feel a little braver now, and he began to walk around the house, looking in all the rooms downstairs.

Looking for what? He didn't know, but he searched the rooms top to bottom anyhow. The smell was bad and the cold in the house was almost unbearable, but he wasn't about to let that dampen his new-found courage.

'Tell me who you are!' He demanded. 'Tell me why you're here? What the fuck do you want?'

He was shouting and walking deeper into the cold and the smell. The stench wasn't entirely unlike diarrhoea, sweet, thick and sickly. But there was also a steely undertone to it, almost like… blood.

He turned into the living room and he saw that the room had been overturned, like he'd been burgled. His furniture had been tipped over, his table had been overturned and his chair had been thrown over.

On the mirror hanging over the fireplace something had been written in the icy sheen over the surface. It had been written in what looked like a mixture of blood and shit.

'ALL I WANT IS WHAT IS MINE…'

He looked at the letters, they had been written in a shaky, hurried text. He turned around again, searching for some sign of an intruder, or indeed a ghost.

There was nothing. He stood, listening to the complete silence. This was a strange occurrence, as it was still early and there should be noises coming from the street. Cars, buses, people, all going about their normal business, but there was absolutely nothing, a complete absence of noise.

He turned back towards the defaced mirror and looked at the message scrawled there. As he read it again, the letters began to run, the frosty ice melting from the mirror as the room was getting warmer and brighter. The smell was receding too, but it didn't go away completely.

He surveyed the scene, turning in a three hundred and sixty-degree circle, taking in the total devastation.

He shook his head as if he was defeated. With his head held low and his shoulders slumped, he looked like a broken man. As he trudged upstairs, he grabbed the photograph that was back on the top of the table in the bedroom.

Jenny's face had started to fade away again. *It's just like a script to a bad film,* he thought as he lay down. He rested the supernatural photograph on his chest and wrapped his hands over it.

'Goodnight Gill, I love you.' He whispered, before falling fast asleep.

Redford University, South London
20 years earlier

68.

FRIDAY NIGHT CAME at last, it was the night of the meeting. John had to admit that he was feeling a little excited... deep down he knew that it was the prospect of having sex with both Gill and Debbie in the same night, *and maybe even Jenny too!*

Gill had phoned him earlier, to test the waters between them after their argument last night, but she couldn't resist telling him how excited she was about the meeting tonight.

Also, bizarrely, Tony Corless had rang him to express his excitement too. He hadn't even been that close to Tony.

But the strangest call of the day came from Kevin.

'John mate, I am *so* nervous about what's going to happen tonight. I just hope I get to play a good part in the proceedings, but you know what? I'd even be happy just to sit there and watch.'

'I don't know what's going to happen there myself, but I must admit, and I'm sorry for you to hear this man, but I can't wait to see your girlfriend naked again.' John was laughing as the conversation carried on.

'Speaking of which, Jen mentioned that she'd really like to go on holiday after the year-end party.'

'Oh yeah?' John replied, knowing that his non-committal reply would just annoy his friend, because he knew he wanted to tell him something.

'Yeah, but with me John. Just me and her.' Kevin was almost shouting at this point.

'Hey man, that's a great idea, maybe me and Gill could meet you wherever you guys end up. Listen, I really have to run, I've got a ton of things to do, but I'm looking forward to seeing you later tonight.'

'No worries man, I'm going to be there a little later than the rest of you, apparently, Robert has some sort of 'special mission' for me to complete before it all happens.'

'What special mission?' John asked, a little curious and, to be completely honest, a little put out.

'Oh, I don't think it'll be anything too special, just a little surprise for you guys, or maybe even an initiation.'

He laughed a little at that, before terminating the conversation.

The Twelve

69.

FOUR HOURS LATER and John was sat in the back of a taxi heading over to the London Docklands for the official meeting of The Twelve. He didn't quite know how he felt about it now as it seemed to be twelve plus one these days.

Lost in thought, he didn't even notice when the taxi pulled up to the specified dockland location.

His directions, directly from Robert, were to wait outside if he saw anyone else entering the building, he had to enter alone, and of his own volition.

'Can you just hang on here for two minutes pal? I just want to wait until that guy has gone in there.'

Patrick Mahone was entering the building.

'No worries guvnor, as long as you know that you're on the clock.'

John smiled and nodded.

Once Patrick was inside, John got out, paid the cabbie and made his way inside the building through the door his friend had just entered.

The night was balmy and the wind coming off the old river felt great as it passed through his hair. He was feeling rather good about himself. It felt, to him, like he was on the verge of something, something great. Something that was going to change his life forever. The feeling usurped any apprehension regarding what they were all going to do in here tonight. As long as he was with Gill, then he felt safe and sound.

He opened the door to go inside, and was hit by the sheer pitched darkness inside. The meagre light coming from the solitary street lamp outside only penetrated a few metres along the narrow corridor. He looked to see if there were any markers anywhere, indicating to him where he should go, but there was nothing.

He felt fear rising at the darkness before him. He wasn't scared of the dark per se, but just in fear of *this* dark. It was as if he could feel something, some malevolent force watching him, waiting for him.

He felt like an intruder.

Come on John. You did this the other night. It'll be over soon and you can go home with the woman you love, and forget any of this nonsense ever happened.

He heard another taxi pulling up behind him, and he took this as his cue to surmount his fears and get inside.

The walls were tight, the corridor had been made intentionally narrow so that only one person at a time could navigate through it, and there was only one direction a person could go, so therefore no-one could get lost while inside.

He carried on walking blindly through the corridor, through all the twists and turns, until he literally hit a pair of blacked out double doors.

He grasped about in the darkness for a handle, eventually finding one before pushing through and entering the dimly lit changing room they'd all been in the week before.

The same robes were hanging in the same place as last time, all with their names behind them.

Tony, Debbie and Ben were inside, sitting by their robes, looking nervous and uncomfortable as they turned to see John come through the doors.

Patrick was stood with his hands resting on his hips, his back was turned to John looking towards the others. 'What's with the black tunnel there?' He asked laughing, 'I felt like I was in a frigging birthing canal.'

'Maybe that's what it's all about.' John interrupted. Patrick turned around to look at him, giving him a confused smile as he did. 'You know, reborn onto the path to a better life?'

Debbie laughed. 'Woah, get you brain box. But I think you're wrong, remember this was organised by Robert and Carl. Neither of them tend to think any further than their dicks. Do we need to start to get undressed yet?'

'That's rich coming from you, I don't think I've ever seen you thinking further than any man's dick.' Tony replied, his tone sounded a little too aggressive for it to be fully a joke.

John picked up a scroll of paper that was by the double doors he'd just emerged from. 'Apparently not, there's a note here, it says we're not to get changed into the robes or drink our drinks until everyone's here.'

He wondered if that meant Kevin too.

Within the next ten minutes the rest of the team had filed into the changing room through the double doors. Gill walked in and John saw, with a stab of jealousy, all the other males in the room, turn and look her up and down. Their faces lusty and anxious.

She gave everyone a shy little wave and came and sat down next to him. 'Hey you!' She offered as a cautious greeting. 'Are we talking properly yet? I don't want to go through this with us not really, you know, together.'

'Listen, we're just about to go at it in there in front of all our friends! Do you think I could do that without talking to you?'

She gave him her best lopsided grin, and he poked her playfully in the ribs before kissing her. 'Now let's get our kit off and get it on eh?'

Eventually they were all there. Ten of The Twelve, all gathered into the changing room, sitting around nervously looking at each other.

A bell began to toll, John counted twelve peels, as the room began to darken into a dim red. Everyone stopped chattering at once and sat down on the benches listening as a voice broke out of the loud speakers. It was the same, unidentifiable voice as last time.

'*I THANK YOU ALL FOR COMING... YOU TRULY ARE THE TWELVE! USING THIS POWER, WE CAN, AND WE WILL SHAPE OUR OWN FUTURES. SACRIFICE YOUR MINDS AND YOUR BODIES TO THE GREAT LORD GLIMM TONIGHT, AND YOURS IS THE PATH TO ENLIGHTENMENT... ALL, PLEASE DISROBE, DRINK YOUR DRINKS AND JOIN US IN THE GREAT HALL.*'

John watched as everyone else began to take their clothes off, this time there was hardly any embarrassed looks around at all.

Naked, except for their robes and their crowns, they all lifted their crystal flutes in a group 'cheers'.

The voice came over the speakers again '*TO THE TWELVE!*' It shouted.

'The Twelve!' Everyone responded before downing their flutes of champagne.

Everyone that was, except for John. He drank less than half of his drink, he'd never been fussy about sparkling wine, plus after what happened last time! He wanted to stay as lucid as possible. He thought he may well need all his wits about him.

With an air of excitement, the ten of them began to file into the main hall. The levels of nervous tensions were off the charts as they did. Everyone was bubbly and ready for whatever adventure they were about to embark on tonight.

John grabbed Jenny's arm just before they entered the main hall. 'Jenny, can I talk to you for one second, just before we go in?' He asked.

She looked a little taken aback, glancing between him and the rest of the group. 'Erm, Yeah. Of course, what's up?'

'Where's Kev? He rang me to tell me that he'd see us here tonight, as a guest of you! He also said that Robert had a 'special mission' for him. What's all that about?'

Jenny gave him an 'I don't know what you're talking about' kind of look. 'It's nothing nefarious John, the guy's cute, and he needs more friends. Robert and Carl said that after tonight's over The Twelve won't have the same agenda, we'll always have a strong kind of bond... but we could start to let others into our lives.' She shrugged, 'I just kind of think that Kev's nice.' She smiled a sweet, almost beautiful smile at him and shrugged one shoulder as she did. '...and I've grown to like him.'

John let go of her arm, pleased with her answer, but it had only answered half of his question.

They all walked into the same large room as last time, with the same large oak table in the centre.

The scene of the crime, he thought.

They all took their designated places as the lights dimmed again, and it became difficult to see.

John was stood next to Gill. He reached down and grabbed her hand, and gave it a little squeeze.

She squeezed back.

Happy with this response he allowed his eyes to roam down her fantastic body beneath her robe. The knowledge that very soon he would be inside of her started a chain reaction in the pit of his stomach, which culminated in a twinge of excitement, both in his chest and, also somewhere lower.

Intense green light burst through from the carvings on the table and the smoke slunk along the floor into the room like a hungry beast hunting for its prey.

The chanting began over the PA. It was only slight, but John could feel the sway of the rhythm capture him as he tried his best to listen to the words.

He wasn't one hundred percent sure that they were chanting the same words as last time, but if not, they were very similar and the whole atmosphere was just as strange as it was last time.

With a hiss of smoke, Robert and Carl made their grand entrance into the main hall from the same far door.

They were both dressed the same as last time too. Robert was adorning his stag crown with his robe only attached at the neck. Naked underneath it, his excitement about tonight's proceedings was not as forthcoming as it was last time.

Carl made his way around the table until he found his allocated place and slotted in with the others.

Robert climbed onto the table.

'The Great Lord Glimm thanks you all for coming tonight, for accepting him into your lives forever. He will be bestowing you all a small gift in his honour later in the proceedings, but for now we need to welcome his thralls back onto the table and allow the celebration of The Twelve to commence.'

He indicated down towards Carl and Debbie, and invited them up onto the table. 'Debbie Baines and Carl Brookes please join your Lord.'

Carl and Debbie, both wearing their robes and crowns, climbed onto the table to join Robert. As they did the green lights began to strobe and the smoke became thicker as the bizarre chanting rhythm over the PA system grew louder and faster.

John was not enjoying what was happening. He looked around at the faces of his friends, they all seemed to be enjoying themselves, despite their vacant looks. All, with the exception of Ben, once again.

The Twelve

John thought that he must have a stronger resilience to whatever was in those drinks, and was glad he had only drunk half of his glass.

Robert had his hands in the air, and was swaying along with the loud rhythm coming from, seemingly everywhere, now. Carl and Debbie were sat cross-legged and obedient underneath him.

'Thralls,' Robert commanded. 'You must now begin your sacrifice to the Great Lord Glimm.'

Carl and Debbie both looked at Robert, and then at each other. Still swaying with the rhythm of the chanting they leaned into each other and begin to kiss. It, very soon, became evident that Carl enjoyed the embrace.

The faces of everyone around the table were growing more and more excited and animated as Debbie and Carl's kiss became more and more intimate.

John felt Gill's hand reach out and touch his leg. He turned to look at her but she wasn't looking at him, just grabbing at him. She was swaying in time with the rhythmic chanting and looked like she couldn't take her eyes off what was happening on the table.

He reached his own hand out to hold hers but she battered it away. Her hand only had one destination.

When she found it, he didn't know if he heard, or felt it, but he knew that she let out a sigh. Her hands curled tight around his hardening shaft, and squeezed, hard.

John was only human, he was also in his early twenties and his body was not going to let a chance like this pass without a positive reaction.

He felt himself go hard.

Slightly embarrassed, he gave a quick scan around the table, where it was evident that everybody had the same idea.

Brenda was being pawed at by Patrick, while Ben and Nicky were all over each other. What made it strange was that none of them seemed to be able to turn away from Robert, Carl and Debbie on the table.

On the table, Carl had turned Debbie over and she was now on all fours, he had mounted her from behind, and was thrusting himself into her. This time she was screaming like she was enjoying it.

She invited Robert into her mouth, savouring the double entry she was receiving in front of everyone.

It was this level of erotica that had had such an effect on everyone else in the room.

The voice over PA system cut through the rhythm of the chanting.

'*IT IS NOW THAT YOU WILL ALL SACRIFICE YOUR OWN BODIES TO THE GREAT LORD GLIMM. YOU MAY ALL COMMENCE THE GIVING…*'

None of them, John included, needed asking twice.

Gill was on him in a shot, her kisses were fierce, and she was biting his lips and pulling at his hair as she ravaged him in her lust fuelled frenzy.

John wasn't innocent of playing rough either. He pulled Gill's hair right back to stretch her neck, and he couldn't help the impulse to bite into her flesh. He half knew that it was going to leave a mark, and a deep one at that, but right now, he didn't care. All he knew, all he could think about was fucking Gill there and then in the room.

He'd forgotten about all the others present, and to be fair, they'd all forgotten about him too.

He didn't think his cock had ever felt so hard in his life, he felt like the head of his erection could explode any second. Gill's hands were all over it, before her mouth took over.

He felt another, third hand explore him, and he looked down, pleasantly surprised to see Jenny's hand gripping his shaft tightly, she was massaging it roughly into Gill's open and receptive mouth. He turned his head to see what she was doing, and wasn't at all surprised to see Tony entering her from behind.

Both were still watching Debbie, Carl and Robert on the table above them.

John's head was in a whirl; he was dizzy with desire. That was when he felt Gill climb up on the table and pull him close to her with her long, beautiful legs. Jenny pushed his head down, in-between Gill's open legs and John didn't need a second invitation. He buried his face deep within his girlfriend's warm wetness, enjoying the smell, the feel and the taste. After a small while Jenny pulled at his hair, tugging him away from his enjoyment, and towards her. She kissed him hard on the mouth, her tongue tasting and cleaning all of Gill's juices from his own lips.

She pushed him away, laughing, Tony, behind her was laughing too as Gill wrapped her legs around his waist and pulled him towards her. He felt Jenny's hand on his erection once again, feeding it into Gill's soaking wet pussy.

He was having the time of his life.

He opened his eyes for a second, just in time to see Carl roughly push Tony away from Jenny, before pushing his long, thick erection into her himself. Tony didn't look like he minded one bit, he looked like he was really enjoying it.

He turned to see Patrick forcing his way into Debbie, as she was bent over the table. His face concentrated on the job at hand, but enjoying it never the less.

He himself was pounding into Gill in perfect rhythm with the chanting that had come back through the PA system. He was enjoying himself a little too much and could almost feel his climax rising. Two strong hands gripped him on his shoulders, making him lose his impetus, he turned angrily around to see the frenzied, sweaty face of Carl stood behind him. His black hair had flopped over his face, and his mouth was pulled down into a rictus of... Passion? His eyes were wild and for a moment John feared that he was going to do to him what Robert had done during the last meeting.

He sighed a sigh of relief when he was pulled away from, and out of Gill and into the arms of the waiting Debbie.

She turned around and raised her behind towards him, offering herself up. Her face turned back towards him. 'For the glory of GLIMM!' She whispered.

John could see Gill riding on top of the sweat glistening bulk that was Carl. She looked lost in some sort of wild ecstasy; before he had the chance to get jealous, or even before he knew what he was doing, he was looking at Debbie's pretty face pulling a sexual contortion as he slipped, deep inside her.

The room began to spin and everything became a blur as the rhythmic chanting and the smoke began to amplify. Robert was stood on the table looking down at everything that was happening below him, he had a satisfied look on his face as he masturbated.

Then suddenly, everything stopped. The lights went out and the room was thrown into pitch darkness. John realised that he was no longer inside Debbie. A strange feeling of loneliness and cold overcame him. He also felt more than a little ashamed.

He strained to see where Gill was through the darkness, but he couldn't see a thing. It was as if someone had thrown a thick, dark veil over him, that didn't allow any light to permeate inside.

The lights began to brighten slightly, but the smoke seemed to thicken, confusing him even more than he already was. As a slight panic set in, he strained to look for Gill, and he thought that he could just about make out a silhouette that could have been her, lying on the floor. The silhouette was writhing around in a kind of self-induced frenzy.

As the smoke temporarily cleared, he could see that it was Gill, he could also see that Jenny was writhing too, as was Tony and Ben and Nicky… They all were, all of them except him. They were all touching themselves, rubbing on wet clitorises or thick penises, in a sexual frenzy.

'*PLEASE REFRAIN FROM REACHING SEXUAL FRUITION YET. AS A THANK YOU FROM THE GREAT LORD GLIMM FOR YOUR BODILY SACRIFICE, YOU WILL EACH RECEIVE A SPECIAL GIFT THAT YOU ARE TO KEEP WITH YOU, ALWAYS.*'

The smoke began to clear again, and the chanting amplified once more.

Carl and Debbie were having sex again on the table. They were back in the same position and it looked like they hadn't moved in all the time John had had his… What?

The sexual experience of his life?

Hallucination?

What the fuck had just happened to him?

Carl and Debbie's rhythm increased in time with the fast chanting now. Carl's face was turning red, as was Debbie's chest. They were both close.

Everyone in the room began to get up from their writhing about on the floor and started to sway in time with their sexual rhythm.

Suddenly, Debbie screamed a blood curdling scream. She was joined by Carl.

At the same moment, Robert re-emerged from a small door, he was smiling an eerie smile.

John hadn't even noticed that he had been absent from the room.

D E McCluskey

He was wheeling in a gurney, on it lay The Great Lord Glimm's gift to the members of The Twelve.

Present day

70.

JOHN AND DETECTIVE Addison were sat in an unmarked police car outside Jenny's apartment, the time was two-thirty am. They'd been outside the apartment for over an hour.

John was nervously fingering the photograph he was holding. He was trying his best not to look at it, as every time he did Jenny's face would be slightly more blurred than before.

He was worrying that even if they did get to warn her and convince her of her perilous situation, he wondered what exactly they could do to prevent it from happening.

'So, the photograph just fell into your lap while you were sat in your living room?' Addison asked, looking at it in John's grasp. 'You really expect me to believe that?'

'You can believe all you want Detective, because that's what happened. I don't know anyone from your station, and even if I did, I don't want the thing. It's a curse.' He was looking down at the picture, hating it, willing it to burst into flames or disintegrate. He knew it wouldn't, and he didn't wish for it to happen, that's was what had got them into all this trouble in the first place.

'Is that her?' Addison asked as a blonde woman alighted from an idling black taxi and began walking towards the apartments, she looked tired and was pulling a small suitcase on wheels, behind her.

'I can't say for sure, it looks like it might be, I haven't seen her in a long time, but I don't think there's going to be many other people getting out of taxis with suitcases at this hour.'

As the woman wearily approached the apartment, Addison got out of the car, in a manner that would appear unassuming and completely non-threatening. He kind of idled about until she was within five feet of him, he then held out his police badge towards her.

'Excuse me, are you Miss Jenny Weaver?'

The blonde woman looked at him with a tired, confused expression on her face, from his position in the car, John could see she was agitated too.

Addison did have time to notice that she was indeed a very attractive woman.

'Erm, yes. Yes I am. Who are you?' She asked, cocking her head to one side, trying to read his badge credentials.

'My name is Detective Addison, I'm assigned to the London Met. I'm currently investigating a series of incidents and I need to ask you a few questions if I may.'

'Incidents? Excuse me Detective, but as you can see I've just gotten back from a few days holiday. I'm tired and I start a new job in the morning. Can this wait?'

Addison pulled an apologetic face. 'I'm afraid not Miss Weaver. To sound out a small cliché, this really is a matter of life and death. I'll try to be quick, I promise.'

Jenny pulled an exaggerated sigh and made a bit of a show of dumping her bags onto the pavement outside the apartments.

Addison pulled out the photograph that John had handed him, from his inside pocket. 'Can I ask you to confirm if this is you in this photograph? Now I know the image is a little blurred, but I really need your confirmation on this.'

Looking a little more than concerned, Jenny leaned in to study the photograph. As she did John got out of the car and walked towards them, just as she took hold of it.

'Hello Jenny. Long-time no see eh?'

She looked up from studying the photograph, to see who this newcomer, who knew her name, was. She pulled a confused face as she tried to recognise him in the yellow glow of the overhead fluorescents.

'Do I know you?' She asked taking a closer look.

A flash of recognition registered on her face and she smiled her familiar, gorgeous smile. 'John? John... oh, shit it's gone...' She looked at him, clicking her fingers with her head bowed, trying to remember his name. 'Ryder! Is that really you?' She beamed her smile again.

'Yeah, it's Rydell, but yeah, it's me. How are you Jenny?'

She nodded as she heard his name. 'Rydell, that's it. Oh, my God. I'm fine, just fine. I didn't know you were a policeman these days. Oh, how's Gill? I heard somewhere that you guys got married.'

'Oh, no, I'm not a policeman, I'm just helping out on this case. Gill is actually one of the reasons why I'm here.' John bowed his head before he continued to speak. 'Gill's dead, she died a few weeks ago.' He paused, not for dramatic effect, but to allow him to take in a shaky breath. It happened all the time when he talked about Gill. 'We think she was murdered. That's why we're here.'

Jenny acknowledged the sorrow and pain on his face and her own fell into shock. 'Murdered? Oh, my God, John. I'm so sorry... I didn't know. How did it happen?'

'That's what we're here about Miss Weaver.' Addison interrupted the reunion, he could see that the situation was escalating a little.

Jenny stepped back, away from the two men. Her eyes flicking from one to the other, there was an air of accusation between them. 'Hey, now, you don't think I had anything to do with this… this murder, do you?'

John continued, ignoring her question. 'Gill isn't the only one involved in this investigation Jenny. Carl, Robert, Patrick, Ben, Nicky, Debbie… we also think Brenda, Tony and Lynda have all been murdered too, but they haven't been confirmed yet.'

Jenny's eyes widened, 'What?' She asked, her voice had shot up about four octaves.

'Let's not jump to any conclusions here,' Addison interjected. 'We don't know if there's been *any* murders yet. All the scenes are still inconclusive from forensics.' He smiled a congenial smile towards, the obviously shocked, Jenny. 'Maybe it would be better if we were all to go inside Miss Weaver? I do think we have quite a bit to talk…'

'You can't think that I'm a suspect.' She shouted, out of the blue.

Addison smiled to himself and shook his head. *Too many people watching rubbish police dramas on the telly…*

She gave him a stern look and then rummaged through her jacket pockets for her apartment keys. 'I can't believe that about everyone from university. What happened to them? Are you allowed to tell me?' She was directing her questions at John. Then she thought about it for a second or two. 'And… what's it got to do with me?'

'We think they might have been murdered… we also think that you and I may well be targeted next.'

All colour drained from her pretty face.

'Me? Why me? What have I done?' Panic was setting into her voice.

Addison lifted his hands into the air, and shot John a harsh look. 'Let's not jump to any more conclusions

The Twelve

here eh? Please calm down Miss Weaver, that's why we're here. We need to get to the bottom of this and find out why someone might want you all dead. Now, let me ask you again, formally, Miss Jenny Weaver, is that you in that photograph?'

Jenny took another look at the faded, blurred out photograph in her hand. She then looked at John. The corners of her mouth turned down a little and sadness pierced her eyes.

'Yes Detective. That's me in the photograph.'

'Thank you. Now, if we could all go inside and conduct this investigation, I'm sure you don't want your neighbours knowing all your business.' He moved towards the door and indicated for everyone to enter inside.

Jenny's skin looked white, completely drained of blood and colour as they made their way inside the expensive apartments. The few days in the Seychelles working on her tan for her fitness videos had been ruined by one conversation.

John helped her with her travel bags as he followed in behind her.

Five minutes later they were all sitting in her freezing cold apartment. She was fiddling with the heater trying to find out why the room was so damned cold. She had also opened a window to get rid of the stink, the same stink that John had quite gotten used to.

'I'm so sorry about this smell, I don't know what it could be,' she shouted in from the hallway where the thermostat was located.

John was stood just inside the living room door watching her getting more and more frustrated with the heater.

'Jenny, the boiler's not going to fix this cold, and no matter how many windows you open, that stink is not going anywhere. It'll only go away when it wants to.' He explained this to her in a deadpan voice, he knew what was causing the issue, just not who, or why.

'But, but it wasn't like this…' She shouted at the vent and gave it a smack, '…when I moved in, or even when I went on holiday. Why won't you wo…'

Much to the surprise of the two men in the room with her, she burst into tears. Both looked at each other wondering what to do. Addison indicated for John to go and give her some comfort. He walked over to her, wrapped his arms around her and gave her a warm hug.

'John, what's happening here?' She sobbed into his arms. 'My… my life's just getting on track and then… then you two turn up. My fucking apartment's broken, everyone's dead, and you, you tell me that I'm going to be next!'

She sobbed hard into John's arms and he did his best to manoeuvre her over to the settee to sit her down, before she fell down.

The clock on the wall read three am.

Detective Addison stood and eased the photograph from her hands. 'I'm so sorry to have to do this Miss Weaver, but can you take another look at this photograph? I need you to think back to the day this was taken. Can you do that?'

She took it back from him in her shaking hands, and looked at it again. As she did more tears welled in her eyes and began to trickle down her face in rapid succession.

'Oh, my God, John, I remember this now. It was taken on the day when we all first met you. You were… our number twelve.'

Addison looked at John quizzically, as if he'd been holding in some relative information on the case.

'Number twelve?'

'Yeah, I was the last one to be recruited into The Twelve. That was what we called the little group we had going, the one I told you about. Once I was in, there were enough of us to go ahead with the ritual.'

'This is what you were telling me about in the car? The sex orgy?'

John looked a little abashed. 'Yeah, the sex orgy.'

He sat back on the couch next to Jenny, she'd stopped crying now and was looking at him, hoping that he was going to tell her that everything was going to be OK. That the police were going to leave, and that it was all just a joke regarding her dead friends. John put his arm around her and pulled her towards him, in a comforting embrace.

Still with Jenny in his arms, he turned towards Addison, memories were forming, synapses in his brain were lighting. 'For the ritual, we were all wearing robes. We were all naked beneath them, we also had crowns on our heads too. Debbie and Carl were supposed to have sex on the table in front of us all, and then they were both supposed to make their way around the table and have sex with everyone else in the room.'

'That was our bodily sacrifice,' Jenny interrupted, shaking her head. The tears had momentarily stopped and she was remembering now too. John gave her a confused look, but something passed between them, a kind of understanding.

He let go of Jenny, shaking his head, more memories were coming back to him now, just not everything. 'Something's missing though, something else happened. Something after the sex.'

Jenny looked at him, Addison noticed her face reddening a little as if she was remembering something too, a memory he guessed she wouldn't be too willing to part with.

'There was sex, a lot of it if I remember,' she continued, surprising Addison a little with her candour. 'I even remember a little thing between me and you.' She spoke softly, touching John tenderly on the hand.

It was John's turn to go red.

Addison stood up and took out the notepad that he'd had tucked away in his jacket pocket. He licked the nib of the pencil he was holding and looked at the two of them on the settee. 'Right, let's start this again from the…' he began, but stopped abruptly turning his head and looking around him.

A loud, scratchy whisper echoed from all around the room, or maybe even the whole apartment.

'Gliiiiiiiiiiiiiiiiiim!!!'

'Who was that? Miss Weaver, do you have a roommate?'

Jenny looked petrified. 'No!' She replied.

The temperature in the already cold room dropped by maybe another fifteen degrees in an instant. The lights flickered and dimmed. Jenny looked around the room in confusion, as did Detective Addison.

'What's happening?' Jenny gasped.

John was still sat on the couch, he looked alert, but the fear in his face was almost tangible.

He had an idea what was happening.

The mirror over the faux fireplace frosted up. Thin tendrils of ice speeded their way to the centre of the glass. The smell in the room intensified to a level that caused Jenny and Addison to gag reflexively. John, who had gotten used to the smell was OK with it, but Addison had to put his jacket over his nose and mouth to keep the smell away, and to prevent him from vomiting.

'Thiiiiiiiiiiiiiiiiiirteeeeeeeeeeeeen!!!'

John, in a moment of pure clarity, shot up from the couch and began to stare into the mirror. He could only just about make out his face within the frost. He gazed into the mirror, looking towards Jenny's reflection. There was something about the way she looked, it was

The Twelve

almost as though she looked like all the others in the photograph.

Blurred out!

'Thirteen.' John whispered. 'Thirteen!'

He turned around to look at Jenny and Addison who were still reeling from the stench and the cold that had invaded the room.

'There were thirteen at the last meeting'

Jenny dropped her hands away from her face and stared at him questioningly. He turned away again and looked back into the mirror, looking to see Jenny's reflection again. She seemed a little *more* blurred this time, almost gone.

Just like Gill, he thought.

Recollection dawned on Jenny's face as she looked at him, 'Oh my God... The Great Lord Glimm's gift to us all. Something we needed to keep with us at all times.'

John reached out to touch Jenny's arm. She recoiled from his touch as if he were a poisonous snake ready to pounce.

'John, we did something bad at the last meeting, didn't we?'

'The Great Lord who?' Addison interjected, he was writing as much as he could in his little notebook, but his fingers were not behaving due to the extreme cold. 'What was that name again?'

They both ignored the detective, both lost in a little world of their own. John couldn't bring himself to remove his stare from her, and she was reluctant to break the bond too. Things were coming back to them, things, and images, smells... feelings were flowing from their repressed minds. In his head, he could hear the rhythmic chanting, he grasped Jenny's hands and she began to sway. Closing his eyes, he could see the crowns adorned with animal effigies. The largest of them all was a stag.

The stag was pushing a gurney towards a large wooden table. John was stood at the table, Jenny was stood, naked on his left-hand side, and on the other was…
Gill.

Back in the apartment, the lights dimmed around them. Both John and Jenny were swaying in the centre of the room, the music beating into their heads. A rhythm that they couldn't resist, couldn't break free from.

Addison was stood and was staring, wide eyed and slack jawed towards the doorway of the room.

The darkness was spinning around them now, suddenly they were twenty years younger, and twenty years more foolish. Green light and smoke billowed all around them. The stag, they couldn't see his face, had brought their gift from the Great Lord Glimm. As they looked down upon it a huge, dark, shadowy figure loomed over them.

'ACCEPT YOUR GIFT FROM THE GREAT LORD GLIMM.'

The voice boomed from everywhere, it was so loud John and Jenny had to cover their ears. The room around them began to shake and the cold bit into their naked bodies.

Both of them fell onto the floor of the apartment, hitting the expensive shag-pile heavily. The cold from the vision had seeped through into reality, as had the gloom.

John looked up to see a petrified looking Detective Addison staring towards the doorway of the room, he followed his gaze and saw it for the first time.

His tormentor. The murderer of his wife, and therefore his life.

Jenny could see him too… she was on her knees and weeping towards the sinister shadow.

In the gloom of the hallway he was almost difficult to see. He wore a black hooded top over dirty

The Twelve

jeans. Underneath the hood, silvery eyes glowed in the infinity of darkness within the empty space.

The figure stepped forwards into the dim the light of the room. Slowly raising his hands. Jenny and John both noticed the white, dead looking skin.

Slowly, he removed his hooded top and raised his head to face them.

Both Jenny and John gasped as one...

'Kev!'

Redford University, South London
20 years earlier

71.

THE GREAT HALL had fallen completely dark, but the pulsating rhythm of the chant continued. Everyone was swaying in time with the mesmerising sounds. The lights were beginning to slowly brighten and the thick smoke was dissipating.

Carl was screaming a blood curdling scream as he lay on his back on the table, he had climaxed with Debbie, but he looked like a possessed man. He was showing no sign of flagging. His erection continued to throb and it looked to be covered in blood.

Debbie was screaming too; she was also laid on her back covered in a sheen of sweat from her exertions. Her legs were held tight together but there was blood running down her thighs streaming from the centre, from the parts that had just taken such a beating from Carl and the rest of the males.

The strobing light picked up the distinguished figure of Robert wearing his stag crown and his robe swooshing behind him, as he entered the hall. He was wheeling a gurney into the room. Something on the top of the trolley was moving and wriggling, but no-one seemed to even notice, they were all lost within the strange incantations booming from wherever the loudspeakers were situated.

John couldn't quite make out what was on the top of the gurney, his eyes had begun to go fuzzy and dim,

The Twelve

and he could feel himself beginning to move, involuntarily, with the chanting.

As Robert got closer Carl ceased his writhing and sat up, as he was commanded to do. He climbed off the table and lifted whatever was on the trolley, onto the table. After a brief battle, he managed to secure it and limit its writhing.

Due to the darkness of the room, the strobing of the light and the increasing fuzziness of his brain, John couldn't quite get a clear image of what was happening. He was just about lucid enough to make out that it looked like a person being strapped to the table, a man by the size and the shape of him.

The chanting suddenly stopped.

The strobing light stopped too, once again bathing the whole room in a veil of darkness.

With a huge flash of pyrotechnics, the green lights from inside the table flashed bright and everyone stopped their swaying to look, including John.

Robert was bathed in the bright green light as he stood on the table, seemingly alone. Carl and Debbie were now back on the floor in the circle with the rest of them.

Someone else was laying prone, strapped to the table. Whoever it was they were wriggling and struggling to try to free themselves of the bonds.

John's eyes were still adapting to the sudden light, but in the near silence he could hear the person breathing, not shouting. The breathing sounded fast, like the person was scared, maybe even excited, but also as though he or she hadn't been expecting to be tied down to a table and stood over by a naked man in a robe and a stag crown.

Robert began to speak; he was whispering but his voice resonated around the whole hall as if it were coming from the loud speakers. The faint noise of a whirling wind could be heard too, as if there were a storm in the distance, but coming this way.

'The Great Lord Glimm is here now.' He spoke as if telling an assembly of six year olds a ghost story. 'He's with us as we speak. His seed and spirit is within our members Carl and Debbie. His gift to us is also our gift to him. He is here for your undying devotion and your loyalty. In return he will grant your wish.'

Carl and Debbie climbed back up onto the table on either side of the stricken person.

'The Great Lord Glimm asks that you carry with you for the rest of your lives, his token of thanks. Thrall Carl, he asks if you would please reveal the gift.'

Carl knelt on the table and pulled the hood from the person who was lying on the table next to him. As he did the green lights from all around dimmed and a spotlight fell onto the figure, revealing the identity to the group. No-one around the table flinched as they saw who it was.

No-one except for John.

Kevin!!!

John's thoughts were fuzzy as his head and brain felt like they were floating in a thick soup, but the surprise of seeing his friend splayed out on the table before him, shocked him to the core.

He looked around the room and saw absolutely no reaction on the faces of those around him. Even Gill, his girlfriend, who'd met Kevin on many occasions, just stood there looking at him, her face a blank canvas.

John was fighting an internal battle. He was struggling with what his mind was telling him was reality, but his consciousness was telling him was a dream. He couldn't grasp the concept of right from wrong. He was existing in a semi-fantasy world that was scaring the living hell out of him.

'Debbie, the Glimm within you requests his gifts. You know what you must do.' Robert spoke in that deep voice that didn't quite seem to be his own.

Acting as though she was on auto pilot, Debbie knelt at Kevin's head and undid the gag that was currently over his mouth. She then took a tender moment to caress his hair, before pulling it quite fiercely towards her. A loud ripping noise ensued, and a deep painful scream emanated from all around the room.

It was Kevin screaming as he began to struggle to free his bonds.

'WHAT THE FUCK ARE YOU DOING? THIS WASN'T PART OF MY MISSION!!! GET THE FUCK OFF ME, GET ME OFF THIS TABLE YOU PSYCHOS... NOW'

Lying on the table next to him was a straight, cut throat, razor. No-one had noticed it there before.

Slowly, Debbie proceeded to pick it up, looking at it as if she'd never seen it before, as if it had just appeared out of thin air.

'You know what you must do Debbie.' Robert whispered.

Nodding slowly, she grabbed a handful of Kevin's hair and cut it off with the razor.

'WHAT THE FUCK!' He screamed again.

Blood began to pour from the shallow cuts made on his head as Debbie continued to shave him. Hair and flesh fell out in large clumps onto the table.

He began to thrash in his restraints, all his violent protestations resulted in were deeper gashes into his scalp and more and more blood pouring onto the table.

John watched as if he was in a dream, a very bad one, but a dream nonetheless. With one eye closed he watched Kevin's hair fall into the carvings on the table, as they fell in, clouds of smoke appeared as it burnt in the green light. The streams of blood from Kevin's head were also running into the green lights, via the grooves of the carvings in the wood.

The mixture of burned hair and heated, almost boiled blood, smelt like meat that had been left to go rotten, mixed with excrement.

Somewhere in the room, Kevin was still screaming.

Robert now stood over his bloody face as Debbie moved away still holding the dripping razor. He raised his hands into the air as if in prayer, and then bent down to reach under the rim of the table, there his hands found a large wooden baseball bat that had been concealed.

Kevin watched, not really understanding what was happening, but his eyes grew wide when he saw what Robert was holding in his hands.

'Robert… Come on man, this has gone too far mate. Let me go, please,' he begged. 'Come on man. I'm not going to say anything to anyone, just let me go, this is too far. TOO FUCKING FAR!!!'

The panic in his voice was real. His wide, scared eyes never once left the bat in Roberts' hands.

Robert raised it into the air again, and shouted:

'Hickula, tragantie a billinctus, shakker, toogorey'

Debbie and Carl raised their hands and touched the bat, as they did, they both begin to chant the strange words too.

This continued for a few seconds, the chanting was only interjected with the pleading, begging and crying from Kevin to be let loose.

Everyone in the room was swaying to the chants once again, as rhythmic music, mingled with a vague bass fuelled track, filtered through the loudspeakers. Most of them had their eyes closed, and were waving their hands in the air.

John was the only one in the room with his eyes wide open. Although his hands were in the air and he was swaying too, he didn't look as lost as the others. He was

The Twelve

semi-aware of what was happening, but completely incapable of doing anything to prevent it.

Suddenly the chanting stopped.

Robert's face changed in the light of the spotlight on them. It became a mask of hate and pain but mostly violence. He looked like a different person. As he raised the bat into the air once again, Carl and Debbie moved away to either side of him, it looked as if this part of the ritual had been rehearsed.

Kevin looked up with horror as the bat was held above Roberts' head like the sword of Damocles.

Robert closed his eyes and whispered, *'HICKULA, TRAGANTIE A BILLINCTUS, SHAKKER, TOOGOREY'*

The bat was brought down savagely. A direct hit to Kevin's mouth and chin. The blow ruining his face with one hideous crunch. Not just breaking his cheek and his jaw, but shattering them.

His screams were unmerciful and muffled as his mouth and face caved inwards.

To John's unravelled mind everything that was happening on the table seemed like it was in the distance, shrouded by a wispy red cloud. He watched with a vacant look on his face as the bloody fountain erupting from Kevin's mouth, sprayed all over him, Gill, Jenny and Tony. None of them even noticed they were now covered in blood. As he looked down and saw it all over his naked body, it began to make pretty pictures in his mind. He smiled a little, even though he was sure something bad had just happened. He could hear moans and cries of pain, but that all seemed so far away.

'THE GREAT LORD GLIMM INVITES YOU ALL TO RECEIVE YOUR GIFT' Robert shouted in that same voice, dropping the bat from his grasp. *'ONCE THE POWER OF THE GLIMM IS INSIDE YOU, YOUR*

CONTRACT WITH THE GREAT LORD WILL BE SEALED.'

Kevin was moaning in pain as thick, black blood from his ruined face gushed out of his mouth between his broken teeth, split lips and ruined jaw. His puffed-up eyes kept rolling back towards the inside of his head, and then flicking back again as he waved in and out of consciousness.

Robert was holding a bag in his hands, held high above his head.

'YOUR GIFT FROM THE GREAT LORD GLIMM AWAITS YOU. COME AND RECIEVE.'

Carl was stood at the edge of the table helping Patrick climb up onto it. Once he was on the table Patrick stood before Robert with his head bowed low. Kevin was twitching and writhing on the table trying to grab at Patrick's feet.

Robert put his hand on Patrick's head and closed his eyes, he mouthed a silent prayer then removed his hand again. He pulled a very small sack out of the bag he was holding and handed it to Patrick. He accepted the offering, bowing his head as he did. He bent down towards the twitching, bloody body below him, he knelt at his head and considered the freshly shattered face.

Kevin's mouth flapped as he tried to plead with Patrick to help him.

Without even flinching, Patrick put his hand inside Kevin's ruined and bloody mouth. His fingers gripped one of his smashed teeth, and he pulled.

Kevin screamed again as fresh blood began to stream from his mouth.

Patrick stood holding the extracted tooth in his hand. In a kind of trance, he put the tooth into the small sack, whispering unheard words to himself. He held the sack in his hands looking at it as if was the most precious object he'd ever seen.

The Twelve

Gill, her face vacant, made her way up to the table, and with the help of Carl she climbed up. Robert put his hand on her head and prayed, he also gave her a small sack, and she too bent and extracted a tooth from Kevin's face. Delicately putting the tooth into the sack, she climbed off the table, and took her place next to John.

He looked at her, even though he had a silly smile on his face, he felt lost, his thoughts were bleak, dark and semi-lucid. 'What have you just done?' He asked, before bursting into a fit of giggles.

'Carl, would you come up here and bless me, as I receive my deserved gift?' Robert asked. His voice had now returned to normal. Carl climbed up and put his hand on Robert's head. He too took a small sack and helped himself to one of Kevin's teeth.

'Now I will return your favour.'

Robert blessed Carl.

Next up was Debbie, then Nicky and then Ben. Each of them in turn accepting a blessing, a sack and then taking a tooth out of the now unconscious Kevin's face.

Tony made his way up to accept the blessing, then Brenda, and then Lynda.

Finally, Jenny got up onto the table.

As she did Kevin's eyes began to flutter as if he'd woken from his sleep and recognised her, or something about her. She accepted the blessing and then bent down to her boyfriend's face.

His eyes flicked open wide and he looked at her. She hesitated for one second, gazing into Kevin's bruised eyes. Then she looked past him with a wicked, almost sly smile on her lips.

His eyes were wide and pleading and his swollen flapping lips chattered as he tried to connect with her again.

Jenny then reached into the bloody mess that was his mouth. A guttural, animalistic scream emanated from the boy and rang around the room. She plucked out a tooth and placed it into her small sack.

As she stepped down from the table, she smiled at John. 'It's your turn now number twelve,' she whispered to him.

John could see the helplessness in Kevin's eyes, but he himself was just as helpless to do anything about it. As if lost in the worst dream of his life, he climbed up onto the table and stood before Robert with his head bent.

Robert put his hand on his head and whispered, most of the words were ineligible to John, but he did manage to pick out the same words they had all been chanting. Robert then reached into his larger bag and removed the last of the small sacks.

John, still under the influence of the chanting and whatever had been in the drinks, accepted the small sack and looked down towards the mush that used to be his friend's face.

'Accept the offering of Lord Glimm,' Robert commanded.

John suddenly felt a change happen within him. He was feeling a lot more lucid, almost as if the effects of the drugs were wearing off. With a sickening feeling in his stomach, he knelt next to his friend holding his small sack in his hand. He looked at his smashed features, his nose was a bloody pulp, and his two eyes were puffed up so badly that it took John a small while to be able to notice that he was actually looking at him.

Kevin tried to move what was left of his mouth, it seemed he no longer had any control over the opening and closing of his jaw, but could only move it from side to side in a clicking, sickening fashion. He was trying to speak to John, but his split lips and hanging jaw wouldn't allow him, all that came from him was a pathetic mewling moan.

With hands that were not trembling as much as they should have been, he slowly pulled his friend's lips apart, revealing his smashed and devastated gums.

'*TAKE THE OFFERING!*' Robert demanded a little louder now.

John looked Kevin in the eye once more. The minute movement of his friend's mouth was causing fresh, dark, almost clotted blood to spill down his cheeks. Holding in a balk, he reached his fingers inside the black, bloody maw at the bottom of his battered face.

Kevin moaned again, or was it a whimper? John couldn't tell, he didn't *want* to know.

Reluctantly he pulled the last tooth from the hole, and put it into his small sack.

Looking down at the package in his hand, it was covered in his friend's blood. His hands were dripping with it, and it was all over his torso. He braved one last look at his stricken friend, and was just in time to see one solitary, pink tear run out of his bloodshot eye and down the crooked landscape of his broken face.

Clutching his bloody package to his chest, John returned to his position at the side of the table. He'd returned to the circle of his friends.

'*THE GREAT LORD GLIMM IS SATISFIED THAT YOU ACCEPT HIS GIFT. HE COMMANDS YOU TO KEEP THIS WITH YOU, EVERYDAY OF YOUR LIFE... YOU MUST ALL NOW SWALLOW THE GIFT.*'

Carl and Debbie made the rounds of everyone at the table, offering them a small glass with a thick looking dark liquid in it.

'*DRINK THE LUBRICANT AND SWALLOW THE PACKAGE. THE MATERIAL WILL NOT DIGEST, IT WILL NOT PASS THROUGH YOUR BODY. YOU WILL CARRY THE GREAT LORD GLIMM'S GIFT WITH YOU... FOREVER*'

They all swallowed the packets one by one in the order that they had accepted the gift. Patrick was first to swallow, Gill second, followed by Robert. Next up were Carl and Debbie, then Nicky and Ben. Tony, Brenda and Lynda swallowed theirs and then Jenny.

When it came to John's turn he faltered for a moment. The small grain of sanity that had seeped back into his head prevented him from following through with the swallowing of the tooth. He couldn't do it; it just wasn't in his nature. That and the fact that this was one of his friend's teeth made it even more abhorrent to him. He drank the lubricant liquid down in one swig but used a slight of hand trick to stash the tooth into a fold in his robe.

As soon as it appeared that all The Twelve had swallowed their gifts, John watched Robert climb back up onto the table and kneel over Kevin's head.

He waved his arms towards everyone, drawing them closer, around the table. Everyone shuffled forwards. John's sanity and his whole world view were turning in his head. He could see three Kevin's now lying on the table, as a multitude of colours began to flutter before his eyes. He looked for Gill, but all he could see were strange animals on people's heads. A fox, a rabbit, a badger, a bird… all of them looking apparently right at him, or even through him.

He thought that the chanting had started up again, but the last shred of sobriety he had left in him, was slipping away, and he couldn't quite be sure.

Was it in his head?

He was aware of Robert stood on the table waving his hands around. All he wanted to do was get away from here, he wanted to drag Gill away with him too.

And Kevin.

Poor Kevin.

The Twelve

He swayed, and as the hypnotic effects of whatever was in the thick lubricant began to take hold of him, he was sure that he saw Kevin sit up and look at him. As he did his eyes began to shine a bright silver in the dark of the room.

His friend then smiled at him, his mouth was the Abyss. Fire, lava, black demons and damnation straight from Hell were spewing forth from it. John witnessed it all with a vague, dawning horror. As he marvelled at the strangeness of it all, something was thrust into his hand. He didn't know who gave him it, and even as he looked down at it, he couldn't quite recognise what it was.

Gill's face flashed before his eyes, her grin was deliciously lop-sided. She looked happy and this made him happy.

She was waving something in his face, it looked a little like the thing that he had been given. The item was as long as his hand, and it looked sharp on one side.

It felt good as he gripped it, like it belonged there.

'THE INSTRUMENTS OF YOUR DESTINY ARE IN YOUR HANDS. PLUNGE THEM DEEP INTO OUR BODILY SACRIFICE, SEAL YOUR FATE. THE GREAT LORD GLIMM WILL WALK BESIDE YOU IN ALL THAT YOU ENDEAVOUR...'

Kevin was still sat up on the table looking at John, his smile was still horrific and his eyes were still shining silver. The chanting started up again from the PA system, louder and faster than before. The green lights emitting from the carvings on the table strobed brightly as the smoke rose from them.

The sickly smell from the hair and blood within the lights hit John's nostrils and he felt a strange reaction ripple through his whole body. He felt sick, like he was about to vomit. He looked towards the image of his friend sat on the edge of the table, in his drug induced haze he began floating about his vision. It was quite a unique sight.

John was still watching in a crazed state as Robert stepped up behind Kevin and took hold of his head with one hand. A far away blood curdling scream ripped through John's head as Robert pulled Kevin's head back and brought his dagger around to the front of his neck. He watched with amazement and wonder, as all kinds of colours spilled out of the deep gash where Roberts' dagger sliced.

A voice from all around the room rose above the chanting.

'COME NOW AND COMPLETE THE SACRIFICE. PLUNGE YOUR DESTINY INTO MY GIFT… COMPLETE THE CIRCLE OF THE TWELVE. SACRIFICE THE THIRTEEN.'

The volume of the chanting over the speakers increased at least ten-fold, as did the tempo of the rhythm. There was a frenzy in the room, which was akin to someone throwing a bloody piece of chump into a shark tank. Every member of The Twelve dived forwards towards the body of Kevin lying on the table with his blood gushing from his neck.

Each was fighting to get the next blow in, to sink their dagger into their sacrificial flesh, to each claim a destiny that they thought they deserved.

Even John was caught up in this melee, he swiped his dagger towards his friend's body time and time again.

Each member's weapon was covered in blood. Each member of The Twelve were covered in blood.

The thrusts continued to rain in hard, fast and furious. Each one seeming to relate, in almost perfect timing, with the ever-increasing tempo of the chanting

A soothing blackness engulfed John; he and the rest of the members suddenly stopped what they were doing. One by one they fell to the floor, seemingly spent.

The Twelve

John's head began to swim and his vision blurred. He opened his hand and his dagger slipped from his grip.

Before he, himself fell, he just had time to see Robert walk among the fallen, busy picking things up.

He heard whispered voices that he thought were speaking directly to him.

'*I KNOW.*' It whispered. '*I KNOW IT'S IN YOUR ROBE.*'

John didn't know what the voices meant or where they were coming from, but he was feeling far too hazed to even try to understand. He fell to the floor in a slow motion. While he was there he looked around and saw *all* the other members lying down.

The lights to the room went off and darkness descended.

There was peace.

The time was three-fifteen am.

Present day

72.

THE SHOCK OF seeing his old friend again caused John to reel back and he fell onto the couch.

Jenny was rooted to the spot.

Kevin had been the missing link; he was number thirteen. The unofficial thirteenth member of The Twelve. The recollection of all they'd done that night came back to hit them all at once.

Jenny's eyes began to well up with tears. She lifted both her hands to her mouth to stifle the sobs, and to hide her shame about her betrayal.

'Kev, oh Kev. I'm so sorry. I never knew what they had in store for you, I…' she couldn't finish her sentence.

Kevin glided deeper into the room, his head was bowed low. Addison stepped up to him, he was holding his small notebook in his hands. 'Excuse me but you still haven't answered my question. Who you are and how you did you get into this room?' Kevin waved his hand towards him, dismissively and the policeman's legs buckled and he collapsed to the floor. His eyes were wide open and alert, he was still awake and lucid, but he couldn't move a muscle.

Kevin turned his attentions to Jenny. As he did he pulled back his hood completely.

From his low vantage point this was quite simply the most gruesome sight Addison had ever witnessed in his life, and he'd seen some terrible things.

The boy's head was shaved almost bald, thick deep cuts pocked the skin of his white, fish-belly cranium. Dark blood trickled out of these cuts down towards his filthy neck. The black blood was in deep contrast to the white of his skin. Where his throat had been slashed, deep folds of skin were falling away and hanging loosely around his neck.

But it was the thing's mouth that gave Addison the most cause for concern. It was a mash of inflated, bloated, white scarred skin. The swollen gums emphasised the crooked tombstone teeth inside it. They looked like they'd fallen out and a child had forced them back in again.

Black, half congealed blood spilled out of his mouth every time he moved, merging with the thick blood pouring out of the gash in his neck.

It was a horrific nightmare vision.

As he advanced on Jenny he opened his hooded top. He was naked underneath, and a sickening stench flooded the room. It smelt like old rotted fish. There was a massive tear in the flesh of his stomach where a thick flap of skin hung loose. As he advanced on her, wounds began to appear in his skin. One, then two, then five, then ten, then thirty, his torso began to resemble a tray of mince in a butcher's shop.

'You betrayed me Jenny Weaver. You told me you liked me. You wanted to go away, on holiday with me. But all you wanted to do was to use me, seduce me, lure me into your sick perverted games. It was your meeting, the meeting where you all killed me. Yes, you all killed me... in the name of The Great Lord Glimm.'

At the mention of this name Jenny's panic broke. She began to wail. 'I never wanted to kill you. I never wanted to, it was Robert, he was the main one, he made the first cut.'

'It's funny how you can remember it now, Jenny Weaver. For twenty years, you and the others kept it hidden in your subconscious. Oh, Tony's drugs in the wine and in the lubricant helped, but not one of you held any remorse for what you done. Not *ONE* of you even remembered me. *I WAS NOT MISSED.*'

This rant sent John off thinking.

To his shame, he only now realised that he'd not seen Kevin at the graduation ball. He had never once thought about what had happened to him after university, and he'd never once even considered getting back in touch with him again and seeing how he was, how his life had turned out. All that had been resolved tonight.

How could one person be eradicated from another person's memory so completely?

'Kev... I, I did think about you... I did really like you.' Jenny cried. Her sobs racking through her body, shaking her uncontrollably causing clear, running mucus to pour from her nose.

In her fear, she never even noticed.

'No, Jenny Weaver, you liked the idea of a successful life. I was a means to an end for you, and for the whole of The Twelve. I know that. You and your friends saw me as an easy target, someone who would not be missed. And you were right, were you not? The only people who missed me were my parents. The Twelve didn't even notice the brief investigation into my sudden disappearance, did you? No, you all went back to your perfect lives in the popular circles of university.'

At the mention of his parents Jenny began to cry again. She put her head in her hands and sobbed.

John had a strange dichotomy running through his head, on one hand he wanted to go to her and put his arms around her, convince her that everything would be OK. On the other hand, he thought about how cold a person

The Twelve

she was, and the rest of them, and how much of a complete shit *he* was.

'We were horrible people,' he muttered. 'Horrible and nasty, vile people.'

Kevin advanced on Jenny once again. He stood with her, face to face. His ruined and broken nose inches from her perfect but snotty nose.

His face was malevolent and dangerous.

Jenny's was scared and tired.

'You have something of mine Jenny Weaver. I want it back and I want it now. I have the others right here and I need yours to add to the collection.'

He opened his bloody mouth and ten black, rotten and disgusting looking teeth fell out into his awaiting hand. He held the teeth up to Jenny's face and clinked them together in his grip. The small tiny noise they made as they grinded together hurt John's ears.

Jenny tried to close her eyes and look away, but found that she couldn't. The grotesque figure of what used to be Kevin put his hand around her head, to a casual observer it would have looked as if he was about to embrace her. His dark thick blood dripped onto her clothes but his glowing, silver eyes held hers.

With a jolt, he ripped her clothes from the top of her body, the gym top and her sports bra underneath falling to the floor. Her skin was glistening in the cold air, her sweat mingling in with the cold of the room causing her to steam. Her nipples were tight as he pulled her closer. John could see that she was trying to scream, trying to get away from this hellish spectre, but she was helpless.

Kevin's hand traced its way from her mouth down to her stomach, leaving a trail of his filth in its wake.

John's eyes widened, as he realised what Kevin was about to do.

'No, please don't, no, please... please.'

Kevin's fingers plunged into her stomach. Dividing her flesh as if it was soft plastic. There was a sickening ripping sound; neither John nor Detective Addison had ever heard anything like it in their whole lives.

Jenny could plead no more. She was literally ripped open in front of them.

John wanted to close his eyes, he didn't want to see what was happening. All he could think about was Gill, how scared she must have been when Kevin, an entity that she had known and liked in life, performed this act on her.

A tear trickled down his cheek. It was a tear for Kevin's miserable life, for Gill's horrific death, but mostly it was a tear for himself, and everything that he had lost.

Jenny's eyes widened and turned pink as they filled with blood, a bloody tear appeared in the corner of her eye and then began to flow down her cheek.

Both men were staring, they were helpless voyeurs, mere witnesses to these grisly proceedings.

As Kevin's hand delved deeper, blood began to trickle from the side of her mouth. She looked as if she was trying to speak, attempting to say something. All she succeeded in doing was to spit blood out at her assailant, blood mixed with saliva.

Is she mouthing the word sorry? Addison thought as he watched this sickening bloody pantomime act out in front of him from his low-down viewpoint.

Kevin's arms were deep into her stomach now; the only reason she was still stood was that she was holding onto his ghostly frame. Her head was thrown back as if she were reaching orgasm, the only one thing halting that image was the copious amount of blood dripping from her face. Where Kevin's hands had entered into her torso, no blood had yet spilled, it was as if his arms were acting as a kind of plug.

Suddenly his hands stopped moving inside her. His face changed, and he looked jubilant as if he'd found something, something that he'd been searching for. He slowly pulled his hands out of her body. The sheer volume of fresh pain caused Jenny to jerk her head back again, more violently this time. The violence had the effect of removing the plug to her wound as Kevin's hand exited her body with a disgusting squelch.

The blood and the displaced innards of his searching began to spill out of her, in a steaming pile, all over the floor of the living room.

Kevin's gore covered hands held something up to his face, it was what he'd been looking for. Jenny's wide bloodied eyes also focused on what he'd found.

Then, her used and discarded body crumpled onto the floor. Oozing her lifeblood, she fell onto the still steaming pile of her own innards.

John had a flashback to the night of the ritual. The way Kevin's blood and hair burnt when the small streams ran into the lights, causing the foul stench.

He shuddered at the thought.

Kevin was still looking at the small, bloody sack he had in his hands, this was the reward he had been looking for.

This was what he wanted.

He held it up to examine it, and his face changed. He looked almost happy. He opened the small sack up with enthusiasm and removed the contents.

From the floor, Addison strained to see what was in the bag. Although part of his curiosity was professional, to want to know what all the killings were about, but a small part of it was just to look anywhere other than at Jenny's twitching, almost dead body lying in the pile of her own intestines and organs. She couldn't have been more than two yards away from where he was lying.

The sack contained a single tooth.

Kevin dropped the small, old, expensive sack onto the floor and then bent down to where Jenny was lying face down in gore.

He held it up to her face.

John watched as her eyes swayed a little, before they focused on the tooth she had carried with her for twenty years.

He put the tooth with the others still in his hand, and moved in closer to Jenny's dying face. He opened his bloodied, mouth, the smell that wafted through the room when he did this caused the two men to gag once again.

He smiled and his lips tore. More blood poured from his open wounds, intermingling with the blood on Jenny's face and floor. He took the tooth and then showed her his empty hand, all the other teeth were gone. He opened the ruin of his mouth and flashed her a ghastly sight. The teeth had all been inserted back into his hideous, bleeding gums.

He still had her single tooth in his fingers, he held it in between his dirty forefinger and he rolled it around and around. Her eyes were trying to keep focus on it, but they kept rolling around to the back of her head as she dipped in and out of consciousness. Once he knew that he had her full attention, he made a gruesome show of pushing it back into his mouth. As the sharp root of the tooth cut the surface of his gum, a squirt of fresh blood splashed over Jenny's dying face, causing her to blink. He then opened his mouth fully and smiled.

There was only one small gap left in his row of crooked teeth.

Her eyes then rolled to the back of her head once again, for the last time, as she died, silently, with a hole

The Twelve

in her stomach, on a bed of her own rapidly cooling intestines.

Kevin allowed her to die without a second thought.

Then his head turned to look towards John.

John knew that his time would come, the funny thing was, was that he was kind of welcoming it. 'Just a few moments of pain Gill, and I'll be with you forever,' he breathed.

'John Rydell, you were my friend, my only friend,' the monster whispered as he advanced on him. 'Stand up!' He commanded.

John stood up from the couch where he'd witnessed that awful scene. As the spirit that had been Kevin got closer to him he closed his eyes, resigning himself to his fate.

Kevin was now face to face with him, and John could smell the stink of death and decay that radiated from his presence, he assumed, from his ancient wounds. His heart beat faster and his whole body flushed with adrenaline in anticipation of what was to come.

'You have something of mine... and I want it back... now.'

It was hard for John to speak, his throat felt bloated and blocked, but with sheer determination he managed to croak. 'Kev, I... I didn't swallow your tooth. I slipped it into the lining of my robe. I couldn't, I...'

Kevin held up his ghostly hands as if to quieten him. 'I know you didn't. The Great Lord Glimm whispered to us before you blacked out. He knew you didn't swallow it. The thing you have is different, John Rydell. You were my friend. I do believe that if you could have helped me then you would have. It was in your eyes.'

John could feel himself on the verge of tears. He closed his eyes and allowed them to flow. *How could I have been such a shit for all these years, not knowing or caring about what happened to Kev after university?*

Kevin looked at him as if he had just read his mind. 'It wasn't your fault John Rydell, the drugs that Tony Corless used were designed to alter your mind.'

John noticed that the stink had begun to receded, and that the room had become noticeably warmer. He opened his eyes and regarded his old friend.

His ruined face was gone, replaced with a face that John instantly recognised, a face that he could bring himself to look at. It was the face of Kevin, his friend from twenty years ago.

'What do you want from me then?'

'You have in your possession a photograph. I require it back. It is to prove to the powers that my mission is over, that it was a success. I have retrieved my missing possessions and fulfilled Glimm's promises to The Twelve.'

With a shaking hand, John took the photograph out of his pocket and looked at it again. All the faces were gone now, all of them except his. He was now officially the only member left of The Twelve.

'This is yours?' He asked.

'Yes, given to me by The Great Lord Glimm himself.'

John's face didn't mask his confusion.

Kevin looked at him, this time when he smiled the absence of blood and gore was rather comforting. 'Robert didn't know what he was doing. The sacrifice to Glimm was perfect, one who came of their own volition, but he got the chants and incantations wrong. The ritual he performed was designed to *PREVENT* whatever wish the recipient deposited into the bowl. Robert desired to become a judge in the Old Bailey, at the top of his profession, he made that on his own. I was there to prevent it from happening. Carl was about to move to a

The Twelve

big football club in a big money move, I was there to prevent it, Debbie's club, Ben's deanship, Nicky's role in a sitcom... need I continue?'

John was shocked. 'What about me? Did you prevent me from my partnership?'

Kevin shook his head.

'No, John, I didn't. You didn't swallow the tooth, and I know that you'll be pleased to know that your dagger did not once make contact with my body, you were drug addled and frenzied, but your dagger didn't pierce me. You, my friend, didn't murder me.'

'So, I'm free to go?'

'Once you give me my photograph, you are free to leave.'

John looked at the picture, all the blurred-out faces, all the lost lives, screamed out to him as one. Once again, he pondered on the significance of it.

Why this photograph?

'Why this photograph? Of all the photographs that were taken of The Twelve, why this one?'

He handed it over to the ghost, glad for it to be out of his possession. Kevin accepted it and looked at it himself. He smiled a sad smile.

'This was the day that sealed my fate. It was the day that The Twelve were complete. It happened right after this photograph was taken, and you kissed Gill for the first time. Right then I was murdered. You never put your knife into me, but once this camera clicked, I was already as good as dead.'

John bowed his head, remorse deeply instilled within him. He lifted his head to look at Kevin's face once more, there were tears in his eyes.

'I regret what I had to do to your wife John, but she swallowed the tooth. Once she did that, she had sealed her own destiny.'

John just looked at him and shook his head. 'Your mission has to be a failure, I don't have your tooth.'

The spirit of Kevin looked at him, his face softened as he slowly shook his head in return. 'It wasn't about the teeth John. It was about revenge. You are free of your debt to me, look to see me no-more John Rydell.' With that, Kevin began to disappear.

'Wait.' John shouted.

'Yes John Rydell?'

'I need to know something that's been playing on my mind for a while. I need to know what Gill wished for.'

Kevin looked at him, his face was almost transparent and expressionless. 'Why do you need this information John?'

His eyes held Kevin's.

The spirit closed his eyes, and fell silent for a few moments. Eventually, he opened them. 'I will tell you John Rydell.'

John's heart began to beat faster again. He was going to find a huge missing piece now, maybe a little something that would bring him closer to Gill once again.

'Gill wished to be the best mother she could for whatever children you both had. Goodbye John Rydell.'

Kevin's apparition vanished without a trace. The room instantly heated up, back to the normal temperature, and the smell disappeared completely.

John was stunned to silence.

He fell to his knees; tears, freely flowing from his eyes as he stared into nowhere.

Detective Addison discovered that he could move again. He got up slowly and looked around the room, taking in the bloody mess that was the remains of Jenny Weaver.

He looked over towards John, who was now lay in the foetal position, with his back against the couch he'd recently been sat on.

He was crying.

He cried for the loss of Kevin's life and how easily he had been forgotten, he cried for the other nine and their gullible following of someone who didn't know what they were doing. He couldn't find it in him to cry for Robert, he thought that maybe he should, but that would be another day.

Most of all John cried for him and Gill and what they could have been, he cried for their unborn children.

Redford University, South London
20 years earlier

73.

'HURRY UP GILL,' John shouted into the bathroom of Gill's flat. She had been inside there for almost an hour getting herself ready. *I don't know why she takes so long, she's gorgeous anyway,* he thought.

Eventually she made it out. 'Whit-whoo, look at you,' she cooed as she looked at John stood in her bedroom wearing a full dinner-suit complete with bow-tie and wing tipped collars.

As he turned to look at her, he lost his breath. Gill was a sight to behold. Her dress was long, almost down to her ankles, but it was tight. The dark green material hugged onto her fantastic figure anywhere, and everywhere it could. She had a small black stole around her shoulders that matched her shoes and her bag. Her make-up was on-point and her hair… he couldn't even begin to describe her hair.

She smiled at him, a famous lop-sided grin. 'Are we ready then lover-boy?'

'Can't we just stay in tonight, and I'll ruin that dress for you?'

She giggled just as the beep from out on the street indicated that their taxi was here.

The journey to the graduation ball was short, and John couldn't keep his eyes off her. Gill noticed that there was something about him tonight, something giving him a nervous edge.

The Twelve

As they got to the ball-room it was already busy. Taxis and limos were pulling up and smartly dressed people were alighting, all of them ready to party. This was a celebration, their studying days were over, for now, and tonight was a night of fun.

As they got into the ball-room John's colleagues from the computer sciences class called him over. Gill was busy talking to several students from her law classes.

They came together again on the large table as the meal was about to begin. He looked around him and recognised some of the faces from their old club, The Twelve. He raised his glass towards Tony Corless who was sat on the next table. He looked awful, his eyes were red and he had a vacant smile plastered on his face. Patrick was on the table behind him, Ben and Nicky were over the other side of the room…

John frowned a little as Robert walked in, he was linking a young girl, who looked far too young for him. On seeing him, he instantly lost his appetite and he grabbed Gill's hand under the table. *What did we see in these people?* He thought, before dismissing it completely and continued having a great night with friends, and the girl he loved. The girl he hoped would say yes to the question he was going to ask her tonight.

As the food came out, John suddenly felt like something was missing, someone was missing. He looked around at all the faces of his friends and acquaintances, they were all here, but he still had that niggling feeling.

'Number twelve?' A voice asked from behind him, and he snapped his head around to see who it was. The waitress was stood over a man on the opposite table. 'You ordered the number twelve? The vegan meal?' She asked again.

John relaxed, the strange feeling that he had, passed, and the night was a success.

Gill said yes…

Present day

74.

ADDISON TOOK JOHN outside the apartment, he was still inconsolable. As he steered him towards the car, he didn't want to go in, and Addison didn't really want him to. He knew he had to call this in, he had to call something in, but he just couldn't think what he was

Once John was secure he climbed into the front seat and picked up the handheld microphone. As he did he spared a short glance into the rear-view mirror. What he saw there chilled him to the bone. The spirit of Kevin was sat in the back seat, he had his hood up and he was staring dead ahead, his silver eyes were glistening.

Addison turned slowly to look at the hateful thing he had just watched tear apart a young woman. As he completed his turn, Kevin turned his head to look at him.

Fear filled Addison and he found that he couldn't talk. After all he had witnessed tonight and everything he'd heard, this was the final straw.

'Detective Addison, there is one more thing to do, and my mission here is complete. The Great Lord Glimm will then allow me to finally cross over.'

Although Addison was in shock, he managed to stutter. 'Wh… What is it? What do you need?'

'I need to be interred.'

Anderson thought about this for a while, shaking his head. 'I can't help you with that, you died twenty years ago.'

The back window frosted up in an instant and writing began to appear. It was an address in London's docklands.

'If you go here, there is a room. In the room, there is a large circular oak table. Underneath the table there is a sack. Inside you will find human remains.'

Addison was shocked, but his instincts kicked in. 'The remains, are they… yours?'

'Yes.'

'How do I justify looking in this building and stumbling across your remains?' Addison asked, his initial horror ebbing now with professional intrigue.

'Use John's testimony. Pull together all the deaths, and put them on The Twelve. John will give you the location of the building, I will put it back into his mind. He will remember that The Twelve were supposed to meet there for the ritual, but he changed his mind at the last minute. John never made it to the ritual, he is innocent of all crimes. Is this understood Detective Addison?'

All Addison could do was stare at the apparition in the back seat.

'Do we have an agreement Detective Addison?'

'Yes! Yes, we have an agreement.'

'Take my remains to my parents, they will bury me and I will then cross over. You have my word, and the word of The Great Lord Glimm, that this is over Detective. Look to see me no more.'

With that he vanished, leaving Addison stunned, alone in the car.

75.

JOHN ARRIVED AT his house. The ride from Canary Wharf had been mostly silent. 'Thanks for the lift back,' he said sullenly as he unbuckled his seatbelt in preparation of leaving the car.

'Listen, this investigation isn't over, I'm going to have to quantify some of the stuff I've seen tonight. I can't write up a report blaming eleven murders on a ghost. I'd be out on my heels as soon as they read it.'

'I know, we need to get together and develop something rational, something believable.'

'We will, I have a feeling that you'll start to remember things soon. Right, well, I'll be in touch over the week or so. I have some leave coming up that I think I need to take. My brain has never felt so… lost. I'll get in touch when I'm back and we can do it then. Away from the watchful eye of Mrs Addison.'

John looked at the policeman, it hadn't really occurred to him that he might have been married.

'Right then, I'll wait for your call.'

He got out of the car and closed the door behind him. As he walked away, he heard the window pull down behind him.

'John?'

He turned around and looked at the detective, he wasn't used to him calling him anything other than Mr Rydell.

'My name's Dave by the way. Dave Addison.'

John smiled as the window pulled up and the car drove away.

76.

AS HE ENTERED the house, John braced himself for the biting cold, but there was none. Nor was there any nasty smells, except for the week-old washing in the sink that had been neglected. That smell he could live with.

He looked all around the house and smiled a small melancholic smile.

There was enough Gill left in here for him to remember her by. 'Maybe I won't sell you after all,' he whispered.

He closed the door behind him, locking out all the nasty, horrible events that he had been a part of over the last few weeks. He needed some time alone to process the depravity that he had, partially, been the cause of.

He closed the door, locking him inside with his memories of Gill.

Maybe I'll ring Mick tonight, see if he wants to go for a drink.

Slowly he climbed the stairs and entered into his and Gills bedroom. Without undressing, he crawled into the bed, pulled the covers tight over his head, and cried.

He cried himself to sleep.

D E McCluskey

The Twelve

D E McCluskey

Acknowledgements and author notes

I started to write this story a while back, as I had the compulsion to write a scary, dark ghost story. I love the kind of films where the protagonist is doing something in the forefront of the scene, while somewhere, deep in the background a shadow will move, only slightly, but with real menace.

That's what I intended to do here. I wanted my ghost to be the kind of ghost who would skulk in the shadows, only show itself when the characters were either asleep, or they had left the room, but then when it wanted to, it would unleash its unholy wrath on the intended victim.

Initially I wanted this to be a graphic novel. I scripted it and even went as far as commissioning a fantastically talented artist for it (thanks Janine). We did the first ten pages before Janine turned around to me and said that she thought the scope for this tale was just too big to be a graphic novel. In its initial, raw state, the graphic novel would have been more than 200 pages, it would have bankrupted me, and probably gone unnoticed by the majority of the potential audience, as there is still, for some obscure reason, a stigma against graphic novels… Till my dying day I'll never understand that.

The Twelve

I have brought out the ten pages as a preview graphic novel for this book, check out my facebook page for details:

www.facebook.com/dammagedcomics)

So, I cut my losses and began to develop it into a novel. I sat down and re-read the tale, noticing many narrative errors, errors that would have been glossed over in a graphic novel (fixed in the script) but were too glaring for a novel. I sat myself down and rewrote it.

The original tale was about thirty-five thousand words and then when I finished the rewrite, it was sixty-five. I never knew that there was so much more tale to tell. So, I had the first complete draft, and I was well happy with it. Then I asked around for someone to edit it for me.

Tony Higginson was my first editor, he read it, he told me that he loved the story, the structure and the pacing of it, but it was a million miles away from being finished. I looked at him as if he was daft, which he is, but he was serious.

What felt like six hundred thousand rewrites later… this is the end product.

I hope you enjoy reading it as much as I enjoyed writing it…

A few acknowledgements…

My troupe of proof readers, who let me know of all the plot inconsistencies and my splelling (sic) mistakes. Paula Heaton, Stella Read, Naomi

Gibson, Abbie Roylance, Natalie Webb (Coady) and finally Lauren Davies, who has had to live with this book for the last year and a half… constantly!

I need to thank my sisters for their unending support. Annmarie Barrell and Helen Robertson

I need to thank Matt Shaw for putting me right on the art of writing, Tony Higginson for honing the dark art and the million cups of Earl Grey, and Janine Van Moosel for the fantastic cover artwork (plus the graphic novel preview).

Well, if you've gotten this far, then it looks like you've read this thing, and for that I thank you, that's why I do it.

Please stick with it, there's a lot more to come!!!

Thanks again for reading…

Dave McCluskey
Liverpool. UK
May 2017

The Twelve

Made in the USA
Columbia, SC
11 November 2018